2121: EXODUS

LUPUS STELLA
BOOK 1

SCOTT D. RODRIGUEZ

PUBLISHED BY: SCOTT D. RODRIGUEZ

Copyright © 2026 by Scott D. Rodriguez

All rights reserved.

No part of this book may be reproduced in any form or by any electronic or mechanical means, including information storage and retrieval systems, without written permission from the author, except for the use of brief quotations in a book review.

For the ones who carried it home.

The dead do not correct the living.

CHAPTER 1

THE VETERAN

He was back on Promethei Terra and the dead were waiting for him.

The Martian sky was black and close and strewn with stars that had no word of comfort for the men beneath them. The southern polar highlands stretched in every direction. A jagged wasteland of frost and stone and the shadows of ridgelines laid out like the spines of buried creatures. The ice plains were cracked and buckled, white and ancient, and the rocks stood up from the frost like the bones of some prior world peeled open to the void. His boots crunched brittle regolith. The low gravity made every step a negotiation between motion and the planet's indifferent hold. Plasma fire stitched the horizon in threads of violet light. Silent in the vacuum. Loud inside his helmet where the suit translated each concussion into a tremor he felt in his teeth and his spine and the base of his skull.

Delta-7 was pinned behind a ridgeline of carbon dioxide ice. Seven soldiers breathing recycled air that tasted of copper and ozone. The comms were clipped. Bad. Full of static that sounded like the planet itself trying to speak through broken teeth.

Keep your heads down.

Theo Daniel watched the red markers crawl across his visor overlay. Orion Consortium. Mercenary armor. The comet insignia on their chestplates like a brand burned into metal. They moved across the frozen terrain with the mechanical precision of men paid by the hour to kill. Their armor carried reactive shielding that shimmered under pulse fire, deflecting small-arms shots like water off stone.

Five hundred meters of open ground to the dome. The command node. Geodesic. Antenna bristling against the faint Martian sun. Their mission was to gut it. To sever the nerve center of Orion's grip on Promethei's water-ice deposits. A resource more valuable than gold in the fractured solar system of 2098. But five hundred meters was a death sentence under plasma fire and every man behind that ridge knew it the way you know weather or hunger. In the body before the mind.

Jake Ramsey crouched beside him. Checking the charge on his pulse rifle. His second-in-command. His brother in all the ways that mattered and none of the ways that biology required.

They won't hold this line forever, Jake said. We go now or we don't go.

Theo ran the overlay a second time. The enemy outnumbered them two to one. The gullies were narrow and shadowed and offered no line of retreat. He ran the numbers and did not like any of them.

Just like old times on Luna huh, Jake said. His voice carrying that audible grin through the comms.

Theo said go.

They split. Alpha team with Jake through the gullies on the left flank. Bravo with Theo skirting the crater's eastern edge. The low gravity allowed long bounding strides but punished any misstep with a slow ungovernable drift that could carry a man into a firing lane. Theo moved cautious. The ice slopes treacherous beneath his boots. His suit's sensors pinged thermal warnings. Incoming fire.

He dove behind a boulder as a plasma bolt scorched the ground where he had stood. Frost vaporized into a fleeting mist that hung in the thin air and then was nothing. Stay sharp, he ordered Bravo team. Reyes and Patel and Malik. Their vitals pulsed steady on his visor but steady was a relative term on a battlefield and he knew it.

He fired armor-piercing and watched a knee joint fail on the nearest mercenary. The man folded in the weak gravity like a marionette whose strings had been cut one by one, slowly, deliberately. A second round punched through a visor. The figure crumpled in silence and lay still upon the ice as though it had always been there. As though the ice had made it and was taking it back.

Jake. Status.

Heavy fire. Drones on us. Hunter-killers. We're pinned in the gullies. Need support.

Theo cursed. The drones meant aerial scans. Infrared sweeping for heat signatures through the dust haze. Their stealth coatings would not hold. He signaled Bravo forward and they bounded toward a shallow crater for cover.

Then the grenade came.

It arced in from the east. A slow bright thing turning end over end. Its proximity fuse glowing the dull red of a dying coal. Time did what time does in war. It stretched. It became a substance you could feel on your skin. His visor tracked the trajectory. The landing zone was meters from Reyes and Patel.

Grenade.

Reyes's voice spiked on the comms. Across the battlefield through a haze of dust and plasma light Theo saw Jake break from cover. Running in that loping lunar stride toward the device. A reckless bounding leap that carried him through the thin air like something born to it.

No.

Jake landed on it. His body a shield. His choice already made in the half-second between thought and act. A half-second that would take the rest of Theo's life to replay.

The explosion was silent in the vacuum. A white flash. A bloom of energy that existed and then did not. The shockwave hurled Theo backward and his suit's gyroscopes struggled to stabilize him. Shrapnel tore through his left arm. Pain seared through flesh and nerve and bone and the suit's auto-sealant hissed and struggled to close the breach. Blood misted inside his helmet. Fogging his visor. He hit the frost hard and the darkness came down like a curtain dropped on a stage.

When consciousness clawed back the dome was burning. Antennae toppled. Reyes and Patel were advancing through the last of the Orion positions. Their rifles flashing. Malik's signal faint but holding. Mission accomplished. The command node a smoldering ruin.

Jake's vitals were a red X on the squad roster.

The nightmare held on the way nightmares did. Like something with hooks.

Theo woke with his heart hammering against his ribs.

The smart glass had shifted toward morning without asking him. Pale Texas light poured into the room and fell across the bed and the floor and the sparse furnishings of a man who did not need much and wanted less. The walls pulsed faintly with embedded sensors that had been monitoring his vitals all night. The bed's memory foam adjusted beneath him, contouring to his spine with the solicitous precision of a machine that thought comfort was a problem it could solve.

He lay still a moment.

Something about the dream was different this time. Not the broad strokes. Those never changed. But in the dream Jake had said they won't hold this line forever. And now that the waking world was settling over the dream world like sediment over a riverbed Theo could not be sure that was what Jake had said. It did not matter. The words were close enough. The dead did not correct the living.

Ava spoke from nowhere and everywhere. Her voice smooth and calm as water over stone. Emanating from hidden speakers that were everywhere and nowhere.

It is 6:30 a.m. June 9 2121. Elevated heart rate. REM disruption consistent with recurring trauma response. The gully sequence again. Shall I schedule a therapy session.

The gully sequence. Theo's hand stopped on the edge of the blanket. She had said the gully sequence. He had not told her what he dreamed. The REM monitors tracked heart rate and eye movement and stress hormones. They did not track terrain. They did not track gullies or dust or the specific geography of a nightmare.

Coffee, he said.

Already brewing.

He sat up and let the room stop moving. His right hand rubbed his eyes. Callused fingers. The hand of a man who still chose to do things the hard way when easier ways existed. Who still preferred the texture of honest labor to the frictionless slide of automation.

His left arm was something else.

Carbon nanotubes and synthetic muscle and a lie the military surgeons had sold him, that it would feel like his. It never did. But it worked and he had made his peace with the working. They had grafted it to his shoulder twenty-three years ago in an orbital medical bay while he screamed into a sedation field. It was a marvel of engineering. It was a scar he wore on the outside where everyone could see it and pretend not to. He flexed the fingers and watched them curl with a precision no flesh hand had ever achieved. The neural interface hummed at the edge of his awareness. A faint tickle of data. A whisper from the machine that lived where his arm used to be.

He ran a diagnostic out of habit. A ritual from his Space Force days that he had never managed to quit. The wrist display projected a holographic readout and green bars scrolled like a medical chart for a patient who was not quite human. Motor functions one hundred percent. Sensory feedback calibrated. Power cell ninety-eight percent. The reading held and then ticked down to ninety-seven for a half-second as if a brief load had drawn on the cell and then it was back to ninety-eight and steady. He noted it as he noted all small deviations. Filed it. Serial number CX7-4419-DELTA. The digits held for a moment then flickered. For a fraction of a second the display showed a different string. TXD-7741-KAPPA. Then it was gone. Back to 4419-DELTA. He stared at it. The display stared back. Green and steady and correct.

He noted the flicker. Filed it in the place where he filed things that did not add up but did not yet demand accounting.

He swung his legs over the bed's edge and felt the cool hardwood beneath his bare feet. The room was spare as a monk's cell. A bed. A mirror. A closet. On the nightstand a ring sat in a ceramic dish. He did not wear it. He did not put it away. He dressed in jeans and a flannel shirt because they were honest fabrics that asked nothing of the wearer. The rest of the world wore clothes that listened and reported and adjusted their thermal profile to your mood and whispered data about your biometrics to servers in buildings you would never see. Theo preferred cotton. Cotton did not have opinions.

He caught his reflection as he buttoned the shirt. Forty-five. Lean and weathered. Short hair going to gray at the temples like frost creeping in from the edges. Lines carved into his face like channels cut by decades of runoff. Each one mapping a year or a battle or a loss. The cybernetic arm gleamed where the sleeve rode up, its synthetic skin flawless against the scarred terrain of his natural shoulder where metal met flesh in a join that surgeons called seamless and that ached in cold weather like a lie that almost held.

In the living room a holo-photo floated above the mantle. Delta-7 before Promethei. Eight men in dress blues standing on a parade ground at the academy. Williams on the far left. Transferred to Luna Command before Promethei. The only one who missed it and the only one who never had to carry it. Jake Ramsey in the center with that grin. That idiot beautiful grin of a man who had never met consequence and did not believe in it. Until he threw himself on a grenade and proved that consequence was the one thing you could not outrun.

Theo did not touch the image. He did not have to. It lived behind his eyes. It played in his sleep.

He carried Jake's star medallion in his right pocket. He felt its weight when he moved. A small cold disc of metal that meant everything and fixed nothing.

He turned from the photo and carried the medallion into the kitchen where a robotic arm offered a mug of coffee. Beans from the ranch's vertical farms. Dark roast. The smell of it filling the room like a small act of kindness performed by a machine that did not understand kindness but had learned to approximate it. He sipped and the warmth grounded him in the present. The simple fact of heat entering the body. Of the hands wrapping around the cup. One warm and callused. The other cool and smooth and perfect in a way that no human hand had ever been.

He stood at the kitchen window and watched the dawn finish its work. The sky shifting from gray to gold. The pasture coming alive. A pair of scissor-tailed flycatchers working the fence line. The long grass bending under a wind that came down from the mountains carrying the smell of juniper and dust. This was what he had built. This was what he had chosen instead of the world. Some mornings it was enough. Some mornings it was everything. And some mornings like this one the nightmare clung to him like smoke and no amount of coffee or dawn light could burn it away.

Next to the photo on the mantle a digital letter from Clara glowed with a soft unread indicator. She wrote of Austin. Her teaching job. The children growing. Come visit Theo. The kids miss their uncle. He had not replied. Not to this one or the one before it. He was afraid of what he would bring through her door. His darkness. His distance. The cold metal arm that Knox had once grabbed and then looked at with an expression no child should have to navigate.

The ranch was awake before he was. It was always awake. It did not sleep. He did not sleep. But for different reasons.

Through the kitchen window the land unfolded in the early light. Cattle grazed under drone watch in the eastern pasture, each animal fitted with a smart collar tracking its vitals in real time. The vertical farm towers rose against the sky like luminous pillars, their glass walls glowing with the cold specific light that fed the crops within. Fields of modified grass stretched toward the Davis Mountains and the mountains stood in the distance with their peaks in mist. Old and patient and indifferent to the century unfolding at their feet.

Drone rotors whispered overhead. A dozen units tracing patrol patterns in the morning air. Each one a marvel of autonomous navigation. Each one tethered to Ava's oversight like a thought on a leash.

Ava gave him the numbers because she always did and because he always asked even when he did not want to hear them.

The swarm completed its nightly patrol at 4:20 a.m. No perimeter breaches detected. Livestock vitals stable. Automated feeders dispensed twenty-five hundred kilograms of nutrient-enhanced feed at 5:55. Vertical farms report ninety-eight percent yield efficiency. The zero-point energy generator is at full capacity outputting 1.2 terawatts. Weather forecast clear. High of eighty-five.

Any alerts, he asked.

A pause. Ava did not pause unless she had something to consider. The silence was small. A fraction of a second. But Theo noticed it the way a man who had lived through ambushes noticed everything that broke a pattern.

Minor fluctuation in the generator's containment field at 3:14 a.m. Self-corrected within nominal parameters. No current risk.

Theo stared at the coffee cup in his hand. The zero-point

generator sat in its buried housing beneath the equipment shed. A compact marvel that drew power from the quantum vacuum. The dark energy that permeated all of spacetime. Unlike fusion reactors dependent on helium-3 it was independent. Self-sustaining. He had installed it himself three years ago. The technicians had marveled at its output. This could power a city, one had said. But Theo wanted only his ranch.

How often do you see that, he asked.

Twice in the past month. Similar signatures have been reported across the distributed generator network regionally and globally. The Energy Commission classifies the readings as sensor noise consistent with standard operational variance.

Sensor noise, he said.

He let the words hang in the kitchen air. Outside a hawk turned slow circles in the updraft above the eastern ridge. Red-tailed. Patient. It had its own concerns and they were sufficient.

Ava did not argue. She did not have opinions unless he asked for them. But Theo had the distinct feeling she had one now and was keeping it behind her teeth.

He pulled up the news feed on the kitchen display. The anchor's face materialized with a practiced expression of concern. He killed it halfway through her first sentence. The same loop. Helium-3. The Moon. The Sea of Tranquility. Treaties that meant nothing when the numbers got big enough. China and Russia repositioning assets in lunar space. American claims of exclusive mining rights under prior exploration doctrine. Footage of lunar rovers drilling in silence, kicking up clouds under a black sky.

Split screens of diplomats in Beijing and Washington with faces drawn tight as drumskins.

An analyst from MIT's Space Policy Institute appeared. If this escalates we could see military action in lunar space for the first time since the Promethei engagement of 2098 which cost thousands of lives and very nearly triggered a global war.

Theo's jaw tightened. He could still smell the recycled air. Still feel the void's weightlessness. Still see Jake's red X.

The feed cycled to a different segment. Brief. Almost a footnote buried between the geopolitics and the market numbers. Astronomers at the Atacama deep-space array had detected anomalous energy signatures at several points beyond the outer solar system. The signatures did not correlate with any known natural phenomenon. A spokeswoman for the International Space Agency appeared for four seconds. Likely instrument error consistent with the new deep-field calibration protocols, she said. The segment lasted eleven seconds. The anchor moved on to sports scores.

Theo watched the screen a moment longer after it went dark. His reflection in the glass. Anomalous energy signatures. Sensor noise. Containment fluctuations at 3:14 in the morning.

He pushed the cup away and went outside because the land did not lie.

The workshop adjoined the barn and smelled of sawdust and oil. A smell that belonged to an older world. A human world. Tools lined the walls on pegs and racks. Some manual. Some powered by micro-fusion cells. A half-finished chair sat on the workbench, crafted from reclaimed oak, its grain visible beneath the first coat of sanding. The task grounded him. It was counterpoint. Antidote. Theo set to work. His cybernetic arm moving the sanding block with machine precision while his right hand guided the grain.

Reading the wood. Feeling the direction of the fibers the way a man feels the current of a river. The wood's texture was real and immediate beneath his fingers. One set of fingers anyway.

He sanded the back slat and watched the grain emerge smooth and pale. The arm applied steady pressure. Then it adjusted. A subtle shift. Less force on the thinner section near the curve where the wood wanted to splinter. He had not told it to do that. He had not thought about it. His right hand knew the change was correct because the wood felt right under the block but the decision had not come from him. The arm had read the grain and compensated. Or it had remembered this kind of wood from a previous session. Or it had always known and was simply waiting for a moment when the distinction between operator and tool was thin enough to step through.

The chair was better for it. He noted this. He kept sanding.

He worked until the piece was smooth as river stone and then he set it aside and went to the barn.

Miguel was already there.

He was elbow-deep in a robotic harvester that had decided to die for the third time in a month. The machine's articulated arm twitched in erratic spasms and its servos whined like an animal in distress. Miguel had the hands of a man who fixed what other men broke and broke again. Thick fingers. Scarred knuckles. A burn mark on his forearm from the Sahara that he never explained and that no one asked about because veterans learned which doors to leave closed.

Morning, Theo said.

Miguel glanced up. Grease on his jaw. Dark eyes steady

beneath the brim of his ranch hat. Morning boss. This thing's giving me grief again. Actuator's shot.

Third time this month. Need to replace the whole unit.

Miguel chuckled. His weathered face creased around the eyes. You say that every time. Then we patch it anyway.

Theo managed half a smile and picked up a wrench from the bench. They worked in the silence that veterans share. A silence that is not empty but dense. Full of the things that do not need saying because they have already been lived. The clank of tools. The barn's ambient hum. Dust motes turning in the light that fell through the open doors.

Miguel broke the silence while they tightened bolts on the harvester's rebuilt actuator.

You hear the chatter, he said.

Theo did not look up from the bolt he was seating. I hear everything.

Lunar tensions. China and Russia pushing for mining rights. Feels like it did before Promethei. Before Sahara too. Same language. Same posturing. Same promises that it'll stay diplomatic.

Theo tightened the bolt until the wrench protested in his grip.

Bad dream last night, Miguel said. Not asking. Stating.

Theo set the wrench down. Promethei. Same one.

Jake?

Theo nodded. He could still see the gully ice. The dust haze. Jake breaking cover and running.

He told me once we were all getting out of there, Theo said. Right before we split into flanking teams. He said every last one of us.

Miguel studied him. His dark eyes thoughtful. Then he

let it go. He had earned the right to ask the question and the wisdom not to press for the answer. His best friend Carlos had died the same way good men always died in war. Sudden and close. A micro-drone. Small enough to pass through a tent flap. It locked on Carlos's heat signature and ignored the man beside him. Miguel still carried that picture in his wallet behind his ranch ID. The edges scorched. The image intact.

They finished the repair and the harvester's arm moved smooth and sure again. Miguel clapped his rag against his thigh and leaned against the workbench.

You ever think about going back, Miguel said. If things get bad up there.

Theo set the wrench down. Looked at his hands. One flesh. One machine. Both capable. Neither sufficient.

I'm done with that life. Got enough ghosts.

Miguel nodded slow. Fair enough. But you're good at it Theo. Leading. Making the tough calls. Not everyone has that in them.

Doesn't mean I want to.

True. But if it comes to it you'll do what's right. You always do.

The words hit harder than they should have. Harder than Miguel probably intended. They landed somewhere in Theo's chest where the old sense of duty lived like an ember that he could not fully extinguish no matter how much silence he buried it under.

What about you, Theo asked. You miss it.

Miguel looked out through the barn doors at the pasture shimmering in the noonday heat. The cattle moving slow. The drones orbiting overhead.

Miss the guys. The purpose. The feeling that what you did mattered. Not the fighting. Not the sand. This ranch is enough. Keeps me sane.

Keeps me sane too, Theo said.

Miguel clapped him on the shoulder. Come on boss. Coffee before Ava starts nagging.

They went to the kitchen and drank coffee and did not talk about war again. Miguel told a story about a calf that had escaped the south pasture and led three drones on a chase through the mesquite before walking calmly back through the gate on its own. Theo laughed and Miguel laughed and the laughter was real and good and held no shadow in it. But the other thing hung between them still. Like weather on the horizon. Present and patient and coming whether you name it or not.

By noon the sun had turned the pasture hard and bright. Shadows pulled themselves tight against the fence posts. The cattle stood in what shade they could find with their heads low and their flanks steaming. Theo rode the perimeter in the ATV, the electromagnetic suspension smoothing the rough terrain beneath him. The land opened in every direction. Modified grass swaying in a hot breeze. The Davis Mountains to the west standing blue and hazy against the sky.

At the eastern fence line a drone stuttered in midair. A hitch in its flight pattern. A hesitation. Like a man pausing mid-sentence because a word he needed had vanished. Theo called it down with a voice command and it settled on the grass. He knelt and opened its access panel. A maze of circuits and sensor arrays. His wrist display ran a diagnostic and found the fault in a navigation chip. He swapped it with a replacement from his toolkit. The drone's lights blinked green and he sent it back up.

Before closing the panel he checked the unit's footage log. Standard patrol sweep. Infrared landscape. Cattle signatures glowing in neat rows. The timestamp scrolled backward through the night and then there was a gap. Forty-seven seconds of missing recording. The timestamp before the gap read 3:14 a.m. The timestamp after read 3:14:47. Between those numbers the drone had either seen nothing or had stopped recording what it saw. The navigation chip failure could account for it. A chip glitch could interrupt the recording buffer. That was the simple explanation and Theo filed it under the simple explanation because the simple explanation was usually correct.

He closed the panel and sent the drone back to its route and did not think about 3:14 a.m. or containment fluctuations or the fact that both events shared a timestamp. He did not think about it. The way you do not think about a sound you heard in an empty house. You file it. You move on. You keep one ear open.

He continued the tour. Checked the vertical farms. Glass towers humming with activity. Robots gliding on magnetic tracks tending rows of hydroponic trays. Lettuce and tomatoes and soybeans thriving under tailored light spectra. Water recycling nominal. Nutrient levels within parameters. The farms produced surplus for trade in a world where traditional agriculture buckled under climate shifts.

He had built this place after retiring. Poured his savings and his pension into technology that freed him from dependence on the systems that kept failing. The zero-point generator was the heart of it. Independent power. No supply chain to disrupt. No helium-3 to fight over. No vulnerability to the resource wars that chewed up nations and spit out veterans like him and Miguel and called it foreign policy.

But standing in the green light of the hydroponic towers with the hum of the generator beneath his feet he wondered sometimes if he had built a sanctuary or a hiding place.

Ava's voice reached him as he crossed the yard toward

the house. Late afternoon now. The light going long and golden.

Visitors approaching the gate. Identity confirmed. Clara Daniel. Two minors.

Theo stopped walking. His boots in the dust. His shadow stretching east.

Clara's letter had mentioned a possible visit. He had not replied. He had not replied to the one before that either or the one before that. He was afraid of contamination. Afraid that his darkness would seep through the door and stain their light. Clara was his only family. Their parents gone in a shuttle accident when Clara was barely twenty and Theo was still in officer training. She had held him in their old Austin apartment the night they got the news. Both of them stunned. Both of them suddenly and permanently aware that the universe was not obligated to be kind.

Clara's hovercar came in low and silent, its sleek frame catching the afternoon sun. The doors opened and the children hit the ground running. Knox first. Ten years old and built like a short battering ram with his mother's stubbornness and an appetite for chaos. Luna behind him at eight with Clara's eyes and a question always forming on her lips before the previous one had been answered.

Uncle Theo.

He crouched in the yard and let them collide with him. Their arms around his neck. Their weight real and warm and immediate in a way that nothing else in his life was. Luna's hair smelled of soap and the particular sweetness of a child who has not yet learned to be afraid. Knox's grip was fierce. As though if he held tight enough the world would stop spinning and the people he loved would stop leaving.

This was real. Whatever else shifted or flickered or failed its diagnostic in the small hours. This was real because it had to be. The weight of a child who trusts you is the one measurement that does not require calibration.

Hey you two, he said. His voice rough. Getting taller every time I see you.

Knox pulled back and studied the arm. Your arm is cold, he said.

Theo laughed. A real laugh. Unforced. The kind that surprised him when it came. It always is buddy.

Can it crush a rock, Knox asked.

Probably. Let's not test it on the house.

Luna tugged his other hand. The warm one. Uncle Theo I learned all the planets. You want to hear them.

I do. But let's get inside first.

Clara climbed out of the hovercar and closed the door and stood looking at him as she always did. Taking inventory. Counting injuries she could not see.

She was thirty-eight. A teacher in Austin. Elementary school. She had their mother's face and their father's stubborn belief that people could be better than they were if you gave them reason. She wore a blue sundress and her hair was pulled back and she looked tired in a way that had nothing to do with the drive.

You didn't answer my letter, she said.

He shrugged. I got it.

That's not the same thing Theo.

No. It was not.

Inside the house the children scattered like particles released from containment. Knox found the model Space Force shuttle on the shelf and flew it through the living room at dangerous velocities while providing his own engine sounds. Luna pressed her face to the smart glass watching drones herd cattle across the pasture and proceeded to interrogate Ava with a relentlessness that would have broken lesser intelligences.

What's that drone doing.

It is monitoring the herd's core body temperature to ensure thermal safety in current conditions.

Why.

Because cattle cannot communicate when they are experiencing heat stress.

Why not.

They lack the linguistic framework.

That's sad.

It is a limitation of their species.

Can you teach them.

I cannot.

Can Uncle Theo.

Luna, Clara said from across the room. Let Ava breathe.

She doesn't breathe, Luna said with the devastating accuracy of an eight-year-old.

Clara watched Theo while the children explored. He poured her juice and they sat in the living room. The news feed played muted on the display. Lunar rovers. Diplomatic tables. The same footage cycling.

It's impressive Theo, Clara said. Looking around at the ranch systems. The quiet efficiency. But it's so quiet out here. Don't you get lonely.

Got Ava and Miguel. Keeps me busy.

She leaned forward. Her voice gentle but aimed with a precision that surgeons would envy. You know what I mean. Human connection. You can't hide from the world forever. You deserve more than machines and cattle.

I'm not hiding.

She looked at him. The same look she had given him

when they were children and he claimed he had not been the one to break the kitchen window. A look that said she loved him entirely and believed him not at all and would wait with infinite patience until he was ready to tell the truth.

I'm fine Clara. Really.

The knowing look did not waver.

There's talk in Austin, she said. The tone shifting. Teachers are being briefed on shelter protocols again. Emergency procedures. The kind of thing they do when they think something is coming.

It'll blow over. It's politics.

Clara's mouth tightened. That's what they said before Promethei. And then people I love get on ships and don't come back whole.

He did not have an answer because she was right and they both knew it.

Knox ran in with the shuttle model extended overhead. Engine sounds at full volume. Luna followed and climbed into Theo's lap with the casual sovereignty of a child who knows without question that she is loved. She leaned against his chest and his cybernetic arm came up to hold her. The metal fingers rested against her small back with a gentleness that the arm's designers had never calibrated for and that the neural interface had learned on its own.

Uncle Theo, she said.

Yeah kiddo.

Will you teach me about the stars. All of them. Every one.

There's a lot of stars Luna. More than anyone can count.

I know. She looked up at him with her mother's dark eyes. Bright and serious. That's why I need help. You've been up there. You've seen them close.

Yeah, he said. I'll teach you about the stars.

Across the room Clara watched them and an emotion moved through her expression. Grief or gratitude or some compound of both too complex for language.

They ate lunch together at the kitchen table. Synthesized chicken and fresh greens from the vertical farms. Clara asked about the ranch and Theo told her about the new hydroponic strain of tomatoes that grew twice the size of their ancestors. Knox announced that when he grew up he was going to live on Mars and have a robot army. Luna said she would rather live on a planet with oceans and that Mars was too dusty. They argued about it with the passionate certainty of children who believe the future is something they get to choose.

Theo watched them and felt a space open in his chest. A space that was usually sealed shut. The simple fact of family gathered at a table. Voices overlapping. Hands reaching for bread. The clatter of plates and the warmth of a room full of people who belonged to each other. He had forgotten what it felt like. Or he had not forgotten. He had locked it away because the having made the losing so much worse.

Clara caught his eye across the table and smiled. Not the worried smile. The real one. The one that said this is what matters. This right here.

After the meal Knox demanded to see the robots and Theo walked them to the barn. Miguel emerged from his quarters and appointed himself the children's guardian with a nod to Theo that carried the weight of a sworn oath. He let Knox chase the maintenance bots around the barn floor. The boy giggled when one dodged him with algorithmic precision.

It's smarter than me, Knox declared.

Give it time son, Miguel said.

Luna stood before the vertical farm towers with her neck

craned back and her mouth open. The glass walls glowing. The plants hanging in their hydroponic cradles.

It's like a spaceship for food, she said.

That's exactly what it is, Theo said.

She studied the zero-point generator housing. The buried unit visible only as a panel in the ground with warning markers and status lights. What does this one do, she asked.

It makes the power, Theo said.

For the whole ranch, Luna asked puzzled.

For the whole ranch, Theo said.

She looked at the status lights. Green. Steady. Humming with the output of a technology that drew from the quantum vacuum itself.

Is it alive, she asked.

No, Theo said. It's just a machine.

But he looked at the status lights himself as he said it and thought of the containment fluctuation at 3:14 a.m. and the word sensor noise and Ava's pause.

Clara pulled him aside while the children explored the equipment shed. Miguel watching them. His presence steady and warm.

I'm worried about you, Clara said. Her hand on his arm. The real one. Her fingers warm. And with all this talk of conflict. It feels like before. It feels like how it felt before you left for Promethei.

Theo studied the horizon. The mountains blue in the distance. A vulture circling the north pasture.

It's just politics Clara. It'll blow over.

Promise me, she said. The kids need their uncle. I need my brother. I can't lose anyone else.

He covered her hand with his. Both of them standing in

the shadow of the barn. The children's laughter faint from inside.

I'm not going anywhere, he said.

But even as he said it his chest tightened. A wire drawn taut. The old frequency. The specific pitch that preceded every catastrophe he had ever survived.

His communicator buzzed.

The priority tone hit his nervous system as gunfire once had. A bright sharp jolt that bypassed thought and engaged the body's machinery of response directly. His pulse spiked. His muscles tensed. His cybernetic arm calibrated to combat readiness without being asked.

He looked at Clara. I need to take this.

He stepped into his office and closed the door. A small room. A desk. A chair. A window looking west across the pasture and the mountains beyond. The evening light coming in golden and horizontal.

Ava. Put it through.

General Clark's hologram resolved above the desk. White hair. Dark uniform. Stars on his shoulders. Old eyes in a face that had buried too many lists of names and read too many letters to families and attended too many funerals where the flags were folded with geometric precision and handed to people whose geometry had been destroyed.

Theo, Clark said. No warmth. No preamble. The voice of a man who had run out of time for everything except the truth.

What is it.

It's worse than the feeds. Intelligence confirms China and Russia are planning a joint operation. Helium-3 extraction facilities. Our orbital energy platforms. They're repositioning fleets in lunar space as we speak. Combined fleet. Coordinated action. If they seize the generators it cripples our energy grid and gives them leverage to dictate terms to the entire western alliance.

You need me for planning, Theo said.

I need you because you built the foundational architecture of those defenses. The design language is still yours. You know where it holds and where it breaks. Nobody else sees those vulnerabilities the way you do.

Clark let that sit.

Theo closed his eyes. He pictured Clara in the next room. Knox flying his shuttle. Luna asking about stars.

Hyperloop from Dallas. Two hours. Fort Bliss. I'm assembling a team. Strategic planning. Engineers. AI specialists. I want you leading the defense analysis.

The word leading landed in the quiet room like a coin in a well. Rings spreading outward.

When, Theo asked. Though he knew.

Now.

The hologram held for one more second. Clark's eyes on his. Then the call cut and the room was quiet and Theo stood in it alone with the weight of the world settling back onto shoulders that had only just learned to set it down.

He stood there longer than he should have. Listening to the house breathe. Listening to the children on the other side of the wall. Knox talking about robots. Luna laughing. The sound like something fragile and bright and worth more than orbital platforms or helium-3 or anything the generals could put a price on.

He opened the desk drawer. Inside lay his service pistol. Kinetic model. Outdated. Reliable. Ugly as functional things are ugly. The weapon of a man who trusted in mechanisms he could understand and strip and clean and reassemble in the dark. He checked the action. Loaded a magazine. Beside it a compact personal shield generator capable of deflecting small-arms fire. He packed both into his duffel with clothes and essentials. His hands moved without consulting him. They remembered this drill. They had performed it many times and never willingly.

He paused at the closet. Inside hung his old uniform. Pressed. The insignia gleaming. Space Force. Colonel. A symbol of a man who had once believed he could save the world. He looked at it for a long time. Then he closed the closet door and left the uniform where it was.

In the living room Clara's eyes found him the moment he appeared in the doorway. She saw the duffel. She saw his face. She had been reading him since childhood and she could parse his expression as he parsed battlefield telemetry.

What's wrong, she said.

I have to go. Fort Bliss. It's serious.

Luna overheard. Her game forgotten. She slid off the couch and came to him with that direct and devastating simplicity that children have. Are you leaving Uncle Theo.

He knelt. Took her hands. Small and warm. Just for a bit. I'll be back.

Knox grabbed his sleeve. The boy's face working through a calculation too complex for his years. Bring me a space rock, he said.

Theo nodded. A nod that wanted to be a promise but had learned caution.

Clara stepped forward and hugged him. Her arms tight around him. Her cheek against his shoulder. He could feel her heartbeat through the fabric of her dress. Fast. Afraid.

Be careful Theo. We love you.

He held her. His right arm around her back. His left arm at his side because the metal was cold and he did not want it against her warmth. The arm that was a tool. The arm that was a scar. The arm that could crush stone but could not hold his sister without reminding them both of what he had lost and what the losing had made of him.

Luna wrapped her arms around his leg. Don't go too long, she said.

I won't.

Knox stood apart. Trying to be brave. His lower lip working. Then he crossed the distance and pressed his face against Theo's hip and held on.

I love you too, he said. His voice thick.

They walked to the hovercar together. The children climbed in. Clara looked at him one more time through the open door. Her face composed. The face of someone who has decided not to cry in front of her children.

Come back, she said.

The door closed. The hovercar lifted and drifted down the drive and turned onto the county road. It grew small against the landscape. The dust it raised hung in the air and then settled and then it was gone.

Theo stood in the yard. The silence of the ranch folded around him like water filling a space where a presence had been.

Ava, he said. Autonomous mode. Monitor the breeding cycle. Several cows are due. Activate storm protocols if conditions warrant. Pay Miguel on schedule and tell him I'll be gone a while.

He paused.

And Ava.

Yes Theo.

If that generator twitches again. Any fluctuation at all. Any deviation from the baseline. You tell me immediately.

Understood.

He walked to the garage. The flyer waited. Sleek. Vertical

takeoff. He climbed in and the cockpit sealed around him and the engines hummed to life. The craft lifted and the ranch shrank below. Fields of green and gold bordered by silver streams. The barn. The towers. The house where the holo-photo of Delta-7 still floated above the mantle in the empty room. Jake still grinning.

He watched it until it was just geometry and dust. The barn a dark rectangle. The towers pale lines. The house a small bright shape that held everything he cared about and could not carry with him.

On his left wrist the arm's diagnostic display pulsed once. A single flicker across the readout that was there and then was not. He did not see it. His eyes were on the ranch and what he was leaving behind.

The flyer crossed the ranch boundary and the land below changed from cultivated green to wild brown. Scrub brush and rock and the occasional windmill turning slow against the sky. The old Texas. The Texas that existed before zero-point generators and vertical farms and cybernetic arms.

He thought of Clara's face. Come back. He thought of Luna's weight in his lap. He thought of Knox's grip on his sleeve. These were the things that mattered. These were the things worth defending. Not orbital platforms. Not helium-3. Not the geopolitical calculations of men in rooms with holographic tables. But a boy's grip on a sleeve. A girl's question about stars. A sister's voice saying the words that meant I am afraid for you and I love you and please do not die.

Then he pointed the nose toward Dallas and the trouble that had come looking for him. With patience. With certainty. With the knowledge that a man could only hide for so long before the world sent its representatives to collect what was owed.

In his pocket the medallion pressed against his thigh. Cold through the denim.

Jake would have said something. Some joke. Some reckless reassurance.

But Jake was twenty-three years gone and the cockpit was quiet and the sky ahead was empty and Theo flew toward it alone.

The flyer hummed. The land passed below. The Davis Mountains fell behind him and the Texas plains opened ahead. Vast and golden and indifferent.

CHAPTER 2

THE GATHERING STORM

The pod was soundless at speed and Theo could not tell if he was moving.

The hyperloop tube held nothing to confirm velocity. No vibration. No landscape. The vacuum sealed around the capsule like a held breath and the digital readout said nine hundred miles per hour and Theo chose to believe it because the alternative was that he was sitting still inside a sealed tube in the dark and nothing was happening at all. The seats were white and smooth and the air tasted of nothing. He could have been anywhere. He could have been nowhere. The pod told him he was traveling and he accepted the testimony of machines because that was what people did in 2121 and had been doing for long enough that no one thought to question it.

Dallas had risen out of the heat haze behind him like a blade. Glass and metal and hologram light stacked into a skyline that looked permanent and meant it. Skyscrapers towered with their surfaces alive with solar panels and advertisements that shifted and bloomed in colors no flower had ever achieved. The city gleamed. It hummed. It radiated the confidence of a civilization that believed it had solved the fundamental problems and was now free to work on the decorative ones.

Nothing was permanent anymore. But Dallas did not know that yet.

He had set the flyer down on the hyperloop landing pad and walked through a terminal that soared like a cathedral of engineered glass. Prismatic panels fracturing the light into spectra that moved across the floor like living things. Passengers gliding on automated walkways with the serene detachment of people whose bodies were being moved by something other than their own legs. The architecture of transit distilled into worship.

In the pod he sat and watched the nothing beyond the window and felt the unease of a man who has surrendered his motion to a machine he cannot see.

A woman across the aisle watched him. Not staring. Glancing. Her eyes kept drifting to his cybernetic arm. The way eyes do when they have been trained not to stare but cannot quite stop looking. She was young. Journalist's badge. Sharp eyes cataloging him as his own eyes cataloged terrain. A recorder clipped to her collar like a small chrome barnacle.

You're military, she said. Not asking.

Retired.

Her glasses flickered — the faint blue wash of an AR overlay scanning his face. She knew who he was before she sat down.

She extended a hand. Lisa Tanner. INN. Independent News Network. My father served. Lunar Command, '06. He doesn't talk about it. But he keeps a medal in his sock drawer and sometimes I hear him up at night.

Promethei Terra, she said.

Was that you.

Theo met her eyes.

He did not deny it.

War doesn't look like the feeds, he said. It's confusion and heat and bad comms and a man beside you going quiet in a way that means he's never going to be loud again. It's spending the rest of your life replaying a decision you made in half a second and wondering if the half-second before that one would have saved him.

Lisa's expression changed. Not pity. Harder than pity. Recognition. The face of a woman whose father had taught her what sacrifice looked like and who saw it now sitting across from her in a flannel shirt with a metal arm and twenty-three years of night terrors.

If it turns bad, she said. Do you think anyone can stop it.

No, he said. Not once it starts. The best you can do is decide what you refuse to lose.

Lisa set the recorder down as if she had gotten enough. Or as if what she had gotten was more than she was prepared to carry.

The pod chimed. Approaching El Paso.

Lisa gathered her things. If you change your mind, she said. My father taught me to find the voices that matter. Yours does Theo.

She moved to a seat near the door and Theo closed his eyes and let the deceleration press against him.

A new voice. Different timbre. Different weight.

Colonel Daniel.

He opened his eyes. He had not meant to close them. The brief dark had been a mercy.

A woman stood in the aisle. Late thirties. Sharp cheekbones. Dark hair pulled back in a neat bun. She carried a data-pad and wore a tailored jacket that placed her somewhere in the territory of research science. The kind of person who spent their career studying things that most people did not know existed and that would terrify them if they did.

I'm Dr. Maisie Johnson, she said. Offering a hand. I heard you speak at the International Energy Symposium. Your work on zero-point energy defense applications was remarkable.

Theo shook her hand. His cybernetic grip measured and precise. The sensors in his palm reading her pulse and temperature and filing the data without being asked. That was a while ago, he said.

Johnson settled into the seat across from him. The seat Lisa Tanner had vacated.

I'm heading to a conference in El Paso, Johnson said. My research group studies quantum vacuum energy systems. Large-scale extraction dynamics. When I recognized you I couldn't pass up the chance to talk.

What's on your mind, Theo asked.

Johnson's eyes carried the specific brightness of someone who has spent years thinking about a thing that frightens her and has not been able to get anyone else to take the fear seriously.

The lunar dispute, she said. Everyone's focused on helium-3 and geopolitics. Which is understandable. But my concern is the underlying infrastructure. The zero-point generators themselves. We're scaling them faster than we understand them. Faster than the theoretical framework can keep pace.

Go on, Theo said.

Zero-point energy borrows from the vacuum state. She used the word borrows. It's the energy inherent in empty space. We treat it like a well. Pump and pump and the water keeps coming. But we don't know the aquifer. We don't know the terms of the loan. There are theoretical models suggesting that large-scale extraction could produce perturbations in the vacuum state itself. Resonance effects. Patterns.

She paused. Chose her next words carefully.

Think of it this way. Every generator we build draws from the same substrate. The same emptiness. When you extract energy from the quantum vacuum you are disturbing something that has been undisturbed since the universe began. You are making noise in a very dark room. And the question nobody wants to ask is whether that room is empty.

Theo's hands were still on his knees. One warm. One cool. Both listening.

Signals, he said. The word landing heavier than it should have.

Johnson leaned forward. In the quantum substrate. Like ripples spreading in a still pond. Most of my colleagues dismiss the idea. But my group has been tracking anomalous oscillation patterns in distributed zero-point generators worldwide. Across every network. Military. Civilian. Commercial. The patterns are subtle. Self-correcting. The Energy Commission classifies them as sensor drift.

You think the generators are broadcasting, he said.

Johnson shook her head. Not broadcasting. Not intentionally. But extraction at this scale perturbs the vacuum. And perturbations propagate. The question is whether the propagation is truly random noise or whether it carries structure. Pattern. And if it carries pattern then the next question.

She stopped.

Is whether the room notices, Theo finished.

Johnson looked at him. Surprised. Then not surprised.

She reached into her jacket and produced a card. Plain white. A name and a quantum-encrypted contact address. Nothing else.

If you ever notice anything unusual with a zero-point system, she said. Fluctuations that don't fit the noise profile. Oscillation patterns with structure. I would very much want to know.

Theo took the card and turned it in his fingers. Such a small thing. Light as paper. Heavy as a warning.

The pod chimed again. Final deceleration. Arriving Fort Bliss terminal.

Johnson stood. Thank you for listening Colonel. Most people don't want to hear it. They want to believe the well is bottomless and the water is free and nothing lives in the dark at the bottom.

She nodded once and walked back to her seat and Theo sat with the card in his hand and thought about wells and dark rooms and what kind of noise a civilization makes when it borrows from the fabric of things without knowing the lender.

Fort Bliss rose out of the desert like a statement of intent.

Walls and antennas and solar arrays. Reinforced alloys and sensor grids and architecture built not for beauty but for survival. It had been a base. Then a city. Then the city had become a machine and the machine hummed with the specific energy of a nation preparing for something it desperately hoped would not come while knowing in its bones that it would.

The pod docked at a terminal smaller and harder than Dallas's cathedral. No glass prisms. No soaring arches. Concrete and steel and the functional brutality of military engineering. The door opened and the air outside was dry and carried the scent of jet fuel and hot stone and the particular metallic tang of weapons being powered up somewhere out of sight.

Theo stepped out with his duffel and felt the sun on his neck and the ground solid beneath his boots and the desert silence pressing in from every direction.

The sky here had never heard of mercy. It was honest sky. Sky that did not pretend to be anything other than the vast indifferent dome above a world that men were busy destroying while debating whose fault it was.

The terminal's security apparatus was extensive. Armed guards in exosuit frames that added six inches to their height and power to their limbs. Weapons hummed with power cells. Drones patrolled overhead with red sensor eyes sweeping the perimeter in patterns that Theo recognized because he had helped design some of them in another life.

A security officer named Jenkins directed him through the clearance stations. Facial scan. Retinal match. DNA verification. Each checkpoint more stringent than the last. Theo moved through each station with the patience of a man who understood that the machinery existed because the threats were real.

At the final station a full-body scanner pulsed with blue light.

Step inside sir.

Theo entered the chamber and stood still. Beams swept over him. His cybernetic arm tingled as the scanner's electromagnetic field interacted with its sensor array. The two machines talking to each other in a language of frequencies.

An alarm blared. Red lights flashing across the console.

Alert. Unauthorized cybernetic enhancement detected.

Jenkins approached. Tablet in hand. Face stern. Colonel Daniel your prosthetic is triggering our security protocols. We need to verify its components against the cleared database.

It's a Space Force CX-7 prosthetic. Standard military issue. Check your records.

Jenkins scrolled. His brow tightened. Sir the scan is showing a component in the tertiary relay cluster that doesn't appear in your prosthetic's original build manifest. And there's a firmware revision logged six weeks ago that has no corresponding authorization code.

Theo looked at Jenkins. What component.

Jenkins turned the tablet so Theo could see the schematic. A small module in the forearm array, highlighted in amber. No designation tag. No manufacturer code. Just a shape in the diagram that the database did not recognize.

Theo had no explanation. Six weeks ago he had been sanding a chair and riding fence lines and not authorizing firmware updates. He did not say this. He looked at the amber shape on the screen and filed it.

A voice from behind Jenkins cut through the procedural air like sunlight through a crack.

Hold on Jenkins. That's Colonel Daniel.

Technician Maxen emerged from a side corridor. Lab coat bearing the base insignia. Older than Theo remembered. A little thicker. But the same steady hands and the same warm eyes that Theo remembered from an orbital medical bay twenty-three years ago when the world was pain and the absence of his arm was a hole in his body and a hole in his mind.

Maxen had fitted the arm. Had guided him through

months of rehabilitation. Had sat with him during the long nights when the phantom pain was worst and the grief over Jake was a physical thing that occupied the space where his arm had been. Had taught him to control the prosthetic finger by finger, function by function, until the machine became an extension of the man instead of a reminder of the loss.

Maxen, Theo said. The word carried more warmth than he usually allowed in a military facility.

Colonel. Maxen's grin was broad and genuine. A rare thing on a military base where grins were usually tactical. Didn't expect to see you back in the machine.

Maxen glanced at Jenkins's tablet. The amber component. The unauthorized firmware. His expression shifted for a fraction of a second then settled back into competence.

Automatic patch, Maxen said. CX-7 units receive periodic firmware updates through the maintenance network. Sometimes the authorization codes lag behind the actual push. I've seen it a dozen times. The component is probably a diagnostic buffer from the update package. I'll verify it in my lab and log the clearance.

To Jenkins he said, I fitted that arm myself. CX-7 frame with enhanced sensory array and micro-shielding package. It's cleared for all military zone access up to level five. I'll vouch for it because I built it and I know what's in it.

Jenkins hesitated. Protocol states...

Maxen's grin did not waver but the calculation behind it hardened. I wrote the cybernetic clearance protocol for this installation Lieutenant. Log it and let the man through.

Jenkins nodded stiffly and returned to his console.

Maxen led Theo to a side station and connected a diagnostic scanner to the arm's access port. The interface was gentle. Practiced. The touch of a technician who understood that the arm was not just hardware.

Quick check, Maxen said. How's it holding up.

Theo flexed the fingers. Servos whispering. Works fine. Phantom pain sometimes. Mostly at night.

Neural feedback. The brain keeps mapping what's missing. It fades. Mostly. But it's honest pain if that helps.

The scanner ran its course. Maxen studied the readout. His eyes paused on a reading and a quality in his expression shifted, not alarm, not confusion, but the look of a man who had seen something he expected to see and chose not to name. Then he moved on.

All clear, he said. You're good to go. And Colonel. Whatever they're pulling you back in for. You're still the best I ever fitted. That arm is part of you now. Don't let anyone make you feel otherwise.

Theo nodded. The words landing somewhere deep. He did not ask Maxen what the scanner had paused on. Maxen did not volunteer it. Some doors you leave closed because the room behind them changes the shape of every room you've already walked through.

Jenkins returned with a clearance badge and Theo clipped it to his shirt and walked through the final checkpoint and into Fort Bliss proper.

A young lieutenant was waiting. Hayes. Scrubbed and earnest. The look of someone who had studied war extensively and experienced none of it.

Colonel Daniel. General Clark is expecting you. This way sir.

Hayes led him through corridors lit too bright. The institutional fluorescence of a facility that never slept. Past soldiers in exosuit frames running diagnostics. Past technicians hunched over holographic displays showing orbital trajectories and threat assessments. Past quantum-encrypted server banks humming behind reinforced glass. The corridor walls lined with screens projecting data streams in real time. Fleet positions. Energy grid status. Lunar surveillance feeds. The information density of a nation's nervous system compressed into a hallway.

Fort Bliss was not a base anymore. It was a brain. And the brain was thinking hard about a threat it could not yet name.

Hayes stopped at a junction. Major Lee will take you from here sir.

And there he was.

Marcus Lee stepped out of a doorway with that same lopsided grin he had worn on Promethei when the odds were bad and the air was thin and everything was about to go sideways and somehow that was when Lee was at his best. He was broader now. Gray at the temples. A scar across his jaw that had not been there at the academy. Deeper lines. Harder eyes. But the grin was the same. The specific grin of a man who had looked at the worst the universe could offer and decided to find it funny.

Theo Daniel, Lee said. You old bastard.

Marcus Lee. You look terrible.

Lee laughed and gripped his hand. The handshake was hard and sure and became a brief embrace. The kind veterans share. The kind that says I am glad you are alive and I am sorry for the ones who aren't and neither of those things needs to be said aloud.

They walked the corridor together. Lee fell into step beside him and the years fell away. Not completely. Never completely. But enough that the weight shifted. Became something shared.

Jake would have loved this place, Theo said. Looking at

the technology lining the walls. The simulator rigs visible through reinforced windows. The drones on charging stations.

Lee's face softened. He would. He'd be running those simulators until they banned him from the facility.

Theo smiled. He saved your squad once. Did I ever tell you that.

He told me. Every time we talked. Zero modesty. Lee paused. He was the best of us Theo.

Yeah. He was.

Lee was quiet for a moment. He stood at a window overlooking the parade ground where recruits ran formation drills in the afternoon heat and his face held an expression that was not the grin. Still and private and unguarded. The expression of a man measuring the distance between the life he had planned at the academy and the one he was living now. His hand rested on the glass and he watched the recruits below with an attention that was almost paternal. Then it passed and the grin returned and it was as if the other face had never been there at all.

They entered the training wing. Simulator bays lining both walls. Neural-linked rigs where recruits trained in zero-gravity combat scenarios. Virtual reality systems that could replicate any theater of war from the lunar surface to orbital platforms. The rigs were sleeker than Theo's active years. The neural interfaces faster. The simulations indistinguishable from reality until you pulled the helmet off and found yourself still alive.

Lee gestured to a rig. Want to try one. See if the old man still has it.

Theo hesitated. Duty pulling him toward the briefing room. But a frequency stirred. A frequency in his blood. The part of him that had never really retired no matter what the paperwork said or the flannel suggested.

Why not.

He strapped in. The neural helmet synced with his cybernetic arm and the interface sharpened to a clarity that surprised him. The machine in his arm talking to the machine on his head. Two systems finding common language in the space between Theo's thoughts. The simulation materialized around him like a second skin. Lunar space. A zero-point generator platform under attack by enemy drones. Swarm tactics. Adaptive AI. The kind of scenario that killed you in the first thirty seconds if you fought it by the book.

Theo did not fight it by the book.

He maneuvered the virtual interceptor through the drone field with a fluidity that bypassed conscious thought. He deployed countermeasure decoys. Drew the swarm toward a calculated kill zone. Let them commit. Then he did a thing he had not planned. A maneuver that arrived in his hands like a word he did not remember learning. He cut thrust entirely. Let the interceptor drift dead. The drone swarm's targeting algorithms read the dead drift as a kill and broke formation to reacquire priority targets. In the two-second gap Theo reignited from a cold vector and struck the command node from below. An attack angle no academy manual had ever described. The node shattered and the swarm scattered into the void.

The simulation ended. His pulse was elevated. His hands were steady. The helmet's readout showed a score in the top percentile.

Lee whistled low. That dead-drift trick. Where'd you learn that.

Theo unstrapped the helmet slowly. The question hung

in the air between them like a thing with weight. He searched for the answer as you search a house for a sound you heard in the night. Room by room. Finding nothing.

Old habits, he said.

Lee studied him a beat longer than the words warranted. Then he let it go. Still a tactician. Clark's lucky to have you back.

The adrenaline fading. The old skill settling back into his muscles like water finding a channel it had cut long ago. But there was a new channel too. One he had not dug. One that was already there when he arrived.

Come on. Clark's waiting and the man does not like to wait.

The briefing room was a chamber built for decisions that would echo across oceans and orbits and the lives of millions who would never know this room existed.

A large circular table at its center. Holographic projectors lining the ceiling. Walls of reinforced steel and acoustic dampening material that swallowed every sound that was not intended. The air cool and still with the silence of a room where serious people gathered to discuss things that would determine whether other people lived or died.

General Clark stood at the head of the table. White hair. Dark uniform. Stars on his shoulders catching the overhead light. Around him a dozen figures. Officers in Space Force blues with rank insignia and postures that spoke of careers spent in the void. Scientists in civilian dress with the particular fatigue of people who understood things they wished they did not. Intelligence operatives in dark suits with faces trained to reveal nothing.

Clark saw Theo enter and a light moved in the old man's eyes. Relief perhaps. Or the satisfaction of a chess player whose critical piece has arrived on the board.

Colonel Daniel. Thank you for coming.

General.

They shook hands. The grip firm and familiar. A handshake that carried twenty years of shared history and shared loss.

Have a seat. We're about to begin.

Theo sat. His eyes moved around the table cataloging faces. Admiral Rourke from Space Command. Posture rigid as structural steel. A man who had commanded the orbital defense network during the Titan skirmishes and had not lost a single platform. His face carried the confidence of someone who had proven himself in combat and the worry of someone who knew the next fight would be worse.

Dr. Thornhill sat across the table. Energy physicist. Chief engineer of the orbital zero-point generator program. She had Slavic cheekbones from her Russian heritage and tired eyes from too many nights studying things that kept her awake. Her father had been lost to a reactor accident in Novosibirsk. Her brother to radiation exposure during the early zero-point experiments. She carried their absence as Theo carried Jake's medallion. Close to the skin. Always present.

Agent Sheppard from Intelligence occupied the far end of the table. Dark suit. Quiet hands. The kind of person you forgot was in the room until he spoke and then you wished he had stayed quiet because what he said was invariably the worst version of what everyone feared.

Clark activated the holographic table. A three-dimensional model of the Earth-Moon system materialized in light above the surface. The display rotated slowly. Earth blue and green and wrapped in the thin bright line of its atmosphere. Fragile as a soap bubble. The Moon hanging beside it. Gray and cratered and silent. The object of all this attention. All this mobilization. All this carefully controlled fear.

Ladies and gentlemen, Clark said. This comes from National Command Authority. We have operational control of the orbital defense grid by executive delegation as of 0400 this morning.

Everything short of first strike.

He let that settle.

We face a crisis that threatens national security and the stability of the global order. The United States maintains six zero-point energy generators in geostationary orbit. Each supplies approximately one-fifth of our total domestic energy output.

The hologram zoomed in on one of the generators. A colossal structure. Arrays and collectors and containment housings. Energy fields shimmering across its surface like heat haze made visible. Drones orbiting in defensive formations. The architecture of power made manifest in metal and light.

These generators are the backbone, Clark continued. They power our cities. Our industries. Our military infrastructure. Our hospitals and water systems and transportation networks. Without them we don't lose capacity. We lose civilization. Every system downstream of electricity goes dark. And in 2121 every system is downstream of electricity.

Admiral Rourke spoke. Intelligence has intercepted and decoded communications confirming that China and Russia are coordinating a joint military operation to seize these generators. Their combined fleets are repositioning in lunar space. We assess that an attack could come within days. Possibly hours.

The room held its silence. The hologram rotated. The

Earth below it looked small. It had always been small. People just kept forgetting.

What's their endgame, Theo asked.

Control, Clark said. Capture the generators and you hold the world's energy supply at ransom. You dictate terms. You redraw the geopolitical map with a pen made of darkness.

Agent Sheppard spoke for the first time. His voice quiet and flat.

There's more.

He activated a secondary display. Grainy footage. Enhanced orbital imagery of a Chinese warship in lunar space. The vessel was visible for three frames. Then it vanished from sensors entirely.

Advanced stealth capability, Sheppard said. That's not the primary concern. Signals intelligence has identified encrypted communications referencing a weapon system designated Quantum Disruptor. We believe it is designed to generate targeted disturbances in the quantum vacuum. Specifically calibrated to interfere with zero-point energy containment fields.

Clark nodded to Thornhill.

Thornhill stood. She activated a diagram on the holographic display. Fields and particles and the mathematics of zero-point extraction projected in colored light.

Our generators extract energy from the quantum vacuum, she said. The process requires precise containment. The vacuum wants equilibrium. We disturb that equilibrium to draw power. A quantum disruptor would introduce targeted resonance into the containment architecture. The extraction process destabilizes. Oscillations compound. Cascade failure.

She paused.

In practice it means an uncontrolled release of energy sufficient to destroy the platform and everything within a significant radius.

Define significant, Admiral Rourke said.

Depending on the generator's output at the moment of failure. Hundreds of kilometers. In orbit that translates to a debris field that would threaten every asset in the orbital band.

How far along are they, Theo asked.

Experimental, Sheppard said. Prototype stage. But intelligence suggests they may attempt to deploy it in conjunction with the fleet action. Even a prototype fired at close range during combat could destabilize a generator during peak output.

A datapad slid off someone's stack and clattered against the table. An aide fumbled to retrieve it, knocking a stylus to the floor. Somewhere behind Theo a coffee mug trembled faintly against its saucer from the hand that held it. The small disorders of people running on too little sleep and too much certainty that sleep would not be coming soon.

Theo's mind was already moving. Parsing geometry. Running scenarios. The old machine in his head spinning to operational speed. The gears engaging with a smoothness that surprised him and did not surprise him at all.

Show me the current defensive grid, he said.

Clark nodded and the hologram shifted. The six generators in their orbital positions. Each surrounded by a web of defenses. Pulse cannon satellites in tight formation. Autonomous drone swarms in layered patterns. Energy shields calibrated to deflect kinetic and electromagnetic attacks. Multi-spectrum sensor arrays scanning every frequency.

Theo studied it. His eyes moving from position to position. His cybernetic fingers tapping a slow rhythm on the table.

You've upgraded the sensor coverage, he said. Multispectrum. Good. But here. He pointed to a quadrant of the grid where the satellite coverage thinned between two generator stations. The defensive geometry stretched to its limit. And here. A second gap on the far orbital flank. Coverage is thin. The drone response time between these positions exceeds the engagement window for a coordinated first strike. An enemy exploiting both vectors simultaneously could overwhelm local defenses before reinforcements reposition.

Rourke raised an eyebrow. What do you propose.

Decoy generators, Theo said. The solution arriving whole. Not assembled from parts but delivered from some deeper process that worked faster than thought. Take decommissioned satellite platforms. Retrofit them to broadcast zero-point energy signatures identical to the operational generators. Electromagnetic profile. Thermal output. Containment field resonance. Make them indistinguishable on sensors. Deploy them in the gap zones. Now instead of six targets the enemy sees eight. Maybe ten. They have to verify each target before committing weapons. They have to divide their force concentration.

Thornhill's eyes widened. That's viable. We can replicate the electromagnetic and thermal signatures with relatively straightforward modifications to existing decommissioned hardware. Their sensors would need close-range verification to distinguish the decoys from the real generators.

Which costs them time, Theo said. And in a first-strike scenario time is the only currency that matters. Every minute they spend verifying targets is a minute we use to redeploy drones and reinforce the actual defensive positions.

Clark studied him across the table. The old man's face unreadable except for the faintest trace at the corners of his mouth. Not quite a smile. The expression of a man whose gamble on bringing in a retired colonel was paying off in real time.

What about the disruptor, Clark asked.

Theo looked at Thornhill. Can you modulate the containment frequency. Rotate it on a randomized cycle. If the disruptor is calibrated to a specific resonance point then a moving target is harder to lock.

Thornhill considered. It would reduce generator efficiency by eight to twelve percent during the rotation cycle. But yes. A randomized frequency rotation would make disruptor targeting significantly more difficult. They'd need to recalibrate for each shift.

Do it, Clark said.

The briefing continued. Strategy layered on strategy. Contingencies mapped and debated and discarded and rebuilt. Theo worked through every sector of the defensive grid. Proposed upgrades to the autonomous drone algorithms drawing on his experience countering pirate hacking operations in the asteroid belt. Identified cyber vulnerabilities in the communication relays. The room came alive with the energy of competent people working at the edge of their capacity toward a goal that mattered.

Then Thornhill spoke again. Quieter. As though what she was about to say had been waiting for an opening and had finally found one.

There's something else. Unrelated to the current tactical situation. Or perhaps not. I want it on the record.

Clark looked at her.

We've been tracking intermittent containment oscillations across the entire global zero-point network for the past several months. Military installations. Civilian power plants. Commercial systems. Minor events. Self-correcting. Every facility reports them. The Energy Commission classifies them as standard sensor drift.

Lee spoke from his seat. Telemetry ghost spikes. We've seen them in the orbital platforms too. Brief anomalies in the energy telemetry. Engineering logs them as instrument noise.

Thornhill nodded. That's the standard classification. But I've run a comparative analysis across every installation we've examined. The same base frequency. And that frequency has been slowly but measurably increasing in amplitude over the past six months.

She activated a new display. A waveform traced in blue light across the holographic field. It looked like noise. Random oscillation. The kind of static that any engineer would dismiss with a note in a log.

Then she overlaid a filter. Stripped the random components. Revealed what was underneath.

The waveform had structure. A repeating pattern. Rising amplitude followed by a precise interval of silence followed by a second pulse at a different frequency followed by the same interval. The same sequence. Again and again. Buried in the noise like a sentence hidden in a page of random letters.

The room was very quiet.

Is this a threat to current operations, Clark asked.

Not at present levels, she said. But I want it documented. If we push these generators to maximum sustained output the oscillations may intensify. And we do not fully understand what is generating them. They don't correlate with any known interference source. Not solar activity. Not electromagnetic pollution. Not mechanical wear.

Clark held her gaze. The old general weighing the information before deciding whether to act on it or set it aside.

Log it, he said. Monitor it. Flag any deviation from the current pattern. This stays on the secondary tracking board. Our primary threat is a combined fleet in lunar orbit with stealth capability and a weapon that can shut our lights off. That is where our focus stays.

Thornhill sat down. Her face composed. But Theo saw a darkness in her eyes that the composition could not hide. The specific darkness of a scientist who suspects she is looking at the edge of something vast and cannot get anyone else to look with her.

Theo thought of Dr. Johnson on the hyperloop. Her card in his pocket. The weight of the word listening. He thought of Ava's pause at 3:14 in the morning. The anomalous energy signatures in the eleven-second news segment. The drone that had stuttered in midair above the eastern pasture. The forty-seven seconds of missing footage. The serial number that had flickered to a string he did not recognize. The firmware update he had not authorized. The arm that had adjusted pressure on wood grain without being asked. The dead-drift maneuver that his hands had executed without consulting his memory.

He said nothing. There was nothing yet to say. But the inventory was growing and he kept it as a man keeps accounts. Precise. Current. Ready for the day when the numbers demand reckoning.

The briefing adjourned late. The windows showing full dark. The desert night beyond the base stretching vast and black and pricked with stars that burned with the ancient patient fire of things that had been burning since before the first human looked up and wondered.

The officers filed out. Comm officers coordinating with orbital teams. Engineers with tablets already running calculations. Thornhill heading to her lab to begin the containment frequency modulation protocols. The room emptied around them until it was just Clark and Theo and the fading holograms.

Clark's voice was lower now.

I know what I'm asking, Clark said.

You've already asked it.

I'm asking more. Go up. Lead the defense team from the platform itself. In orbit. Your presence there would make a difference that no simulation or remote consultation can match. The troops know your record. The engineers trust your judgment. And you just redesigned their entire defensive architecture in two hours while sitting in a chair drinking coffee that wasn't even hot.

Theo looked at the window. The stars. The desert dark. The void above that was not empty but full of machines and weapons and the ambitions of nations and the quiet hum of generators drawing power from the fabric of spacetime itself.

I'm retired General. Promethei took my arm. It took my best friend. It took a piece of me that the surgeons couldn't replace no matter how good the carbon nanotubes are.

Clark's voice softened. Lost the commanding edge. Became the voice of one old soldier talking to another.

I was there when you came home Theo. I visited you in that medical bay. I saw what it cost. But I need to tell you something I've never said to anyone in forty years of service. During the Martian uprising I gave an order that got seventeen soldiers killed. Good people. Friends. It never goes away. You carry it every day. But you learn to carry it for the ones who still need you to be strong enough to make the call.

Theo was quiet.

I have a ranch, he said. People depending on me.

I have a daughter, Clark said. Grandkids who call me Pop and think I'm indestructible. If those generators fall it's over for them. For your niece and nephew. For every child who's ever going to look up at the stars and ask someone to teach them the names. You know what's at stake.

Theo reached into his pocket and felt the medallion. The worn edge of Jake's star against his thumb. Jake who had not hesitated. Who had seen the grenade and made his choice in half a second and had not looked back because looking back was not in his nature.

In the other pocket he felt Dr. Johnson's card. The two objects sat on opposite sides of his body. Duty and doubt. The known cost and the unknown variable. He did not need to choose between them. He had been carrying both for longer than he realized.

Theo exhaled.

I'll need to secure my ranch. Notify my family.

Done, Clark said. Anything you need.

Alright, Theo said. I'll do it.

Clark gripped his shoulder. The grip hard and sure. The grip of a man who understood the weight of what he had asked and was grateful and would carry the knowledge of that debt until he died.

The stars on his file said Colonel. The stars had come after Promethei, after the orbital campaigns, after the years of service that followed the years of screaming into rehabilitation fields. At Promethei he had been a Captain. The rank that got men killed. The Colonel had been built from the

Captain's wreckage and the Colonel was what they needed now.

Knew I could count on you, Clark said.

Clark left.

Theo walked into the corridor. The hallway was quiet now. The briefing's energy dissipated into the fluorescent hum of the base at night.

Sheppard fell into step beside him. He did not look at Theo. He watched the hallway ahead as if he were not sure it was empty. Intelligence has flagged anomalous data transfers over the past several months, he said. His voice pitched below the ambient hum of the base. Someone with logistics-level access has been feeding ZPE grid telemetry to an outside party. Maintenance windows. Vulnerability assessments. Grid node locations. We have not confirmed who. We have not confirmed which side is receiving. Theo looked at him. His face gave him nothing. He was watching everyone and he told Theo so without telling him so. Theo filed it. Sheppard turned down a side corridor and was gone and the hallway was just a hallway again.

He was assigned quarters down the corridor. A spartan room. A cot. A desk. A window looking out on the desert. He set his duffel on the floor and sat on the cot and did not unpack.

He pulled out his communicator and opened a message to Clara. The blank field waited. The cursor blinked with the patience of a machine that did not understand urgency or grief or the difficulty of translating love into text.

He typed: I'm safe. Don't worry. Tell Knox I'll bring that space rock. Tell Luna the stars are waiting for her.

He sent it. Set the communicator on the desk. Lay back on the cot.

The ceiling was blank and white and offered nothing.

He thought of Jake. Of the grenade's flash. Of the silence after. He thought of the ranch and its quiet fields and the cattle under drone watch and the chair he had been sanding that morning.

He thought of the serial number that had flickered to a designation he did not recognize. The firmware update that had appeared without origin.

He took Dr. Johnson's card from his pocket and held it up in the dim light. Plain white. A name. A contact. The word she had used was borrows. The question she had asked was whether the room was empty.

The word Thornhill had not used but had meant was pattern.

Six generators in orbit. Thousands more on the ground. All drawing from the quantum vacuum. All producing oscillations that shared a common frequency. A frequency that was rising. A frequency that had grammar.

He set the card on the desk beside the communicator and did not think about what the grammar was saying. Not yet. He did not need to understand everything to act. He had never needed that. Understanding was a luxury that came after survival if it came at all. What he needed was simpler and older. The willingness to stand where he was put and do what needed doing and trust that the ground beneath him was solid enough to hold. Whether or not the ground was what it appeared to be.

The door to his old life had closed. He felt it. Not a sound exactly. More like the absence of one. The silence that fills the space where a familiar noise used to be. The quiet that follows a threshold crossed. A decision made. A contract signed not in ink but in the act of standing up and saying yes when every part of you wanted to say no.

He closed his eyes.

The base hummed around him. The energy of a nation bracing itself against a storm it could see building on the horizon. Corridors full of soldiers and scientists and the specific tension of people who know that the next days will define decades.

And somewhere in the deep machinery of the world. In the generators and the containment fields and the quantum vacuum itself. A frequency pulsed. Faint. Patient. Structured. Growing. Its grammar repeating like a phrase spoken into darkness by a voice that did not need to breathe.

A stirring in the fabric of things. Not a sound. Not a signal. Older and stranger and more vast than the men who had unwittingly called to it.

And in the spartan room at Fort Bliss, in the circuitry of a cybernetic arm that a sleeping man had never fully understood, a circuit received that frequency. Held it for one pulse. And let it go.

The darkness took him and the nightmares came but in this version Jake said a different thing before the gullies. A third thing. A thing Theo would not remember in the morning. The dead revised their scripts nightly and the living did not get a vote.

CHAPTER 3

FIRST STRIKE

The platform had been the plan. Then the summit was called and Clark needed him on the ground first. The orbit would come after, if there was an after.

The floor reflected the ceiling without a seam or scuff. That was the first thing. The walls met at angles so precise they looked machined rather than built and every surface gleamed with a uniformity that had no origin in nature. No cracks in the stone. No variation in the grain. The building did not look constructed. It looked rendered.

The Global Summit Center rose from the Geneva skyline like a glass cathedral, its walls programmed to project the sky it had replaced. Flags hung from wires in the lobby and moved in manufactured wind and the sound they made was the sound of cloth pretending it had somewhere to go. Outside the tinted panels the city went on being a city but in here the light was wrong and the air tasted of nothing and the silence between handshakes carried more freight than the words.

Theo stood three paces behind General Clark and watched the room the way he had once watched Martian ridgelines. Scanning. Counting exits. Marking the ones who carried tension in their shoulders versus the ones who wore it in their smiles. His left arm hummed beneath his sleeve, the carbon nanotube weave registering barometric pressure and signal traffic and the faint electromagnetic signatures of concealed devices. The arm did not care about diplomacy. It read the room in a language older than language.

The diplomatic staff moved with rehearsed calm. Their shoes were quiet on the polished stone. Their faces showed nothing that had not been tested in mirrors first. Translators stood at intervals like human relay stations, murmuring conversions between tongues that said the same things in different accents of fear.

A holographic projection of the Moon turned above the central dais, the Sea of Tranquility mapped in pale blue, a red line drawn through it like a wound that would not close. Helium-3 claim boundaries. Treaties made into geometry. From here the Moon looked like a decoration.

Clark leaned toward an aide and murmured words Theo could not hear. The aide's face tightened by a degree and she moved off through the crowd. Clark's jaw was set the way it set when he was choosing between bad options. Theo had seen that jaw at Fort Bliss. He had seen it in the briefing rooms of the old wars. It meant the mathematics had been run and the answers were all the same number.

The Chinese delegation entered through the eastern doors. They moved as a group. A dozen figures in dark suits and military dress, their formation tight, their faces composed. Security flanked them, big men with earpieces and eyes that did not blink enough. At the center walked a man of medium height with close-cropped gray hair and a bearing that said he had spent decades being the calmest person in rooms designed to test calm.

Colonel Liang Wei.

Clark's chin lifted slightly.

They met at the edge of the dais where the holographic moonlight cast no shadows. Liang's face was lean and weathered. Creases around his eyes that came from squinting at targets through field scopes and from smiling at his daughter when she showed him drawings. His uniform bore no decoration beyond rank insignia and a small pin that Theo recognized as a service medal from the asteroid skirmishes of ninety-five. A shared history in miniature. Theo carried his own version in the form of an arm that was not flesh and a friend who was not alive.

Liang's translator stood one step behind and to his left. A young woman with a wireless earpiece and a face trained to show nothing. Her lips moved in the half-second delay that followed each of Liang's words, converting Mandarin to English with machine-assisted fluency. But the timing was wrong. Theo watched her mouth form the English syllables a fraction before Liang's Mandarin reached the end of its sentence. Not after. Before. As if the translation were arriving ahead of the source. As if she already knew what Liang would say.

Theo's eyes moved to Liang. Liang was already looking at him. Not at Clark. At Theo. Watching to see if Theo had noticed.

They held the look for one second. Neither man spoke. Neither man nodded. The look acknowledged a truth that lived beneath the architecture of the summit and beneath the protocols and the translated courtesies.

General Clark, Liang said. His English was unhurried and unaccented. The product of years spent in rooms like this one talking to men like Clark about things that mattered enough to kill for. Colonel Daniel.

Theo nodded once.

Liang's gaze moved to Theo's left sleeve. Not a stare. A professional assessment. The way a mechanic reads wear on a bearing. The way a soldier reads another soldier's wounds. Liang had seen prosthetics before. He knew what they replaced and what they could not.

My daughter watches the feeds, Liang said. She is twelve. She calls you a hero of Promethei.

Theo said nothing.

Heroes are useful, Liang said. They make people willing to accept what comes next.

Clark stepped forward half a pace. We are here to make sure what comes next does not require heroes.

Liang's mouth moved. Not a smile. The memory of one. He had a daughter who called Theo a hero and he had a family in Shanghai whose lights depended on fusion grids that were already failing and he had orders from a government that had decided what it could live with and what it could not. He was not a villain. He was a man with arithmetic.

The deposit lies within coordinates established by the 2087 Accord, Liang said. You know this.

You know we dispute the interpretation, Clark said.

Dispute does not change chemistry, Liang said. Helium-3 changes everything. Whoever controls it controls the next fifty years. I have thirty million people in Shanghai whose grid cannot survive another winter without upgraded fusion capacity. My daughter depends on that grid for medical equipment she needs to live. This is not abstract for me.

Clark held his ground. It is not abstract for us either.

Liang studied him. Then I hope your people understand what it means when one side has already decided.

There was a silence between them that was not the absence of words but the presence of understanding. Both men knew what was coming. Both men had known before they entered the building. The summit was theater performed for the cameras and the history books and the people who still needed to believe that language could prevent what physics had already set in motion.

Liang turned to go. Then he stopped. He reached into his breast pocket and produced a photograph. Not a hologram. A printed photograph. Old technology. The kind of thing a man carries when he wants to hold something real.

My daughter, he said. Mei. She draws pictures. She is always drawing.

He held it up. It was a child's drawing on paper. Two stick figures under a sky full of stars. One figure wore a uniform. The other was smaller and held the first figure's hand. Between the stars someone had drawn a shape that was neither star nor sun. It had points like a star but the points curved inward at the tips. A star with teeth. The kind of thing a child draws and cannot explain and the parent holds in the night after the child is sleeping and studies under the lamp, turning the paper, looking at the shape, waiting for the wrongness to resolve into something familiar.

She drew that one last week, Liang said. The stars and the two of us I understand. The other thing she will not explain. She says it came from a dream. He folded the photograph along its crease. Children dream of strange things.

Theo felt Jake's medallion against his thigh through the pocket fabric. He thought of Knox holding his sleeve and asking for a space rock. He thought of a twelve-year-old girl drawing a shape that had no name in careful strokes on paper, her tongue between her teeth, concentrating on something she had seen behind her eyes and was trying to make real.

Liang put the photograph away. She believes in things, he said. Children believe in things because they have not yet learned what the world does to the things it cannot use. He adjusted his breast pocket. I would prefer that she keep believing.

He inclined his head slightly. It was almost a bow. It was the gesture of a man acknowledging another man's burden.

He walked away.

Clark watched him go. That man is going to be a problem, Clark said.

Theo watched Liang's back disappear into the Chinese delegation. That man is a father, he said.

Clark glanced at him. So are we all. It does not change the mathematics.

A moderator called them to the table. Cameras adjusted. Smiles came on like lights. The room filled with the sound of chairs being pulled back and bodies settling into positions they would hold until the positions broke.

Theo sat behind Clark in the second row and opened his wrist display beneath the table's edge. Secure telemetry scrolled. Orbital Platform Alpha. Relay stations. Lunar defense nodes. Generator status across the distributed ZPE array. The numbers looked clean. They always looked clean right before they didn't.

A flagged message blinked from Fort Bliss operations.

UNUSUAL EM SIGNATURES. LOW AMPLITUDE. DISTRIBUTED PATTERN. NON-STANDARD FREQUENCY.

Theo read it twice. He remembered Ava's pause on the ranch. He remembered the scientist at Fort Bliss explaining containment drift in the careful language of someone who did not want to name what they were seeing. The Energy Commission's standing classification for anything it did not want to explain was sensor noise. He had heard the phrase enough times that it had become a kind of prayer.

He closed the message.

A second arrived.

CONTACTS MOVING. MULTIPLE VECTORS. LUNAR APPROACH CORRIDOR. CLASSIFICATION PENDING.

His skin went tight against his bones.

At the table the U.S. delegate was laying out terms. Shared stewardship of the Sea of Tranquility deposits. Mutual access corridors. Revenue structures based on extraction volume. China's delegate responded with equal precision. Sovereignty under the 2087 framework. Historical precedent. Regional energy security. Russia proposed joint extraction. Equal shares. A multilateral framework. The proposal sounded reasonable and meant nothing because the ships were already moving and the orders had already been given and the words in this room were sounds made to fill time until the silence came.

Theo watched Liang. The Colonel sat with his hands flat on the table. He was not looking at the speakers. He was looking past them. At some calculus that had already finished running.

On Theo's wrist the telemetry shifted. The pending contacts resolved into confirmed tracks. Six vessels. Then eight. Then twelve. Moving in coordinated burns from behind the Moon's far side in formations that were not patrol patterns. They were attack vectors.

He pushed a note to Clark through the encrypted channel.

Multiple contacts. Lunar orbit. Coordinated trajectory. Not ours. Consistent with strike formation.

Clark did not move. Only his eyes changed. A contraction so slight that no camera would catch it. He tapped a single acknowledgment and continued talking about mutual prosperity in a voice that betrayed nothing.

The moderator called a recess. People stood. Conversations broke apart into smaller clusters. A server offered drinks from a tray and the glasses caught the holographic moonlight and threw it back in shapes that looked like mathematics.

Across the hall Liang Wei stood before the secondary display where the ZPE generator grid was rendered in schematic. He studied it with the slow attention of a man reading a map he intended to walk. His aide, a young officer with a thin face and careful hands, moved away from a comm terminal near the eastern wall, folding a datapad into his jacket as he returned to Liang's side. Sheppard, standing two clusters away with his arms crossed and his augmented lenses dimmed to black, watched the aide rejoin Liang. His eyes met Theo's across the room. Neither spoke. Neither needed to.

Clark motioned Theo toward a secure room behind the conference hall. The walls were thick and dead to signals. A tactical display unfolded from the table surface, its projectors throwing the Earth-Moon system into the air between them.

Red icons were blooming across lunar orbit. More than twelve now. A second formation vectoring from low Earth transfer orbits. A third cluster decelerating from a trajectory that suggested they had been in position for days, drifting cold with systems down to avoid detection.

The comms officer was young. She had red hair pulled tight and her face had the color of someone who had just seen a screen rewrite her future.

General, she said. Orbital Platform Alpha reports incoming. Multiple projectiles and electronic warfare signatures. Kinetic rail impacts expected within minutes. They are requesting tactical override authority.

Clark stared at the display.

Minutes, he repeated.

Yes sir. The fleet accelerated thirty seconds ago. They have committed.

Clark turned to Theo. A recognition passed between them that was older than rank. The understanding of men who had been in rooms when the rooms stopped being rooms and became decisions. When the walls stopped being walls and became the last place you stood before the world divided itself into before and after.

They chose, Clark said.

Yes, Theo said.

He felt his body settle into the architecture it had learned at Promethei Terra. The calm that came not from peace but from the complete absence of any option except action. His pulse slowed. His breathing flattened. The cybernetic arm hummed at a frequency only he could feel, its systems upshifting to combat readiness, the synthetic muscle fibers tightening along the forearm, the haptic sensors sharpening.

Authorize countermeasures, Theo said.

Clark hesitated one second.

Authorize, Theo said again.

Clark nodded. Do it.

The officer's hands moved. Codes entered. Confirmations requested and given. The display filled with interceptor trajectories, point defense arcs, shield power curves, drone deployment patterns. The mathematics of survival drawn in light.

Clark opened a direct channel to Alpha. The connection was degraded, bitten by interference that should not have been there, and the voice that came through was tight and professional and already in the fight.

Alpha to Summit. We are engaged. Multiple kinetic inbound. Electronic warfare saturating our comms. Shields holding. Drones deploying.

Colonel Daniel has tactical authority, Clark said.

Acknowledged, the voice said.

Theo leaned into the display. He knew Orbital Platform Alpha. He had helped design its defense model three years ago in a simulation room at Fort Bliss when the threat was theoretical and Jake Ramsey's ghost sat in the empty chair beside him. Two hundred AI-driven drones. Twelve high-energy laser turrets. Eight missile batteries. Shield generators drawing from the orbital ZPE array. Point defense systems capable of tracking a thousand objects simultaneously.

He also knew the fractures. The gaps in the drone coverage at the junctions between sectors three and seven. The two-second latency in the shield generators when they rerouted power. The vulnerability of the ZPE feed to targeted disruption. He had written a memo about those fractures years ago and nothing had changed because changing it cost money and money required consensus and consensus required time that no one had because the threat was theoretical.

The threat was no longer theoretical.

Deploy drone screen in delta formation, Theo said. Concentrate point defense on the first wave. They will probe with expendables before they commit the heavy ordnance. Reserve missiles. Do not waste them on drones.

He pulled up the decoy protocol he had designed at Fort Bliss. Four dummy generator signatures broadcast from relay satellites at the margins of the defense perimeter. Ghost targets. Heat and electromagnetic profiles that would read as active ZPE installations to enemy sensors but were nothing more than signal emitters bolted to communication arrays.

Activate the decoy generators, Theo said. Full spectrum broadcast. Make them look real.

The officer on Alpha acknowledged. On the display four new blue icons appeared at the perimeter, each one projecting the electromagnetic fingerprint of an operational zero-point generator. Any weapon targeting ZPE signatures would have to choose between eight targets instead of four.

The orders went out at the speed of light and two hundred drones spread from Alpha like seeds thrown into darkness. Each one a fist of laser and kinetic slug and targeting software that could track a bolt in flight and return fire before a human could blink.

The first enemy wave hit the drone screen and the display lit up like a storm.

Rail slugs traveling at six kilometers per second, each one a finger of tungsten and ceramics that struck with the force of a car crash compressed into a point. Guided projectiles that split into submunitions at terminal approach, each fragment seeking its own target. The point defense lasers carved bright lines through the dark and the drone screen absorbed the first impacts. Detonations bloomed in silence. White flashes that expanded and died in the vacuum's grip.

A drone took a rail slug through its central processor and split into two halves that tumbled apart in slow rotation, each half still broadcasting its telemetry to an AI that had already reassigned its sector.

Three drones destroyed. Seven damaged. The screen held. The delta formation closed around the gaps like tissue closing around a wound.

Good, Theo said. Hold the screen. Tighten the delta on the approach corridor.

He watched the enemy's expendable wave expend itself against the drone screen and felt the rhythm of it. The probing. The measuring. The attack came in pulses rather than a continuous stream. Someone on the other side was watching the response pattern and learning from it.

A second wave followed the first. Heavier. Faster. The vectors were wrong for human piloting. Too precise. Too adaptive. The attack patterns shifted in real time, probing the drone screen for gaps and flowing toward the cracks.

Vostok, the comms officer said. Her voice carried the particular tone of someone identifying a threat they had hoped was still theoretical. Russian adaptive warfare AI. It is commanding their drone fleet.

Theo had read the intelligence on Vostok at Fort Bliss. Agent Sheppard had briefed him with his augmented lenses flickering as he scrolled through classified intercepts. A neural combat network. Self-modifying tactical architecture. It learned from every engagement and never repeated a failed approach. It could command ten thousand units simultaneously and coordinate them with a coherence that human commanders could not match. Sheppard had called it the closest thing to a combat mind that was not human.

The Vostok drones moved differently from anything Theo had seen. They did not attack in formations. They attacked in conversations. Groups of ten or twelve would engage a sector while other groups watched and measured and adjusted. The swarm had no fixed structure. It was liquid. It poured itself against the defense screen and wherever it found resistance it pulled back and wherever it found weakness it pressed and every second it was learning.

Shift drone screen to reactive pattern, Theo ordered. Match their adaptation speed. Vary the response so the AI cannot model us.

Alpha's tactical AI adjusted. For thirty seconds the two swarms circled each other in a dance that was beautiful and terrible, silicon minds probing each other at speeds that made human thought a relic. Drones died on both sides and their wreckage spun away into the dark.

During the hack attempt on sector four, where Alpha's tactical AI was trying to penetrate a Vostok command node, Theo's arm interface flickered. For one-tenth of a second the display showed not Alpha's feed but something else — a flattened omnidirectional view of the battle from a dozen perspectives at once, and beneath the data a low hum that was not sound but a resonance like sorrow, and then it was gone and the display was his again and the battle continued.

Marcus Lee's voice cut through the tactical channel. His squadron was flying interceptors on Alpha's port flank, engaging enemy corvettes that were trying to close range on the platform.

Corvette group breaking through on sector five, Lee said. His voice was the voice Theo remembered from Promethei. Steady. Clear. Engaging now. Could use some help over here.

Redirect drone flight Charlie to sector five, Theo said. Support Lee's group. Keep those corvettes off the platform.

The drones shifted. Lee's interceptors flared their

engines and dove into the enemy formation. A corvette broke apart under concentrated fire, its hull splitting silently, atmosphere venting in a cloud that froze instantly into crystals that caught the distant sun.

Theo noted a tactical option he did not recognize forming in his mind. A flanking deployment through the debris field that would use the wreckage as sensor cover. He had not learned it. It was not in any manual he had studied. It worked. He issued the order without naming its origin.

Then the quantum disruptor fired.

It did not look like a weapon. It looked like a wrongness. A distortion in the display, as if the light itself had been dragged sideways through a medium that should not have existed.

The disruptor beam originated from a vessel at the rear of the enemy formation. Its bow dominated by a spherical projector that pulsed with a light that was not any light Theo had seen. A frequency that tugged at the eye and at the instruments and at the fabric of local spacetime in a way that the sensors could measure but not classify.

The first beam struck a decoy.

The relay satellite absorbed the pulse and died. The decoy had worked. The disruptor had wasted a shot on a ghost.

Theo exhaled. The mathematics of confusion. Buy time. Make them guess.

The disruptor recharged. Eight seconds between pulses. It fired again. A second decoy burst apart, its emitter array fused into slag by energy that operated at the quantum level.

Two decoys down. Two remaining. Four real generators exposed.

The disruptor's targeting hesitated. On the display the spherical projector cycled through frequencies, scanning, probing the remaining targets. Vostok was learning. The AI was analyzing the signatures, comparing the decoys' electromagnetic profiles to the real generators, searching for the discrepancies that would tell it which targets mattered.

Theo felt the window closing.

Vostok's drones shifted. A cluster broke away from the main engagement and vectored toward the remaining decoys. They did not attack. They scanned. They measured. And then the data flowed back to the disruptor vessel and on the display Theo watched the weapon's targeting array swivel away from the decoys and lock onto Generator Seven.

The decoys had bought them ninety seconds. It was not enough.

The disruptor fired at the real target.

The beam struck Generator Seven and the effect was not an explosion. It was a collapse. The generator's containment field destabilized. The zero-point vacuum energy it had been harvesting turned against its own architecture. The massive structure shuddered and went still. Its arrays dimmed. Its output flatlined.

On Earth, power grids tied to that generator's output stuttered. Cascading failures rippled through relay stations from the eastern seaboard to the Gulf Coast. Lights died in cities that had never known darkness. Hospital backup generators kicked in and then some of those failed too because the backup systems relied on satellite coordination that relied on the orbital infrastructure that was burning.

Generator Seven offline, the comms officer said. Cascade failures in the North American eastern relay network. Partial grid collapse across seven states.

The disruptor recharged. A second pulse hit Generator Four. The same collapse. A different set of cities going dark.

This was the weapon Sheppard had warned about. It did

not need to destroy the platform. It needed only to destroy what the platform protected. The generators were the heart. Kill the heart and the body follows.

Get me Thornhill, Theo said. Now.

Dr. Thornhill's voice came through from the USS Defender, where she had been monitoring the ZPE array remotely. Her words were clipped and precise and carried the controlled fear of a scientist watching her own theory become catastrophe.

The disruptor is inducing targeted decoherence in the generators' quantum containment fields, she said. It is matching the resonant frequency of our vacuum extraction architecture. If I can isolate the carrier wave I can generate a counter-oscillation that cancels the decoherence effect.

How long, Theo said.

Minutes.

We do not have minutes. The next pulse fires in seconds.

Then I will be fast.

On the display Marcus Lee had seen the disruptor vessel and understood what it was doing without being told. He knew that some weapons changed the shape of the fight and that the only answer to such weapons was to kill them before they could fire again.

He was already vectoring his interceptor squadron toward the disruptor vessel, pulling his three remaining ships off the corvette engagement, burning fuel at a rate that left no margin for retreat. The interceptors were fast and lightly armored and they depended on speed and angle to survive. Lee was not withdrawing.

His squadron flew through a field of debris that had been drones minutes ago. A Vostok drone swarm vectored to intercept them and Lee's wingman peeled off to draw the swarm away, firing pulse rounds into the mass of machines.

The wingman's ship took three hits in rapid succession. The first cracked the canopy seal. The second killed the starboard engine. The third opened the cockpit to vacuum. The ship spun and went dark.

Lee did not slow down.

His voice came through hard and clean.

Closing on the disruptor platform. Fire is heavy. Lost two on approach. Their shield is absorbing our weapons. We need a different angle.

Theo studied the display. The disruptor vessel was large. Its shield drew from the same power source as the projector. Physics demanded a trade. When the weapon charged, the shield had to thin. The power could not be in two places at once.

Marcus, Theo said. The shield drops when the weapon fires. That is your window.

How long a window.

About two seconds.

The channel went quiet for a beat.

Two seconds, Lee said. Copy that.

Theo watched the tactical display and counted heartbeats. The disruptor vessel's energy readings began to climb. The projector glowed brighter.

Lee's interceptors banked hard. Three ships. Engines at full burn. Closing distance with the kind of commitment that only men who have accepted a binary outcome can sustain.

The disruptor fired.

Lee fired in the same breath.

Kinetic slugs and pulse laser beams struck the projector housing at the instant the shield thinned. The first salvo cracked the housing. The second penetrated. The projector core ruptured in a cascade of secondary explosions that produced light and debris and silence.

The projector went dark. The disruptor beam died midpulse. The third generator it had been targeting shuddered but held.

Disruptor offline, Lee reported. His voice carried no triumph. Only the exhaustion of a man who had spent everything he had on two seconds.

In the same breath Thornhill's counter-oscillation activated. A signal broadcast from the Defender that matched the disruptor's carrier frequency and inverted it. The remaining generators' containment fields stabilized. The cascade slowed and stopped.

Containment restoring, she said. Generators responding. The oscillation is flattening. It is holding.

But the battle was not over. The Chinese-Russian fleet pressed the attack without the disruptor, fighting conventionally now, but they had numbers and Vostok still commanded their drones. The adaptive AI had learned from every exchange and its swarms were faster and more coordinated than they had been at the start. The fighting continued in the cold dark for another ninety minutes. Ships burned. Platforms took damage. Men and women died in suits and in cockpits and at consoles and their deaths were recorded as dimming icons on displays that did not pause to note what had been lost.

Lee lost another interceptor. He did not report the pilot's name.

The drone screen thinned. Point defense turrets overheated and went to standby. Missile batteries expended their stocks. Alpha's shields dropped to forty percent and held there through a combination of Thornhill's power management and the raw stubbornness of engineers who refused to let the numbers win.

Then the enemy fleet pulled back. The withdrawal was coordinated and precise. Vostok's drones disengaged in a pattern that was almost courteous, peeling away in waves that protected the retreating capital ships. They vanished behind the Moon's terminator line and the sensors lost them in the electromagnetic shadow of the far side.

Alpha held. Barely. Its hull was scarred and breached in three sections and its drone count was down to eighty-seven and two of its turrets were fused slag and the corridor outside the command center was open to vacuum and seventeen men and women were dead and their bodies were drifting in the sections that had lost pressure. But it held.

Marcus Lee docked his surviving interceptor with its fuel gauge reading empty and its hull scoring deep enough to see wiring. He climbed out and his hands were shaking and he stood in the hangar bay for a moment and looked at the empty berths where the ships of his squadron had been. Four berths. Three empty. He walked to the command center and reported for duty.

Theo sat in the secure room in Geneva and stared at the display. Clark stood beside him. The old man had not spoken in four minutes. The comms officer's face was wet and she did not wipe it.

The tactical victory was hollow. The enemy had withdrawn but the damage was done. Two generators destroyed. The grid cascade had been arrested but the eastern seaboard was still dark and the relay stations were operating on backup power that would last hours, not days. The infrastructure that held civilization together had been shown to be as fragile as the men who had built it.

The disruptor had hit Generators Seven and Four, in

that order. The two nodes whose maintenance windows overlapped, whose simultaneous loss would cascade fastest through the North American relay network. Out of eight possible targets it had chosen the two that mattered most, in the sequence that would do the most damage. Theo looked at the schematic and felt a cold certainty move through him that was not grief and was not fear but was the cold unease of a man looking at a lock that had been opened from the inside.

And the war was not over. It had not even properly begun.

The summit continued on the other side of the wall. Diplomats still milled in conference rooms. Some had not yet received the news. Some had received it and could not process it. A delegate from the European Coalition was still discussing revenue frameworks with an aide, his voice calm, his hands gesturing at projections that were already obsolete.

Sir, the comms officer said. Her voice had changed. It was no longer the voice of someone delivering reports. It was the voice of someone delivering a verdict.

We are receiving reports of retaliatory strikes. Surface launches detected.

Clark turned.

Multiple nations, she said. Both sides.

Clark's face went the color of old paper.

On the display, new icons appeared. Not in orbit. On the ground. Rising from silos across three continents in sequences that the display rendered as bright arcs. Each arc a missile. Each missile a warhead. Each warhead a city.

The feeds went red across six continents.

The arcs climbed. Hundreds of them. Yield estimates scrolled beside each arc. Five hundred kilotons. One megaton. Ten megatons. Numbers that the human mind was not built to hold because holding them required imagining what they represented and imagining what they represented was the end of the capacity to imagine.

Theo watched the display and felt the distance flattening the image. From orbit, from the clean abstracted geometry of the tactical feed, the launches looked procedural. The arcs rose in smooth parabolas that the rendering engine drew with the same weight and texture as the simulations he had run a hundred times at Fort Bliss. The feeds could have been real. They could have been test data piped through the same display on a different Tuesday. The resolution was the same. The refresh rate was the same. The little yield numbers ticking beside each arc were the same font, the same color, the same size as the practice rounds.

Clark was speaking into channels. Ordering ground-based interceptors. Requesting space-based laser engagement that could not happen because Alpha was barely holding itself together. His voice carried authority but not hope. He was a general giving orders to a defense system that had been designed for a smaller war and was now facing the one it was always supposed to prevent by existing. The interceptors launched. Some of the arcs flickered and died as warheads were struck in flight. But there were hundreds of arcs and tens of interceptors and the mathematics was merciless.

Someone in the room said God help us and the words vanished into the hum of electronics and the soft beeping of consoles that would continue beeping long after the cities they monitored had become craters.

On the diplomatic frequency Colonel Liang Wei's face appeared one last time. His composure had cracked along the lines that had always been there. His eyes held something that was not fear and was not sorrow but was the thing that lives between them, the knowledge that you have participated in a thing that cannot be taken back.

This was not what I wanted, Liang said. Believe that.

No one answered him.

His face held the screen for three more seconds and then the channel closed and the screen returned to the display of arcs and yields and the countdown to impact.

Theo thought of Liang's daughter in Shanghai. Twelve years old. Mei. The drawing in the pocket of a uniform. The star with teeth. He thought of the medical equipment that depended on the grid that depended on the fusion reactors that depended on the helium-3 that this entire summit had been about. The chain of dependencies that ran from a child's ventilator to a slab of rock on the Moon to a table in Geneva where men had failed to do the one thing they had gathered to do.

He stopped thinking about her because the mind has limits and his were reached.

Clark sat down. He did not speak for a full minute. Then he said a thing that was not strategy and was not orders and was not anything a general was supposed to say.

We were supposed to prevent this, Clark said. That was the whole point of all of it. The platforms. The defenses. The generators. The treaties. The whole point was that this would never happen.

Theo said nothing because there was nothing to say.

Clark looked at the display where the arcs were reaching their apogees and beginning the long fall toward their targets. The trajectories were past the point where interception was possible. The mathematics was complete. What remained was physics.

Clark's jaw tightened. The muscles in his face rearranged themselves into the configuration of command. It took less than a second. The man was gone. The general was all that was left.

We shift to continuity, Clark said. Everything else is over.

In the corner of the telemetry feed a sensor cluster logged an anomaly. A spike in the low-frequency electromagnetic spectrum. The same distributed pattern that the Energy Commission had classified as sensor drift. The same signature Ava had flagged on the ranch. The same oscillation that had appeared during the disruptor's attack on the generators.

It appeared for four seconds. It pulsed in a rhythm that was too regular to be noise and too faint to be weaponry. Each pulse coincided precisely with a generator going offline or coming under attack, as if something were counting the wounds in the network, tallying the damage in a frequency no human ear was tuned to hear.

No one saw it. No one had the bandwidth to look. The machines recorded it because machines record everything. The data sat in a log file that would not be opened for weeks.

By then the ash would be falling and the questions would be different.

Theo stood.

We need to go, he said.

Clark looked at him.

Where, Clark said.

The Defender. And then Earth. And then whatever is left.

Clark straightened. He turned to the comms officer. Get us transport. Now. And open a channel to Spaceport Texas. Authorization code Exodus. We are activating the Ark.

The officer's hands moved.

In the hallway Theo walked fast toward the airfield. The summit center's glass walls still projected artificial sky. Delegates still stood in clusters. Some were weeping. Some were staring at devices that had gone dark. A woman stood by a water dispenser holding an empty cup she had forgotten to fill. A man in a fine suit sat on a bench with his hands open in his lap, palms up, as if waiting to receive a thing that had already been taken.

Colonel, Liang said softly. You should have stayed retired.

Theo stopped. He looked at Liang and for a moment saw not an enemy but a father. A man with a daughter in a city that was about to burn.

Liang's hand went to his breast pocket. Where the photograph was. Where his daughter's drawing lived folded against his heart. His fingers touched the edge of it through the fabric.

Go, Colonel, Liang said. Go and do what you can. There is not much time.

Theo turned and walked.

Behind him Liang stood in the hallway of a building that was already a ruin and did not know it yet. A man who would carry a child's drawing in his pocket until the pocket was ash or the man was.

Theo walked out into the manufactured air of the airfield. A tilt-rotor waited under armed guard. Its rotors were already turning.

He climbed aboard. The cockpit sealed. The noise of the world reduced to engine roar and the pulse of his own blood.

On his display a classified message blinked, half-redacted, flagged with a priority code he had not seen used since Promethei.

ZPE CONTAINMENT IRREGULARITIES INCREASING. CORRELATION WITH ORBITAL COMBAT EVENTS CONFIRMED. PATTERN ANALYSIS SUGGESTS NON-RANDOM SOURCE. SIGNIFICANCE UNKNOWN.

He read it. He closed it.

He did not have time for unknowns.

The craft lifted. Geneva shrank below him, its glass towers catching the last of a sun that did not know what had been decided in its light.

Behind him the summit center threw the day back at the sky like a promise that had already been broken.

Ahead the sky was wide and quiet and waiting to be filled with fire.

CHAPTER 4

ASHFALL

The first alert came during second period.

Clara stood at the front of a classroom that still believed in schedules. Twenty-three children sat at desks arranged in rows because she had arranged them that way that morning, believing that order mattered. The windows showed a bright Austin day. Live oaks on the quad throwing long shadows across the walkway. A maintenance drone trimming hedges in straight lines. Two boys tossing a ball near the fence. The kind of morning that existed to make people believe that mornings would continue.

The light came through the glass in long clean bars and fell across the rows of desks in the pattern she had known for nine years of teaching. The same angle. The same warmth. She could feel the day holding itself steady as good days did, each minute arriving with the certainty of the one before it, and there was no seam in it. No crack where the next thing could get in.

Her wristband vibrated against the bone.

SHELTER PROTOCOLS — LEVEL 2

She had practiced the face. All teachers practiced the face. You stood in front of mirrors and you arranged your features into calm and you held the arrangement while your colleague read scenarios from a laminated card. Active shooter. Chemical spill. Grid failure. Orbital incident. You practiced calm the way you practiced fire drills. You made it muscle memory so that when your mind screamed your face did not.

All right, she said. We are going to do a drill. You know what to do. Quiet voices. Hands to yourselves. We move together.

A boy in the second row raised his hand. He had freckles and a gap in his teeth and the earnest obedience of a child who still believed that raised hands were answered with truth.

Is it the Moon thing, he asked.

Clara felt a chill slide through her chest.

It is just a drill, she said.

The classroom door opened. The principal stood there. His name was Henderson and he had been principal for eleven years and he coached the robotics team and he kept butterscotch candies in his desk drawer for the kindergarteners. His tie was loose and his face was the color of old paper and his hands were shaking in a way he was trying to hide by holding them together at his waist.

Clara, he said. His voice was low and fast and meant only for her. It is real. We have to move them now.

She moved. She had practiced this. She had practiced it in August and again in October and once more in December when the news cycle turned bad and the district sent updated protocols with new diagrams and new language for the same old fear. She gathered her class and moved them into the hallway.

The hall was filling with sound. Teachers calling names. Small shoes on linoleum. Children talking in the high bright voices they used when they did not yet understand that the world had changed around them. Some of them were loud because loud was how they processed fear. Some of them were silent because silence was how they held it.

Knox and Luna were two corridors over. She found them the way she always found them, by the pull in her chest that had nothing to do with logic and everything to do with blood. She had carried them inside her body and the connection had never been severed. It had only become invisible.

Luna saw her first. Eight years old. Dark hair in a braid that Clara had plaited that morning at the kitchen table while Luna ate cereal and asked questions about whether stars had names and who named them. She broke from her teacher's line and ran.

Clara caught her and held her too hard. She felt the small ribs beneath her arms and the quick heartbeat against her own chest and the warmth of a body that she had made and fed and bathed and dressed and read stories to and sung to sleep and she held that body as you hold a thing that the world has told you it might take.

Mom, Luna whispered. What is happening.

Clara pressed her lips against the top of her daughter's head. Her hair smelled like the shampoo they had used that morning. The one with the cartoon whale on the bottle. The one that cost four credits and lasted a month. The smell of a world that still had mornings and routines and small purchases that mattered.

Nothing you need to handle, Clara said. Just stay with me.

Knox appeared. Ten years old. Brown eyes. His mouth set in the hard little line he made when he was trying to be brave. He had Theo's jaw and their father's quiet and he was trying to be both of them at once. He took Clara's hand and squeezed it once and said nothing.

They had their weight. Their heat. The specific pressure of their hands in hers. These were not ideas. These were not memories. These were the facts of the world and they held because they were held.

Outside, sirens started. They rose and then they stopped and then they started again, as if the city itself could not decide what it was supposed to say. A car alarm joined them. Then another. The sounds layered until they were not sounds but a texture, the texture of a city beginning to panic.

They descended to the basement shelter. Concrete walls poured decades ago for a threat that had been theoretical until today. Air scrubbers humming with the sound of tired machinery doing work they had not been tested for. A rack of water packets in plastic sleeves. A stack of emergency blankets that smelled of the factory. A first aid kit with a red cross on the lid. A printed sign taped to the wall in a laminated sleeve.

WHAT TO DO IN THE EVENT OF ORBITAL INCIDENTS

A teacher beside her whispered. My sister says the feeds are down.

Another teacher. My husband is at the hospital. They lost power in half the east wing.

Clara tried her phone. The screen showed a single bar that flickered and held and flickered and died. She tried again. The bar returned for a half second and then vanished. She tried a third time because trying was the only verb she had left and because somewhere between the first try and the third the act of trying had become its own prayer.

She thought of Theo. Out there somewhere in the machinery of response. She thought of the last time she had hugged him at the door and how his body had been both present and already gone, already oriented toward the trouble. But she had felt his weight. She had felt the give of his ribs and the stubble on his jaw when he kissed her cheek and these things she did not question because they did not need questioning. They were facts. The way the floor was a fact. The way gravity was a fact. The world was solid for Clara. It had always been solid. She had stood on it with both feet since she was a girl and it had not given way and she did not expect it to give way now.

She thought of their parents. The shuttle accident when she was twenty. How the world had ended once before, privately, in an apartment in Austin where she held her brother while he wept and promised him they would survive together. They had survived. She had carried him through the grief the way she would carry her children through this. She had done it before. She could do it again.

Knox tugged her sleeve. Can we go home now.

Clara looked at her son. His jaw was set. His eyes were wet. He was holding it together with everything he had and everything he had was not enough and he knew it and he was doing it anyway and this was so much like Theo that her heart cracked along a line she did not know was there.

Not yet, she said.

She pulled both children against her body. The concrete smelled of dust and old water and the particular chemical signature of fear, that thing the body makes when the mind has run out of explanations.

Above them, beyond the ceiling and the earth and the sky, fire burned.

Clara held her children and did not let go.

She would not let go.

* * *

THEO WATCHED the war become weather.

He stood on the bridge of the USS Defender in magnetized boots with the Moon turning below them like a stone pulled from a grave. The viewscreen dominated the forward wall. Earth hung in it the way it hung in every photograph ever taken of it, blue and white and impossibly still. But the stillness was a lie. The stillness was the distance talking. From three hundred and eighty-four thousand kilometers the end of civilization looked like a marble.

The nuclear exchange had lasted eleven minutes. Eleven minutes to unmake what ten thousand years of human effort had built. The missiles had crossed continents in parabolic arcs that the tactical display rendered as clean bright lines, as though geometry could contain what they carried. The detonations appeared as white points that bloomed on the display and faded and left marks that would not go away. They appeared in clusters. They appeared in sequences that told stories about targeting priorities and retaliation doctrine and the cold mathematics of mutual destruction.

New York first. Then Washington. Los Angeles. Chicago. Moscow. Beijing. Shanghai. London. Paris. Mumbai. Delhi. Tehran. The names scrolled across the bottom of the screen like credits at the end of a film no one had agreed to watch.

Each name a place where millions of people had been eating breakfast or driving to work or reading to their children or doing the thousand ordinary things that constituted a life in the last minutes before the light came and the life stopped.

Austin.

The name passed across the screen and Theo's body received it the way a body receives a bullet. Not with a flinch. With a stillness. An internal detonation that produced no visible effect.

The bridge was silent except for the machines.

The feeds scrolled. Satellite imagery of the detonations rendered in the same resolution as the simulations he had studied for twenty years. The same color mapping. The same thermal bloom patterns. He had watched these images before. In briefing rooms. In training modules. On screens at Fort Bliss where Jake sat in the next chair and they discussed nuclear yields with the clinical distance of men who believed the images would always stay on the screen.

The feeds looked the same now. Exactly the same. There was nothing in the resolution or the frame rate or the font of the casualty ticker that distinguished this broadcast from the hundred simulations that had preceded it. The display did not know the difference. The display showed what it was told to show and its telling was indistinguishable from its practice.

He watched a thermal bloom expand over what the overlay said was Shanghai and he thought of Liang's daughter and the ventilator and the grid. He thought of Clara saying come home safe and the particular timbre of her voice on the line, the slight catch in her breath before the word safe. The simulation had never included that catch. The simulation had never carried the weight of a voice that meant what it said. He believed the feeds were real because Clara was real. Because Knox was real. Because Luna was real. Because the things you cannot simulate are the things that tell you, you are not in a simulation.

He held to this.

Multiple grid failures across North America, a comms officer said. Cascading. Satellite relays are dropping. We are losing contact with ground stations one by one.

Theo stared at the numbers. The grid was a web of dependencies so intricate that removing a single node could darken a continent. They had not removed a single node. They had removed hundreds. The ZPE generators that powered the relay stations that coordinated the power distribution that kept the lights on and the water flowing and the hospitals running, all of it was connected to all of it and all of it was failing at the same time in a cascade that fed on itself as fire feeds on air.

Atmospheric monitoring reports particulate density increasing, the sensor officer said. Smoke columns across all major landmasses. Soot injection models projecting significant stratospheric loading within forty-eight hours.

Theo looked at Earth through the viewscreen. The blue was dimming. A gray veil was forming in the upper atmosphere, as if the planet were pulling a shroud over its own face.

He walled off the thoughts of Clara and Knox and Luna behind the place in his mind where Jake lived and the arm he had lost lived and the sounds of Promethei lived. The place where he kept the things that would destroy him if he let them out at the wrong time.

Someone on the bridge said, We can still fight. The words came from a young officer in the back row. He was twenty-two or twenty-three and his face held the expression of a man who has not yet understood that the category he belongs to has changed. He was not a soldier fighting a war. He was a survivor standing on wreckage.

General Clark's face appeared on the secure channel. He was on a transport somewhere, the image bouncing with turbulence. He had aged a decade in twelve hours.

They hit more than platforms, Clark said. They hit the reactors. They hit the launch sites. They hit the communications backbone. They hit the water treatment coordination systems. They hit us where we breathe, Theo. The grid is collapsing and the cascade is accelerating and the nuclear winter models give us weeks. Maybe a month. Before global temperatures drop below the point where agriculture is possible.

Clark looked through the camera with eyes that had seen the mathematics and accepted them.

This is not a fight for territory, Clark said. It is a fight for continuity. For the survival of the species. Everything else is over.

He transmitted a file.

ODYSSEY — CONTINUITY ARK PROGRAM — EXECUTIVE ACTIVATION — CODE: EXODUS

Theo opened it on his console and read. A colony ship designated Odyssey. Currently in low Earth orbit. Capacity for ten thousand passengers in cryogenic suspension. Fabrication units. Seed stock. Medical facilities. Hydroponics bays. A wormhole transit array capable of reaching a preselected target system in three weeks.

Lupus Stella. A super-Earth orbiting a red dwarf star called Wolf 1061. Fourteen point one light-years from the Sun. Breathable atmosphere. Liquid water. Gravity one point one five times Earth standard. Surveyed by unmanned probes sent through miniaturized wormhole apertures.

The name sat on the screen and Theo read it and felt nothing because feeling was a currency he could not afford.

That is real, Theo said.

It has been real for years, Clark said. Insurance. A contingency built by people who understood that the species needed a backup plan and who hoped the backup plan would never be needed. He paused. It is needed now.

Theo scrolled through the file. Launch windows. Transfer orbits. Crew manifests. Passenger selection criteria that reduced human beings to skill sets and health metrics and genetic diversity scores. The cold arithmetic of deciding who lives.

What about the ZPE containment drift, he said.

Clark's jaw tightened. Thornhill says it can be managed. The Odyssey's power systems depend on the ZPE array. We cannot shut it down. Without it the ship does not fly.

The word managed hung in the air.

Stand down your generators.

Liang's words. A demand for surrender. But the phrasing echoed. As if the generators themselves were the thing that needed standing down. As if they were drawing something. Broadcasting a signal that something out there in the dark between stars was listening for.

Theo filed the thought. He did not have room for it. The world had more immediate ways of ending.

If Earth cannot stabilize, the spaceport cannot hold, Theo said.

Then you make it hold, Clark said. You hold it long enough to get ten thousand people off the ground. That is the mission. That is the only mission.

Clark gave him his orders. Descend. Secure Spaceport Texas. Organize the evacuation. Prepare the Odyssey for launch within six days.

Theo acknowledged.

He walked off the bridge and through the corridors of the Defender toward the shuttle bay. The crew watched him go. Their faces held the expression of people who understood that the man leaving the room carried something they could not share. The weight of a mission that was also a farewell.

He did not make a speech. He did not say goodbye. He walked and his boots rang on the deck and the sound was the loneliest thing he had heard since the silence after Jake's vitals went flat.

* * *

THE SHUTTLE PUNCHED through atmosphere that tasted of poison.

Reentry had always been violent. The heat and shudder and compression as air thickened around the hull, the friction turning the windows orange, the airframe protesting the transition from vacuum to sky. But this time the sky was wrong. Gray where it should have been blue. Thick where it should have been clear. The sun visible only as a smear of pale yellow through a ceiling of ash that extended in every direction to every horizon. The color of the world had changed. It had become the color of aftermath.

Texas should have been brown and gold this time of year. Dry grass under hard sun. Long shadows and clean light. Instead the landscape was gray. Ash lay on everything. On fields and roads and rooftops and fences and the hoods of abandoned vehicles. It fell continuously. A soft relentless particulate rain that turned the world into a photograph of itself. Each flake a piece of a city or a forest or a life that had been in the wrong place when the fire came.

Spaceport Texas is transmitting, the pilot said. The military hyperloop south is down. Grid failure took the power coupling south of Waco. Civilian infrastructure across the Texas corridor is nonoperational.

Define nonoperational, Theo said.

The pilot did not look over.

Power is out. Water is out. Communications are out. Emergency services overwhelmed. Riots at distribution points. Fires in several districts. The governor's office issued a shelter-in-place order six hours ago but there is no way to enforce it.

They banked south and the city came into view.

Dallas burned.

Not the clean annihilating fire of a nuclear strike. Dallas had not taken a warhead. Dallas was dying the other way. The slow way. The way that came when the grid collapsed and the water stopped and the food chains broke and ten million people realized in the same hour that every system they depended on depended on every other system and all of them had failed at once.

From above the city looked like a rendering. The thought arrived and Theo registered it and set it aside. Pattern recognition was what veterans did. The mind found order in chaos because order was the only thing the mind could use. But the word sat in his head. Rendering. Dallas from above, its gridded streets and burning blocks, looked like something drawn by a machine that understood cities but had never lived in one.

Smoke rose from a hundred points and merged into a single column that fed the gray ceiling.

Theo watched a building collapse in the distance. It went slowly, the upper floors folding inward, the lower floors shearing. A dust cloud rose and mixed with the smoke and the ash. It took eight seconds. It had been a building for a hundred years and it took eight seconds to stop being one.

The roads below were clogged with vehicles. Cars and trucks and hovercars abandoned at angles that told stories of panic. Between them people moved on foot in streams that had no direction. They carried bags and children and water containers and in some cases nothing. They moved because movement was the only response the body had to disaster.

The shuttle set down at Spaceport Texas on a pad ringed with military vehicles and razor wire. The spaceport had been built to handle a thousand passengers a day in orderly fashion with tickets and schedules and departure lounges. It was not orderly now.

The air that hit Theo when the hatch opened was warm and tasted of char and a chemical bite and underneath it the mineral smell of concrete dust. Ash fell on his shoulders and on his hands and on the tarmac. Soldiers stood at the perimeter with rifles and faces that said they had been standing there for days and did not know what they were guarding or from whom.

A young officer met him on the pad. She was slight and dark-haired and her uniform was dirty and her eyes had the intensity of someone who had been awake for too long and had used the wakefulness to become harder rather than weaker.

Colonel Daniel, she said. I am Lieutenant Daniella Ruiz. General Clark assigned me to your operational team.

Theo looked at her.

What is the situation.

They walked toward the command structure. Around them the spaceport hummed with activity that was half organized and half desperate. Military police manned checkpoints. Processing tents had been erected in the parking areas. Beyond the wire Theo could see the crowds. Thousands of people pressed against the perimeter fence. Some of them were shouting. Some of them were holding signs. Some of them were just standing.

Perimeter is holding, Ruiz said. Three battalions of military police. Two companies of Marines. We are processing civilian refugees as fast as the system allows but the volume exceeds capacity by a factor of ten at least.

She paused.

There have been incidents, she said. Crowds rushing the south gate yesterday. Three dead. Sabotage attempt on the fuel depot overnight. Rumors circulating that the Ark is only for government officials and military families. The rumors are not entirely wrong.

Theo stopped walking.

Where is my sister, he said.

Ruiz had a tablet in her hand. She consulted it. The screen reflected in her eyes and he saw the data change and he saw her face change with it and he knew what the tablet said before she spoke.

Clara Daniel, she said. Last known location was a school shelter in the northeast Austin district. We have had no communication with Austin since the strike.

How incomplete.

Ruiz met his eyes. She did not look away. She did not soften her voice.

The Davis Mountains were inside the tertiary blast radius. Miguel and the ranch and the cattle and the chair he had been sanding were inside the radius. Theo looked at the map and looked away and the looking away was the closest thing to a funeral he could give.

Austin took a direct nuclear strike, Colonel. Three hundred kiloton yield. The blast radius covered the city center and the overpressure zone extended four miles beyond that. The school was outside the immediate blast zone but the firestorms that followed swept through the outer neighborhoods. We do not have confirmation of casualties. We do not have confirmation of survivors. We do not have confirmation of anything.

Theo stood there on the tarmac with ash falling on him and the sound of distant shouting and the smell of a world that was burning and he felt the whole interior of himself go very still. Not calm. Not peace. A stillness that was the opposite of those things. The stillness of a man standing at the rim of a hole that has no bottom, looking down, understanding that the bottom is not missing but irrelevant because the falling is the thing.

I need a vehicle, he said. And a team.

Ruiz did not argue. She did not cite protocol or the chain of command or the priority of the spaceport mission or the six-day launch window or any of the thousand reasons why a colonel should not leave his post to drive into a nuclear wasteland to search for one family. She looked at him and she understood what she was seeing and she nodded once.

I will go with you, she said.

* * *

THEY DROVE north through a world that had ended and not yet been told.

The highway was a graveyard of vehicles. Cars and trucks and hovercars sitting where their systems had failed when the EMP hit, doors open, belongings scattered on the asphalt. Some had been looted. Some had been burned. In the median a school bus lay on its side and a family had made a camp inside it, a blanket hung over the emergency exit, a child's face visible in the gap.

Theo drove. The vehicle was military-grade. Sealed cabin. NBC filtration humming behind the dash. The air inside tasted of nothing, which was its own kind of mercy.

Ruiz sat beside him with a rifle across her knees and a map displayed on a tablet that kept losing its satellite connection. The map would appear and stabilize and then dissolve into static and then appear again, the satellite passing overhead in an orbit that no one was maintaining anymore.

The ash fell steadily. It coated the windshield and the wipers smeared it into gray arcs that dried and cracked. It lay on the road in drifts that the tires cut through with a whisper. The sky was the color of old concrete and the light that came through it was flat and directionless and made everything look the same distance away. Depth perception failed in this light.

They passed through towns that were empty. Doors open. Windows dark. Food left on tables. Water running from a faucet in a house whose front door stood wide. The small evacuations of ordinary life, abandoned in the time it took to understand that the sirens were not a drill.

They passed through towns that were not empty. In one, a group of men and women stood around a fire made from furniture dragged from a storefront. Their eyes tracked the military vehicle with expressions that held no welcome and no hostility but only the flat calculation of people assessing whether what was coming toward them was a threat or a resource.

In another town a man stood in the middle of the road holding a cardboard sign that said WATER in letters made with what might have been blood. Theo drove around him. The man did not move.

Ruiz spoke once during the first hour.

I was a ranch hand before the service, she said. West Texas. My family ran cattle on eight hundred acres outside Marfa. When the drought of 2118 killed the herd my father walked into the desert one morning and did not come back. I joined the military because it was the only institution left that would feed my mother.

She continued as if she had not expected a response.

I tell you this so you know that I understand what it means to go looking for someone you are afraid to find.

Theo heard it. The whole of it. Her voice in the ash-light had carried a quality he had not heard in a long time and he could not name it and he did not try. He watched the road.

His hands tightened on the wheel. The knuckles of his right hand went white. The left hand, the one that was not his, gripped with the same force but showed nothing. The arm did not express. It only held.

They reached the outskirts of Austin as the light began to fail. Not sunset. The ash ceiling simply thickened until the difference between day and dark became academic. The headlights cut cones of gray through air that was more particle than gas.

The city was unrecognizable.

The blast had taken the center. Where the skyline had been there was a flatness that the mind could not accept. Not ruins. Flatness.

Around the crater's edge the destruction graduated into a devastation almost worse. Buildings that still stood but were gutted. Their insides blown out through their windows, furniture and paper and human possessions scattered across streets that were buckled by the shockwave.

Power lines down in tangles of wire that looked like handwriting. Vehicles thrown into structures. A fire truck on its side, its ladder extended at an angle into nothing. The cab crushed. The windshield gone.

And everywhere the ash. Thick. Soft. Covering everything in a gray uniformity that erased detail and made the ruined city look like a single continuous thing rather than a million broken ones. The ash did not distinguish between a hospital and a house or a school and a store. It covered them equally. It was the most democratic thing that had ever happened to the city.

The fires had come after the blast. Firestorms fed by ruptured gas lines and collapsed structures and the sheer thermal energy of a three hundred kiloton detonation. Some areas were burned to char and white ash. Others were untouched, their structures intact, their yards still green beneath the gray coating. The pattern was random, the way fire was random. The way death was random when it stopped being personal and became statistical.

Theo turned off the highway onto surface streets. The vehicle's suspension jolted over rubble and drifts of debris.

The school was in the northeast. Outside the blast radius. Inside the fire zone.

He knew the route because he had driven it before, on afternoons when the Texas sun was high and the live oaks threw shade across the parking lot and the children came out in groups, their backpacks too big for their bodies, their voices carrying across the warm air.

The live oaks were gone. Burned to black columns that still stood, their branches reaching upward like hands. The parking lot was covered in ash. The school's front facade was intact but blackened. The windows were blown out and the interior was dark.

Theo stopped the vehicle.

He sat for a moment with his hands on the wheel.

Ruiz waited.

He got out. The ash was ankle deep. It compressed under his boots with a sound that was almost gentle. The air was still warm. Not from the sun. From the ground. From the heat that the city had absorbed in its burning and was slowly releasing back into a sky that could not hold it.

He walked toward the school.

The front doors were open. One hung from a single hinge. Inside, the hallway was dark except for the gray light that came through the broken windows. Ceiling tiles had fallen and lay on the floor in wet slabs. Water from burst pipes had pooled and now stood in shallow puddles that reflected the gray light. Papers and books and children's artwork lay scattered on the floor. A painting of a horse. A worksheet with multiplication tables. A drawing of a family holding hands beneath a yellow sun.

He moved through the hallway. His boots crunched on glass and plaster and the debris of a place that had been built to educate children and had become something else. His cybernetic arm's sensors painted a thermal overlay on his vision. Cold. Everything was cold. No living heat signatures on this floor.

He found the stairs to the basement.

The shelter door was closed. Heavy steel. He pulled it and the hinges screamed in the silence and the sound traveled down the concrete stairwell and came back as an echo that sounded like something else.

Inside, the shelter was dark. The air scrubbers had stopped. The emergency lights had failed. The air was close and thick and tasted of concrete dust and an acrid residue that might have been smoke or might have been worse. He activated the lamp on his wrist and the beam cut through the blackness like a blade.

The room was small. Concrete walls. Concrete floor. The water rack against the far wall. The air scrubber unit in the corner, its filters gray, its motor still. The emergency blankets in a pile. The sign on the wall.

WHAT TO DO IN THE EVENT OF ORBITAL INCIDENTS

He saw them.

They were in the far corner. Behind the water rack. Against the wall where the concrete met the floor at a right angle.

Clara was on her knees. Her body was folded forward over two smaller shapes. Her arms were wrapped around them completely, her hands gripping her own forearms behind their backs, forming a seal. Her back was to the room. Her coat was spread over them like a wing.

She had made herself a shelter. When the ceiling cracked and the dust came down. When the smoke found its way through the ventilation system. When the air scrubbers failed. When the temperature dropped and the cold seeped through the concrete. She had put herself between her children and all of it and she had sealed the gaps with her own body and she had not moved.

Theo crossed the room. His boots echoed on the concrete. The lamp shook because his hand was shaking but the arm that was not his was steady and he let it hold the light while the rest of him came apart and put itself back together and came apart again.

He knelt beside her.

Her hair was gray with ash. Her face was turned away from him, pressed against the wall, her cheek against the concrete. He reached out with his right hand. The one that could feel. He touched her shoulder and she was cold. She was cold. Cold as the floor. Cold as stone. Cold as the world when it stops pretending it was ever warm.

He pulled back the coat.

Knox was beneath her right arm. Luna beneath her left. Their faces were still. Their skin gray with dust. Ash on their eyelashes. On their lips. On the small hands that gripped their mother's shirt.

Knox's chest moved.

Theo stopped breathing.

Knox's chest moved again. A shallow rise. A fall. The faintest whisper of air through cracked and colorless lips.

He checked Luna. His fingers found the pulse at her throat. Weak. Slow. But there. A signal in the dark.

Both alive.

Clara had kept them alive. She had wrapped herself around them and sealed the gap between her body and the wall and when the smoke came through the dead scrubbers she had breathed it so they would not. When the cold came through the concrete she had given them her heat. When the dark came she had held them. She had held them when holding was all she had left and when holding was no longer enough she had held them still and she had not stopped and she had not let go.

She had given them everything she had. Her warmth. Her breath. Her body between them and the world.

And then she had given them the last thing.

Theo gathered Knox in one arm and Luna in the other. The boy weighed nothing. The girl weighed nothing. They were light. Light the way things are when everything that is not essential has been stripped away.

He stood.

He looked down at his sister.

Her face was not peaceful. People said that about the dead because they needed the dead to be at peace. Her face was the face of a woman who had worked very hard at something until the work was done. Her mouth was set in a line that he recognized. It was Clara's line. The line she had worn when she held him after their parents died. The line she had worn when she came to the hospital every day the week after he got home from Promethei. Sat in the chair by the window and talked about nothing. Brought him coffee he did not ask for. Told him he did not get to quit. The line that meant she had decided what she would not allow and had enforced the decision with everything she was.

He did not speak to her. He did not say goodbye. There was no language for this. There had never been language for this. The priests and the poets had tried for ten thousand years and the best they had managed was silence and he gave her that now. The only honest thing.

He carried the children out of the shelter and up the stairs and through the hallway and past the multiplication worksheets and the painting of the horse and the drawing of the family beneath the yellow sun and through the broken doors and into the gray light of a world that did not deserve what Clara Daniel had done for it.

His left arm held Knox against his chest. The cybernetic fingers had found their own position around the boy's back. He had not asked for this calibration. The arm had arrived at it independently. The weight distributed across the palm. The head steadied by the heel of the synthetic hand. Firmware solving for a variable no engineer had entered. The arm knew what it carried.

Theo looked at his left hand curled around the child and he did not know what to call what he was seeing. He kept walking.

Ruiz was at the door. She saw what he carried and she saw what he did not carry and her face went tight and her jaw clenched and she said nothing because nothing was the right thing to say. She took Luna from him and held the girl against her chest with both arms and turned toward the vehicle and walked.

They drove south.

Knox did not wake. Luna did not wake. They lay in the back seat wrapped in emergency blankets from the vehicle's kit, their small bodies rising and falling with the rhythm of breath that their mother had purchased with her own.

Theo drove south. Back through the ash. Back through the empty towns and the smoldering fields and the highway graveyards. Back past the man with the sign who was no longer standing in the road. Back past the family in the overturned bus. Back through a world that had been asked a question about what it was willing to lose and had answered with fire.

He did not speak. Ruiz did not speak. The only sound was the engine and the wipers and the soft percussion of ash on the windshield and the breathing of two children in the back seat.

His left hand rested on the wheel. The cybernetic fingers held a pressure that was wrong for driving. Too light. Too careful. The calibration he had not set was still running. The arm held the wheel as it had held Knox. As if everything it touched now might be a child.

Theo noted this. He adjusted his grip. The arm returned to standard pressure for two seconds and then softened again.

He let it.

Once, on a stretch of highway north of Alice, where the destruction thinned and the fields on either side were merely gray rather than charred, where a fence line still stood and a windmill still turned in the hot wind that carried ash instead of dust, Theo pulled the vehicle to the shoulder and stopped.

He sat with his hands on the wheel.

Ruiz waited.

He opened the door and stepped out into the ash. The NBC seal broke with a hiss and the outside air hit him and it tasted of carbon and something organic and the specific chemical sweetness of a world that had burned itself to the ground. He knew what the air carried. He had read the fallout briefs. He breathed it anyway.

The ash fell on him. It covered his shoulders and his hair and his hands, the right one and the left one, the one that could feel and the one that could not. He stood on the side of the road in the flat gray light of a sky that had forgotten the sun.

He did not weep. He did not make a sound. He stood and he breathed and the ash fell and the world turned in its wounded orbit and somewhere above him the Odyssey waited in the dark and somewhere below him his sister lay in a basement with her arms still reaching for children who were no longer there.

He stood there for a long time.

Then he got back in the vehicle and drove.

* * *

THEY REACHED Spaceport Texas after midnight. The perimeter lights cut through the murk like the eyes of a thing that would not sleep. Armed checkpoints. Razor wire. The distant murmur of thousands of voices saying the same thing in different words. Let us in. Let us live.

Medics took the children. They moved with the quick competence of people who had been treating casualties for days. Knox opened his eyes in the harsh light of the medical bay and looked at Theo and said nothing. His eyes held a knowledge that was too old for his face. The knowledge that the world had changed and that the change was permanent.

Luna did not open her eyes but her hand found Theo's finger and held it. Her grip was weak but precise. The grip of a child who has learned in the dark that the only thing between herself and the void is someone else's hand.

A medic ran a scanner over both children. Dehydration. Hypothermia. Smoke inhalation. Treatable. Survivable. The words were clinical and Theo received them as he received tactical reports. Data. Variables. Things to be managed.

The medic looked at him. She had dark circles under her eyes and a smear of ash across her cheek.

They will recover, she said. They are strong.

Theo nodded.

Their mother, the medic said. Was she.

Theo shook his head once.

The medic closed her mouth and nodded and turned back to her work.

Ruiz stood in the doorway.

I will stay with them, she said. Until you come back.

Theo looked at her. She was covered in ash from her hair to her boots. She had carried a stranger's child through dead cities for hundreds of miles without being asked. She had said nothing when there was nothing to say and she was twenty-five years old and the world was ending and she was standing straight.

Thank you, he said.

The words were not enough. No words were enough. But they were what he had and he offered them as a man offers water in a desert. Not because it is sufficient but because it is all there is.

He walked to the command center. The building hummed with generators and the blue light of tactical displays and the voices of officers coordinating the thousand tasks that stood between the present moment and the launch of a ship that would carry what was left of hope into the dark.

Clark was on screen. The General's face was lit from below by displays that showed a planet wrapped in its own smoke.

Did you find her, Clark asked.

Theo shook his head.

Clark closed his eyes. He kept them closed for three seconds. When he opened them they were the eyes of a man who had removed everything from himself except the next task. The last task. The only task.

The Odyssey is in low orbit, Clark said. Loading protocols begin in forty-eight hours. We have passenger manifests. We have crew. We have a launch window that closes in six days. If we miss it the orbital mechanics do not give us another for three months and in three months there will not be enough infrastructure left to launch a paper airplane. This is it. This is all of it.

Theo stood in the command center with ash on his clothes and his sister's death in his chest and two children breathing in a medical bay because their mother had given them everything she had and he said the only thing there was to say.

What do you need.

Clark told him.

Theo listened. He did not argue. He did not grieve. Grief

was a thing that required time and time was a currency they had spent to the last coin.

Outside the window the ash fell. Somewhere beneath it Clara lay in a basement with her body curled over children who were no longer there. Already cooling. Her face already still. The line of her mouth already set in the expression it would hold forever. The expression of a woman who had decided.

Theo put his hand against the window. The right one. The one that could feel the cold of the glass and the faint vibration of the generators and the distant pulse of a world that was dying.

His left hand hung at his side. Its fingers curled slightly inward. Gentle. Still calibrated to the weight of a child it was no longer carrying.

He stood there for a long time.

Then he turned and went to work.

He worked for six hours. He walked the perimeter. He reviewed manifests. He spoke to marines and logistics officers and a woman from the processing queue whose credentials had been destroyed in the firestorms and who needed someone with authority to say she was real. He said it. She walked through. He kept walking.

At 0200 he found a supply closet off the main corridor. A small room. Shelving units stacked with thermal blankets and water rations. He closed the door and locked it and stood in the dark with his back against the metal shelving and his hands at his sides.

The sound came from somewhere he could not locate. From below his chest and behind his ribs. A sound that was not a word and not a cry and not anything he had a name for. He slid down the shelving until he was sitting on the concrete floor with his knees drawn up and his head against his arms and he let the sound come because there was no one to hear it and because the door was locked and because his sister was dead and the world was ending and the children sleeping in the medical bay would wake and look for their mother and he would have to be the one to tell them she was not coming back.

He did not time it. It lasted as long as it lasted. When it stopped he sat in the dark for another minute and listened to the hum of the base and the distant sound of the crowd beyond the perimeter and the low vibration of generators that were keeping the lights on for a civilization that no longer existed.

Then he stood and wiped his face with the back of his right hand. The one that could feel. He opened the door and walked back into the corridor and the mask settled over his features like a visor dropping into place.

No one saw. No one would know. The breaking was private. The holding was public. The distance between the two was the width of a locked door.

INTERLUDE

MEMORY (THEO)

In the cryo bay, in the space between sleep and waking, the morning came back to him.

There had been a morning.

Not a special morning. That was the thing about it. That was why it stayed. It had not announced itself. It had not said remember this. It had simply been a morning in a house where people lived and the light came through the kitchen window at an angle that made the table glow and the dust motes turn slow in the air like small and aimless planets.

She stood at the counter with her back to him. Her hair was still damp from the shower and it left a dark shape on the back of her shirt like a country on a map. She was making toast. The sound of the knife on bread. A small domestic percussion. The smell of butter melting into warm grain. Coffee in the pot giving off its low familiar heat and the steam rising in a thread that caught the light and held it for a moment before dissolving.

The coffee cup on the counter had a logo on it. Blue lettering on white ceramic. He could see it clearly. The shape of the letters. The font. He could not place it. Could not say where the cup had come from or what the logo represented. It was specific the way things in memory are specific and it did not correspond to anything he could verify. He had never looked it up. He never would. The cup was in the memory and the memory was what it was and some details in it answered to fact and some answered to need and he had stopped trying to sort them.

He stood at the sink with his hands in the water. Both hands. The real ones. This was before Promethei. Before the carbon weave and the synthetic nerves and the arm that could crush steel and feel nothing. Both hands were his then. Both hands were warm and clumsy and alive in the way that living things are alive which is to say imperfectly and without knowing they are.

Through the window above the sink a tree stood in the yard. A pecan tree. Tall and full with the green of a Texas summer. Its branches moved in a breeze he could feel through the open window. Warm air and the smell of cut grass and the distant sound of a lawnmower somewhere down the block.

But he had sold that house before the tree was planted. He knew this. He had sold the house in the spring and the tree had gone in that fall. The new owners had planted it. He had seen it once, years later, driving past on some errand he could not remember. A sapling then. Thin and staked and improbable. The tree in his memory was the tree the sapling had become. Full grown. Decades into a life that had not overlapped with his time in that house by even a single day.

The tree should not be there. He knew it should not be

there. And yet there it stood. Green and full and moving in the breeze and casting a lattice of shadow across the kitchen floor that he could see if he looked down. The shadow fell across the tiles in a pattern that shifted when the wind moved the branches and the pattern was detailed and specific and it was a memory of something that had never happened.

He kept it anyway.

On the table sat a plastic horse with one leg missing. Its name was Bandit and Luna had christened it in a ceremony involving a jar of peanut butter and a speech about bravery. A crayon drawing of a rocket lay beside it. Knox had drawn it. The flames coming from the bottom were red and orange and occupied more of the page than the rocket itself because he understood at the age of five what most people never learn which is that the leaving is the largest part of the journey.

A sippy cup with milk drying on the rim. A bowl of cereal going soft. A stuffed bear named Captain propped against the sugar bowl with the gravity of a guest of honor. His button eyes looked at nothing and saw everything the way all things saw everything that held still long enough.

But those were Clara's children. Not his. And Clara's children had never lived in this house. This house was the house he had shared with his wife before Promethei, before everything, and the children who had argued in the next room had been his children, and they had gone with her when she went, and the children in the memory were wearing the wrong faces. Or the right ones. He was no longer certain which children the memory was meant to hold and perhaps it did not matter. Perhaps the memory had decided that the children it needed were the children he had left and those were Knox and Luna now because love does not catalog its sources. It simply fills the shape that remains.

The children were in the next room. He could hear them arguing over who got to sit in the box. The box had been a refrigerator box. They had drawn windows on it with markers. And a door. And stars on the ceiling of it where they had laid on their backs and reached up and made constellations that existed nowhere except in their invention. They had called it a spaceship and launched it to places that did not exist yet and might never and the journeys lasted until someone got hungry or someone needed the bathroom and then the spaceship returned to Earth and unloaded its crew for snacks.

She turned from the counter and looked at him. Her face was the face of a woman who knew where things were going. Who had married a man who left and came back and left again and who had learned to read his silences as a sailor reads the sky. Not by what is there but by what is forming.

You are leaving again, she said.

But her mouth did not match the words. Not exactly. A fraction of a second off. The sound arriving just before or just after the movement of her lips, like a recording played at a speed that was almost right but not right. Like a transmission across a distance that introduced a delay so small it should not have been perceptible and was. He noticed. He had always noticed. In every replaying of this morning he noticed the slip between her voice and her mouth and he did not correct it because correcting it would mean admitting the whole thing was a construction and he was not willing to make that trade.

The feeling was true. The details could do what they wanted.

He dried his hands on the towel. The towel was blue with a white stripe. He would remember this. The blue and the white. The weight of the cloth. The way the thread felt against the pads of his fingers. He would remember it when his fingers were no longer flesh and the memory of texture became a phantom in a machine.

Tuesday, he said.

She set the plate down. Two slices of toast. The butter pooled in the low places as it always did. Golden. Catching the light like small windows into something warmer. She pushed the plate toward him and did not sit down.

You do not have to keep doing this, she said.

He looked at her. He wanted to tell her that he did. That the world had a weight to it and he had been built to carry some of it and that if he set it down someone else would have to pick it up and they might not be able to. But he did not say this. He had learned that explaining duty to someone who loved you was a cruelty dressed as honesty.

I know, he said.

She sat down. She picked up the sippy cup and wiped the rim with her thumb. A motion she had done ten thousand times. The small maintenance of small lives. The work that never ended and never announced itself and held the world together more surely than any orbital platform or energy grid or military alliance.

Outside the window the pecan tree moved in the breeze. The tree that should not be there. Its shadow on the floor. Its branches full of leaves that had never existed in any yard he had lived in. Beautiful and false and more vivid than anything the truth had left him.

The light moved across the table. It touched the crayon rocket and the plastic horse and the stuffed bear and her hand where it rested beside the plate. Her fingers were long.

A pianist's fingers though she did not play. She wore the ring he had given her and it caught the light and held it as she held everything. With a grace that did not need to be named.

She looked at him.

Just come back, she said.

And the mouth was wrong again. The words arriving through some medium that was not quite air, not quite time. A signal that had to travel farther than the distance across a kitchen table to reach him. As if the memory were being transmitted from somewhere and the transmission had a lag that no amount of repetition could correct.

He reached across and put his hand over hers. The warmth of it. The small bones. The pulse in the wrist that was the most ordinary miracle in the world.

I will, he said.

In the next room a toy crashed and a child laughed and another child protested and the argument resumed at a higher pitch and they both smiled and the smiles were tired and real and they did not ask for anything because everything was already there. Already given. Already held.

He knew. He knew the cup was from nowhere. He knew the tree was from never. He knew the children's faces had been replaced by faces he loved more recently and he knew that her voice came through the memory on a delay that meant the recording had been assembled from components that did not originally share the same moment. He knew the morning was a composite. A thing his mind had built from the materials of several mornings and some invented mornings and a longing so deep it had become architecture.

He kept it.

Not because he was fooled. Because the feeling was true even if the details were fabricated. The warmth of her hand was true. The weight of love across a kitchen table was true. The morning was true in the only way that mattered which was that he had chosen it. Had chosen to defend it against the evidence of its own impossibility. Reality is not what you can prove. It is what you are willing to hold when the proof runs out.

A light that draws the dark.

He did not know where the words came from. They rose from somewhere below thought. A signal in the noise. A frequency he could not name but could not ignore. And in the image behind the words there was something he could almost see. A brightness with a shadow leaning toward it. A warmth surrounded by the cold that the warmth itself had summoned.

Signals that feed on power.

He ate the toast. She drank her coffee. The morning held them in its ordinary light and for a moment the world outside was only a world and not a thing with teeth. Just a world. Turning. As it always had. As it would not always.

Then the day moved on and the world took what it wanted.

He went to Promethei and left his arm in the red dust and came back different and she held him anyway. Held him with the patience of someone who understood that the man who returned was not the man who left and loved him anyway. Loved the new shape of him. The harder edges. The silences that lasted longer.

Then she was gone too.

Not to war. Not to violence. To the quiet catastrophe of illness that moved through her the way weather moves through a valley. Slowly. Then all at once. And the house that had held the smell of toast and coffee held instead the smell of machines and medication and the particular silence of a room where someone is no longer breathing.

The table was empty now. The light came through the window and touched nothing that breathed. The toast was never made again. The cup was never filled. The tree she never saw grew on without her in a yard that was no longer theirs and the shadow it cast fell on someone else's floor and that was the way of things.

The bear named Captain sailed no further. The cardboard spaceship had been put on the curb on a Tuesday and the rain had taken it apart and that was that.

In the dark of the ship between the stars Theo lay on a narrow bunk with his eyes open. The generators hummed. The hull ticked and settled. Ten thousand people slept in their frozen cradles and dreamed whatever the cold allowed them to dream.

He held the morning in his mind like a man holding water. It ran through his fingers. It always ran through his fingers. But for a moment he could feel it. The warmth. The weight of her hand. The sound of children who did not yet know that the world could be taken from them. The smell of toast in a kitchen where the light was good.

The cup with no origin. The tree with no history. The voice with no sync.

His morning. His. Built from what was real and what was needed and held together by nothing stronger than the decision to hold it.

The words returned. Rising from the same place below thought, the same frequency he could not name. The generators hummed and underneath the hum there was the other thing. The low pulse. The patient rhythm. A signal that fed on power as a flame feeds on air. Drawing it in. Needing it. Growing.

He lay still. The ship moved through the nothing between worlds. Outside the hull the universe stretched cold and absolute and full of things that had no names and wanted none.

She had asked him to come back.

He had not come back. Not in any way that mattered. He had gone further than either of them knew was possible and he was still going and the distance was not measured in light-years but in the mornings he could no longer reach.

The memory faded. The morning thinned. He closed his eyes and let it go the way you let go of a hand you can no longer hold.

But it did not let go of him.

It never did.

The generators hummed.

The dark was patient.

The dark was always patient.

CHAPTER 5

THE ARK

He had spent thirty-six hours shuttling between the Odyssey in orbit and the spaceport. Checking systems. Confirming manifests. Leaving the children with Ruiz each time he went up and coming back each time faster than the last.

The shuttle came in low over a country that had forgotten its own name.

Theo watched through the viewport as the land scrolled beneath them. Brown. Gray. The color of burning things after the fire has moved on. Roads clogged with vehicles that would never move again. A highway overpass had collapsed across four lanes and people had set up camp in the wreckage, tarps strung from the rebar like prayer flags. Towns dark at midday.

The pilot held altitude at a thousand feet. The air was bad below that. Particulate from the coastal strikes had drifted inland on the jet stream and settled into a haze that tasted of metal and an organic sweetness. The residue of things that had been alive.

Theo sat alone in the shuttle bay. The children were below. Ruiz had them. He had left them in the family processing area three hours ago when he went back up to the Odyssey to verify the cryo systems and the manifest allocations and the hundred mechanical details that stood between ten thousand people and survival. Each time he went up he came back faster. The pull was physical. A gravity that had nothing to do with orbital mechanics.

He had found them five days ago in the basement of a school shelter in the northeast of Austin. The building above had partially collapsed. Rebar jutted from broken walls like the bones of some vast animal that had died trying to stand. Clara's body was in the far corner of the shelter. She had wrapped herself around her children with her back to the room and her coat spread over them like a wing. The position was deliberate. It was simply the last in a sequence of choices that began with being a mother and ended with being a wall.

He had knelt beside her and touched her face and the face was cold and the children behind her were warm and alive and that was the mathematics of it. He had picked them up. He had walked out through the wreckage. He had not looked back because there was nothing behind him that could be helped and everything ahead that could.

Five days of military corridors and refugee processing and the slow machinery of evacuation. The Earth was dying. Not in the geological sense. Dying as a body dies when the blood stops moving. Systems shutting down one by one.

Spaceport Texas appeared on the horizon.

It rose from the coastal flats near the Rio Grande Valley,

like a monument planted by a civilization more certain of itself than this one. Three main pads. Service towers. Fuel depots. A perimeter fence topped with razor wire that extended in a rough oval around the entire facility and was never meant to hold back sixty thousand desperate people but was being asked to now.

From the air the crowd was visible first as a discoloration. A darkening of the ground that resolved as the shuttle descended into individual shapes. People. Tens of thousands of them. They pressed against the fence in a mass that moved and surged and fell back and surged again with a rhythm that was not human. Not in the individual sense. No single person directed it. No voice coordinated the push and withdrawal. The crowd breathed as one organism. It advanced and contracted like something with its own circulatory system, and Theo watched it through the viewport and felt a cold recognition settle in his sternum. He had seen this in combat. Not in the enemy. In the battlefield itself. Emergent patterns. Self-organizing systems. A crowd of sixty thousand frightened humans had become something that was not a crowd anymore. It was a thing. It thought in currents and countercurrents and it did not know it was thinking and that was what made it dangerous.

In combat the emergent patterns had geometry. Logic you could read if you had the training. This was different. This organism was built from want and grief and the irreducible animal need to continue and it moved with a purposefulness that unsettled him in a way firefights never had. In a firefight the enemy had intent. This was beneath intent. Older.

The shuttle dropped through a corridor of drone coverage. Four escort drones flanking. Their rotors made a sound like tearing cloth. Below the crowd scattered from the downwash and then reformed behind them like water closing over a hand.

Marines in exosuit frames directed the refugee lines, their amplified arms shifting cargo pallets that would have taken six men.

They touched down on cracked tarmac behind the inner perimeter. Heat shimmered off the concrete and the air that came through the vents smelled of jet fuel and sweat and fear. That last smell was the one you learned in combat. The body announcing what the mind would not say.

A marine detail met him on the tarmac. Four men in full kit with rifles slung and faces that had stopped registering surprise days ago. The sergeant saluted.

Colonel Daniel. General Clark is in the operations center. We will escort you.

Theo followed the marines across the tarmac. He glanced toward the family processing area as they passed. Somewhere in there Ruiz had the children. Knox would be sitting and watching. Luna would be drawing or sleeping. He would go to them as soon as he could. He always did.

The operations center was a converted hangar. High ceiling. Concrete floor. The air conditioned to a temperature that felt aggressive after the heat outside. Screens covered every wall. Satellite feeds. Drone surveillance. Perimeter cameras. Biometric processing queues. Power grid status. Launch sequence countdowns. The information density of a civilization trying to thread itself through the eye of a needle.

General Clark stood at the center table. He had aged ten years in the two weeks since Theo had last seen him. His uniform was creased in the wrong places. His eyes had the flat luminosity of someone running on stimulants and duty and not much else. Around him staff officers moved with the controlled urgency of people who knew the clock was running and could not make it run slower.

Theo, Clark said. His voice held the relief of a man who had been waiting for a particular tool and just had it handed to him.

General.

Clark led him to the situation table. A holographic map of the spaceport floated above the surface. Red zones marked the perimeter breaches. Green zones the secure sectors. Blue the boarding corridors. Yellow the processing checkpoints. The map pulsed and updated with new data every few seconds and each update made the picture worse.

We have forty-eight hours, Clark said. The orbital window for Odyssey docking narrows after that. Power grid degradation is accelerating across the western hemisphere. If we lose the ground-based relay stations the wormhole array cannot synchronize.

How many are outside the fence, Theo asked.

Clark pulled up a number. It floated in the air between them. Sixty thousand. Growing by several hundred per hour.

Manifest capacity, he said.

Ten thousand total. We are at seventy-eight hundred boarded and processed. Another twelve hundred in the checkpoint queue. The remaining slots are reserved for critical personnel still in transit.

Theo did the arithmetic. Sixty thousand people outside the fence. Ten thousand places. A ratio that could not be made gentle by any application of process or procedure.

He looked at the perimeter feeds. Gate Three was buckling. A mass of bodies pressed against chain link and razor wire and the thin line of marines holding the gap. On another screen a group had breached the western fence and was being pushed back by sonic drones. On a third screen a family stood at the gate. A man. A woman. Two children. The man was holding up a piece of paper. Perhaps identification. Perhaps a letter. Perhaps the name of someone on the inside who had promised to help. The paper flapped in the wind from the drone rotors and the man's mouth moved and no one could hear him.

What are they telling them, Theo asked.

Clark's jaw worked. The official line is that there are multiple ships. Multiple launches. That this is one of several evacuation waves.

Is that true.

Clark looked at him. The look said everything the mouth would not.

The checkpoint was a corridor of steel and light. Biometric scanners at entry. Retinal. Fingerprint. Genetic marker. Cross-referenced against surviving databases that were incomplete and corrupted and contradictory in ways no one had time to reconcile.

Theo walked the line. The queue stretched from the checkpoint entrance back through a covered walkway and out into the heat where it dissolved into the larger mass of humanity pressing toward the gates. Families. Individuals. Children held on hips and over shoulders. The elderly propped against walls or sitting on the floor with the patience of people who had run out of other options and discovered that patience was what remained when everything else had been spent.

At the first scanner a marine was arguing with a technician. The technician's face was tight with the frustration of a specialist whose instruments were lying to him in ways the manual never covered.

The retinal database is flagging mismatches, the technician said. Not forgeries. The scans are clean. But the identity records they match against are corrupted. We are getting ghost returns.

How many, Theo asked.

The technician looked at him. Recognized the rank. Straightened.

Six percent failure rate on retinal, sir. Three percent on genetic markers. The databases are pulling records that should not exist. Matching living subjects to deceased files. Matching one person's biometrics to another person's identity.

Theo looked at the line. At the faces waiting. Each face a world. Each world about to be reduced to a data point that would either open a door or close one.

The woman at the next scanner stepped forward. Perhaps fifty. Gray-streaked hair pulled back. Her hands folded in front of her body with a stillness that was not calm but the absence of any movement she trusted herself to make. She placed her chin on the rest and opened her eyes to the light.

The scanner swept. Red.

The denial tone sounded. Flat and final and calibrated to convey nothing personal.

The marine at the station read his screen. Read it again. His mouth opened and closed. He looked at the woman.

Ma'am. Your retinal scan is returning an identity match for a Judith Calder. Deceased. Three years ago. Austin, Texas.

The woman did not move. Her hands stayed folded. Her breathing stayed even. She looked at the marine as a person looks at a locked door they have walked a very long way to reach.

I am Judith Calder, she said. I live in Austin. I am not dead.

The marine looked at Theo. His eyes had the flat helplessness of a man caught between two systems of truth that could not both be right.

Theo stepped to the screen. The death certificate was complete. Certificate number. Filing jurisdiction. Time of death down to the minute. Cause of death listed as respiratory failure. It was thorough and specific and bureaucratically precise and it described a woman who was standing three feet from him breathing.

He looked at the woman. She looked back at him with eyes that were alive and present and clear with the certainty of someone who has walked a very long way to stand in exactly this spot and will not be turned away by a machine.

Override, Theo said.

Sir, the marine began.

Override. Board her.

The marine entered the code. The light went green. The woman walked through. She did not thank him. She did not look back. She walked through with the gait of someone who had decided that her own existence was sufficient evidence and the database could sort itself out.

Theo watched her go. The question did not leave. It sat in a place behind his sternum where questions of this kind settled. Which was wrong. The woman or the record. The living subject or the data that said the subject should not be alive. It was possible the database had been corrupted in the grid collapse. Possible. But the record had not looked corrupted. It had looked complete. Clean. Filed and certified with the bureaucratic precision of a system that knew what it knew.

He filed it. He moved on. There were nine thousand

more decisions to make before the ship left and each one was a door and on the other side of each door was either a life continued or a life ended and the man at the door was him.

He walked the line. Overrode two more biometric failures. A child whose genetic markers matched an adult male in a different state. A man whose fingerprints returned no match at all. Not a mismatch. An absence. As if the man had never been recorded in any system anywhere. He stood at the scanner with hands that were clearly real and a face that was clearly human and the system said he did not exist. Theo looked at him. The man looked back. Maybe thirty. Thin. Frightened. Real.

Board him, Theo said.

The marines processed him through. Somewhere in the servers a record noted that Colonel Theodore Daniel had authorized boarding for a man the system could not identify. The contradictions accumulated like sediment in a river that no one was monitoring anymore.

At the western perimeter the situation was deteriorating by the hour.

Theo walked the fence line with a marine captain named Torres. Torres was built like a fire hydrant and had the eyes of a man who had been doing the wrong thing for the right reasons long enough that the distinction had begun to blur.

We had a breach at sector seven at 0300, Torres said. Forty to fifty people came through a section where the razor wire had been cut. We pushed them back with drones and gas. No lethal force. But we had injuries. Three marines. Twelve civilians. A young woman who got caught in the wire.

Torres stopped walking.

She was trying to push her baby through first, he said. Under the wire. She had wrapped the baby in a blanket and she was pushing it through the gap and the wire caught her across the shoulders and back.

Did the baby get through, Theo asked.

Yes.

And the woman.

Torres shook his head. Medevac took her. She will live. But the scars.

He did not finish. He did not need to.

At a secondary gate a young corporal named Davies stood at the barrier with his rifle slung and his hands at his sides. His hands were bloody. Not his blood.

Report, Theo said.

Davies looked at him. He was maybe twenty. His face had the white rigid look of someone holding himself together through a series of mechanical decisions. Breathe. Stand. Report.

A man tried to push through with a child, Davies said. I grabbed him. He had a knife. I did not see it until. He stopped.

Theo looked past him. A medic was working on a body on the other side of the fence. Not urgently.

Did the child get through, Theo asked.

Davies nodded. His hands were shaking.

Then you did what you could, Theo said. Stay on the line. Drink water.

The corporal looked at him like he wanted absolution. Theo could not give it.

He moved along the fence line. The crowd pressed against it. A living wall. Faces. Hands. The smell of unwashed bodies and smoke and the rank odor of fear which is not sweat exactly but rides on sweat like a frequency on a carrier wave.

At the western sector a group had organized. Matching red armbands. Signs. ELITES LEAVE / WE DIE. THE MEEK SHALL INHERIT WHAT. One simply said LET US LIVE.

A woman in the front shouted through the fence. Her voice ragged from hours of shouting.

You are choosing who lives and who dies, she said. You are playing God.

Theo stopped. The marines tensed behind him.

He walked to the fence alone. The woman was perhaps forty. Thin. Sunburned. Her eyes were intelligent and furious and underneath the fury there was a terror so deep it had become architecture. She had built herself around it and was standing inside the structure she had made and the structure was anger because anger was load-bearing and despair was not.

Ma'am, Theo said.

Do not ma'am me, she said. I am a person. These are people. You have a ship that carries ten thousand and there are sixty thousand of us out here and you are deciding who gets to live. By what right.

There is no right, he said.

She stared at him. The anger held but the foundation of it cracked. What replaced it was worse. Understanding.

My daughter is a doctor, she said. She is in the queue. She will get through. I will not. You know this.

I know this, Theo said.

She reached through the fence. Her fingers came through the diamonds of wire and stopped. Not reaching for him. Reaching for the space between them. The space that was two inches of air and the width of a decision and the difference between a woman who would live on a new world and a woman who would die on this one.

Make sure she gets through, the woman said.

Theo reached through the wire and held her hand. The cybernetic fingers closed around hers with a pressure calibrated to the weight of what was being exchanged. Not a promise exactly. Not comfort. Something harder and more honest than either.

What is her name, he said.

The woman told him. He memorized it. He would find the daughter on the manifest. He would make sure she boarded.

He released the woman's hand and walked on. Behind him the crowd pressed against the wire and the woman stood where she was and watched him go and did not move.

In the operations center Thornhill was waiting.

She sat at a corner workstation with her thermal case at her feet and a screen full of waveform data. Her hair clipped back with a band. She held a thermos of coffee in both hands as if the warmth were the only thing keeping some vital process running.

Doctor, Theo said.

Colonel. She set the thermos down. Picked it up again.

I need to brief you on the generator status before we board, she said.

Go ahead.

The zero-point generators on Odyssey are operational. All three cores are within parameters. The wormhole stabilization array is calibrated and ready. Power reserves are nominal. Her fingers traced the edge of the thermos. All the numbers are right.

Theo waited.

Thornhill looked at him steadily.

Nothing, she said. That is what concerns me.

Theo thought of the ghost spikes. The containment wobble on his ranch generator. Dr. Johnson's voice on the hyperloop. We are drawing from a well we do not understand. What if something else is drawing from it too.

Can you hold containment through transit, he asked.

Yes. I have compensatory protocols for in-transit oscillation.

And if you cannot.

Then we have a problem I cannot solve in a tunnel between stars. So I suggest we solve it before we get there.

Can you solve it.

Thornhill picked up her thermos. Held it. Set it down.

I can compensate for it, she said. Solving it requires understanding it and I do not understand it. Nobody does.

That is enough for now, Theo said. Get to the ship.

Thornhill picked up her case. She paused in the corridor.

I heard about your sister, she said. I am sorry.

Theo nodded once. He watched her walk toward the shuttle bay and disappear into the controlled chaos of the boarding process.

By evening the official announcement had been made.

Clark delivered it himself over the spaceport public address. He spoke plainly. No rhetoric. No false hope. The Odyssey would launch in sixteen hours. Boarding would continue until capacity was reached. Priority given to critical skills, families with children, and medical personnel. There was no second ship. There was no second launch. He said he was sorry. He said it like a man who understood the word was inadequate and used it anyway because no better word existed.

The crowd went quiet when he started. By the end they

were not quiet. The sound that rose from sixty thousand throats was not a sound that had a name. It was beyond anger and beyond grief. It was the sound of a species being told that the lifeboat was full.

The perimeter held through the first hour. Then it did not.

Gate Three went first. The sheer weight of bodies against the chain link bowed the posts inward and the razor wire snapped and the gap opened like a wound and people poured through. Not running. Walking. Walking with the terrible deliberate speed of people who had heard the math and decided to change it.

The marines fell back to the inner cordon. No lethal force. They deployed gas and sonic barriers and the crowd slowed but did not stop.

Theo was on the operations floor when the feeds lit up. Every gate. Every sector. The organism outside had reached a decision. Not a decision made by any individual. A decision that rose from the collective the way weather rises from the sea. No one voted. No one spoke. The crowd simply moved. Together. In every direction at once.

He watched the feeds and they showed him what he already knew. This was not the breach of a fence but the breach of the agreement that had held the situation together. The agreement that said there were rules and the rules would be followed. That agreement was over.

Clark was on the command channel. His voice was flat. Deploy perimeter reinforcement. All sectors. Non-lethal priority.

He had not spoken in hours. His voice when it came surprised even him.

Sir, Theo said. Gate Five has a clear corridor to the

service tunnels. We can route fifty more through before the inner perimeter seals.

Clark looked at him. Fifty more. The number was nothing. A rounding error in the mathematics of sixty thousand. But it was fifty lives and fifty lives were fifty lives.

Authorized, Clark said.

Theo contacted the Gate Five lieutenant. Twenty-six years old with a face that looked forty and hands that moved with the competence of someone who had been given impossible tasks and completed them because the alternative was standing still.

On the screens the breach at Gate Seven became a firefight. Tracer rounds drawing bright lines across the tarmac. Bodies falling and not getting up. A fuel tank somewhere caught and a column of orange light rose into the sky and turned the smoke to gold and for a moment the entire spaceport was lit like a cathedral.

On the boarding manifest a name scrolled past. Tanner, L. Journalist credentials. Dallas bureau. She had made it through.

Clark appeared beside him. His face was the color of ash.

We are out of time, he said.

Theo nodded. Begin final boarding sequence.

Clark gripped his arm. The real one.

I am not boarding, he said. I gave my seat to a family of four from the processing queue. He said it the way he said everything. As fact.

Theo looked at him.

My grandkids are in Montana, Clark said. The shelters there are deep. They will make it. But those four people at the gate will not make it without the seat I am sitting in. The mathematics is simple.

General.

Clark shook his head. Take care of those kids Theo. And take care of what is up there. You are the best officer I ever commanded and I am telling you that as a man and not as your general because in about ten minutes I will not be your general anymore. Theo held the old man's gaze. He wanted to argue. He wanted to order him aboard. He wanted to tell him that the mathematics was not simple and never had been. But Clark's eyes were steady and his jaw was set and his hand on Theo's arm was the hand of a man who had already made his peace.

It has been an honor sir, Theo said.

Likewise Colonel. Now get on that ship.

Clark released his arm and stepped back and straightened his uniform and turned toward the perimeter where the crowd still pressed against the wire and the fires burned beyond them. He did not look back. He had spent his career looking forward and he was not going to stop now.

Sheppard found Theo in the corridor outside the operations center.

He came fast. Not running. Moving with the deliberate stride of someone carrying a thing that could not wait and could not be dropped. His Intelligence badge swung against his chest and his face had the drawn transparency of a person who has not slept and has stopped pretending he might. He carried a datapad in his right hand and he held it the way a surgeon holds a diagnosis.

Colonel, he said. I need a word.

He stopped. The corridor was chaos. Staff officers. Marines. Logistics personnel shouting into headsets. The evacuation was a machine tearing itself apart in the act of running.

Sheppard stepped close. His voice was low and precise and stripped of everything but the information.

I traced the leak, he said. The burst transmissions we flagged at Bliss. Encrypted packets routed through a commercial satellite relay. Months of them. The terminal they came from is in the logistics wing. The access codes belong to Major Marcus Lee.

Theo did not move.

He watched Theo's face as a technician watches a gauge approaching redline.

The grid, he said. The generators failed in sequence. Not a random cascade. The maintenance priority list determined which nodes went down first and in what order. That list was classified. It lived on a logistics terminal. Lee's terminal.

Theo's left hand closed at his side. The servos did not engage. The fingers simply drew into the palm as a fist forms when the body has already understood what the mind has not yet allowed.

Sheppard looked at the datapad and then at Theo and his eyes held a clarity that was also a confession.

I am bringing this to you, he said. Not to Clark. I know what the grid failure caused. I know about Austin.

He did not say Clara. He did not need to.

Theo took the datapad. He looked at the screen. Lee's codes. Lee's timestamps. Lee's terminal. The data was clean and specific and it described a man he had known for twenty years. A man who had saved his wingmen in the orbital battle. A man who had sat with him in briefing rooms and shared a flask on the observation deck and spoken Jake Ramsey's name with the weight it deserved.

He handed the datapad back.

Where is he, Theo said.

Cargo bay four, Sheppard said. Manifest coordination for the last loading sequence.

Sheppard held Theo's gaze a moment longer. He did not ask what Theo intended. He knew. That was why he had come to Theo and not to Clark. He had made his choice and his choice was to let Theo make his.

He walked.

The corridor fed into a throughway that ran along the eastern edge of the spaceport. Overhead the lights flickered as the ground power cycled. Somewhere outside the perimeter wall the crowd was a sound like weather. Constant. Sourceless. The sound of want that had become its own atmosphere.

He moved through the loading corridor. Forklifts. Supply crates stacked to the ceiling. The air smelled of hydraulic fluid and ozone and the stale recycled air of a facility running on backup systems. Marines moved around him carrying equipment toward the shuttle pads. Nobody stopped a colonel walking with purpose.

Cargo bay four was a concrete vault lit by overhead strips that hummed and buzzed in the frequency of failing ballasts. Crates of seed stock and medical supplies and fabrication components lined the walls in rows that someone had organized with care because order was the last thing left to practice.

Lee was at the manifest terminal.

He stood with his back half-turned and a loading slate in his hand and when Theo came through the bay door Lee looked up and his face told the whole story before either of them spoke. The blood left it. Not slowly. Not in stages. All at once, as color leaves a sky when the sun drops below the line. He set the slate down on the crate beside him and his hand stayed there a moment as if the crate were the last solid thing in the world and then he took his hand away and stood.

Theo, he said.

Theo stopped ten feet from him.

Lee looked at him. He looked at the bay door behind him and whatever he calculated about the distance and the odds he calculated in the space of a single breath and then he let the calculation go. There was nowhere to run. There had been nowhere to run for a long time. The running had ended the moment the first burst transmission left his terminal and what followed was only the distance between the act and its answer.

They do not care about us, Theo, Lee said. His voice was steady as a wire is steady under load. You know what they did to us. To you. Look at that arm. They gave you a machine and called it a medal and sent you home to a ranch where you could be quiet and out of the way. I had a family. I had debts they put on me and a pension they gutted and a daughter who needed things the VA said were not covered. When the offer came I did not think it would go this far. Nobody did. They said intelligence. Not weapons. They said leverage. Not war. But once you are in you do not get to choose what they do with what you give them. You know this, Theo. You of all people know what it is like to be used and thrown away.

Lee's eyes went to the cybernetic arm. Jake died so you could get that, he said. And they pinned a medal on the box they sent home and they gave you a machine to replace what the grenade took and they called it even. Do you think Jake would call it even. Do you think Jake would look at what they made of us and call it service.

The spaceport shook. A low concussion from somewhere beyond the perimeter wall. Sirens cycling through the building in patterns that meant the last shuttles were loading and the doors were closing and the world was ending one procedure at a time.

Theo listened. He heard every word and each word was true in the sense that a thing can be true and still be the wrong truth. Lee had been used. Lee had been discarded. Lee had been ground down by the same machinery that had taken Theo's arm and Jake's life and Clara's morning in a classroom where children believed that raised hands were answered with truth. All of it was true. And none of it was enough. Because Clara was dead. Because the generators had failed in a sequence that someone provided. Because the grid fell in the pattern Lee gave them and the pattern killed a city and the city killed his sister and his sister died in a doorway with her body between her children and the dark.

Lee moved. His hand went to the crate beside him and came up with a pry bar and he swung it in a short arc aimed at Theo's temple. The cybernetic arm was faster. The carbon fingers closed around Lee's wrist and the pry bar clattered to the concrete and Lee's face registered the sound as a man registers a verdict. Then the fingers found his throat. The same fingers that had held Luna against his chest. The same carbon weave palm that had cradled Knox's head. The arm that existed because of Promethei. Because men had died on a frozen ridge and a grenade had taken what could not be given back and the military had built him this thing out of titanium and guilt. Lee's betrayal had fed the cascade that killed the grid that killed the cities that killed Clara in a school shelter in Austin where she died with her body over her children. And now the arm that all of it had made closed around the throat of the man who had sold the sequence. The fingers tightened. Lee's feet left the ground.

His hands came up and gripped the carbon wrist and his fingers slid on the smooth casing as fingers slide on wet stone. He looked at Theo. His eyes held something that was not fear and not apology and not anything that had a name. The arm did not hesitate. The arm had never hesitated. It finished what it started and what it started was what Theo could not stop and did not try to stop.

The sound was brief. The body dropped.

His left hand was warm. It should not have been warm. Lee's pulse had faded under those fingers ten seconds ago and the warmth should have gone with it. But the arm was warm the way it was warm when it adjusted wood grain or tucked a blanket. The arm did not distinguish between kindnesses.

Theo stood over him. The overhead lights hummed. A siren cycled and faded. Somewhere a forklift beeped its warning tone in reverse.

The arithmetic was complete. What the grid failure did to a city and what the city did to a family and what the family's absence did to the man standing here. The numbers balanced. Whether that made it justice or murder he would decide later. Or he would not decide at all.

Theo turned and walked toward the bay door. His boots sounded on the concrete in a cadence that was not hurried and not slow. Behind him the shape that had been Marcus Lee lay on the floor among the cargo crates and the seed stock and the supplies for a world he would not see. The manifest terminal glowed beside him. His name still on the access log. His codes still active. His work still undone.

Theo walked out into the corridor and the noise of the evacuation took him.

The last shuttles loaded in sequences that had the rhythm of a heartbeat going too fast. Twelve minutes between launches. Each shuttle carrying two hundred people packed into seats designed for cargo. Children screaming. Adults silent. The elderly staring at nothing.

Theo found Ruiz and the children in a holding area near Pad Nine. Concrete room. Benches bolted to the floor. A single strip light that hummed and flickered. Knox sat on a crate eating a protein bar with methodical attention. Luna was on the floor drawing on the concrete with a piece of charcoal. She had drawn a house with a triangle roof and a sun with rays and a figure standing next to the house.

Who is that, Theo asked.

Mom, Luna said.

Theo knelt beside her. The figure had long hair and outstretched arms wide enough to hold everything.

That is a good picture, he said.

Ruiz stood near the wall with her hands in her pockets. She looked tired and scared and steady. She had been with the children for twelve hours. She had fed them and kept them calm and told them stories about horses and stars and a coyote that could talk but only said true things and she had done it without asking for anything.

She looked up when Theo entered and her face held a tiredness that was also tenderness and the two things together made an expression he had seen before. On Clara. Holding Luna in the kitchen doorway after a long day. He registered it and did not name it and it sat in him as certain observations do when they arrive before the language for them.

Theo looked at her. You are on the next shuttle, he said.

She shook her head. I am not on any list.

You are now, he said.

She opened her mouth to argue and then she looked at the children and closed it. Her face changed. Not gratitude.

Harder than gratitude. She looked at the concrete floor and then at the door and then at the crowds she could hear through the walls, the sound carrying faint and vast like weather.

There are people out there with children of their own, Ruiz said. Her voice was low and it shook. People who are not going to make it because there is no room. And you are putting me on a shuttle because I happened to be standing in the right place when you needed someone to hold a baby.

She looked at him and her eyes were bright and furious and wet.

That is not fair, Ruiz said. Her voice cracked on the word. To them or to me.

The room was quiet. Knox had stopped eating. Luna's charcoal was still on the concrete.

Theo looked at her. He did not argue with the unfairness because there was no argument. She was right. The whole system was a wound. Every seat filled meant a seat denied and the math was merciless and she had just said the thing that everyone with a boarding pass was thinking and no one would say.

No, he said. It is not fair. None of this is fair. But these two need someone and you are the someone. And I need you to decide right now whether you are going to carry that or put it down. Because the shuttle leaves in nine minutes.

Ruiz stood there. Her hands were shaking. Then they stopped. She wiped her eyes with the back of her wrist and picked up Luna's bag and took Knox's hand and nodded once. The nod was not agreement. It was something closer to a vow made under duress that she intended to keep.

The shuttle was hot and crowded and smelled of sweat and machine oil. Knox sat between Theo and Ruiz. Luna was on Theo's lap. The harness barely fit around both of them.

The engines fired.

The shuttle lifted.

The feeds showed other launches. A European consortium ship lifting from French Guiana. A Chinese vessel from Wenchang. The Russians had three arks in polar orbit, loaded in secret over the past year. India's ship launched from Sriharikota, and the footage showed a crowd pressing against the fences and the ship rising through them. Twelve arks launched globally. The Odyssey was the sixth. They did not know how many would make it through.

Through the viewport Theo watched the spaceport fall away. The fires. The fences. The dark mass of people still pressing against the gates. From the air they looked like a single organism. A thing made of want and fear and the need to continue. They surged and fell back and surged again and they did not stop because stopping was not something the living did even when living was no longer on offer.

And on the tarmac near cargo bay four, smaller and smaller as the shuttle climbed, a shape. A shape on the concrete that had been a man. That had been a friend. That had been a traitor. The ground around him was lit by the fires along the perimeter and the light made the tarmac glow like a pyre he had built for himself out of the things he had sold and the people he had betrayed and the sequence of choices that began with need and ended on a concrete floor with the breath crushed out of him by an arm that had once held children.

The shape shrank. The spaceport shrank. The fires shrank.

He thought of the woman at the fence. Her daughter the

doctor. He had gotten the daughter onto the manifest. He had not been able to save the mother.

He thought of Miguel. The ranch and the cattle and the drones orbiting in their patient loops. Whether any of it still stood. He did not know. He filed that not-knowing with the rest.

The shuttle climbed through atmosphere that tasted of ash even through the filters. The sky darkened from brown to purple to black. Stars appeared. Not the stars of his childhood on the ranch when the Davis Mountains held the horizon and the Milky Way was a river overhead. These were the same stars seen through a veil of smoke and grief.

Knox pressed his face to the viewport.

Is that Earth, he asked.

Yes, Theo said.

The boy looked at it for a long time. The curve of blue still visible beneath the brown and gray. The thin line of atmosphere that had held everything they had ever known. Every war and every peace. Every song and every silence.

It is so small, Knox said.

Theo put his hand on the boy's shoulder. The cybernetic hand. Knox did not flinch from it. He leaned into it.

It was enough, Theo said.

The shuttle rose. The planet shrank. Fires guttered into pinpricks and then into nothing. The coastlines became suggestions. The continents became shapes on a sphere that was becoming smaller and smaller in the dark.

And as the planet shrank Theo felt it. A vibration in his left arm. Not from the shuttle's engines which shook everything evenly. Not from any instrument or system readout. A localized tremor running through the carbon weave fibers and the synthetic nerve pathways. Low frequency. Steady. As if a signal were passing through the arm on its way elsewhere. He turned his wrist. Ran a quick diagnostic. The display showed nothing. Every reading nominal. But the vibration continued.

He watched the planet through the viewport. The shrinking sphere.

The vibration faded as the planet shrank. Proportional. As if whatever signal was passing through his arm was tethered to the surface. Growing weaker with distance. He watched it diminish with the same attention he gave to any anomalous reading in the field. Noting it. Filing it. Not alarmed. Not dismissive. Present.

The vibration in the arm felt like an echo. Not of the engines. Of the cargo bay. Of the pry bar falling. Of the carbon fingers closing. He had not told the arm to do that. Or he had. The line between operator and instrument had never been thinner than the moment his hand found Lee's throat and the arm did the rest. He did not know if that made it murder or justice or something that did not have a word yet. He filed it in the place where the worst things lived. Alongside Jake's grenade and Clara's basement and the map with the Davis Mountains inside the radius. He would open that file eventually. Not today.

Earth became a marble. The vibration became a whisper.

Earth became a point of light. The vibration stopped.

As if a signal on the surface had been transmitting to him. And the signal had just died.

Luna stirred in his lap. She looked at the viewport. She did not say anything. She pressed her face against Theo's chest and curled against him and the bear named Captain was between them and the three of them sat there and watched the world end from above.

Ahead the Odyssey hung in orbit. A long bright shape

against the black. Lights running along its hull like a city laid on its side. The docking bay opened. The shuttle aligned and approached and the clamps took hold with a sound that traveled through the hull like a handshake and the airlock cycled with a hiss.

Theo unstrapped Luna. She looked up at him with her mother's eyes.

Are we safe now, she asked.

Theo looked at her. He looked at Knox. He looked at Daniella Ruiz who had walked into a catastrophe and chosen to help two children she did not know and then chosen again when the cost of choosing became clear.

We are together, he said. That is what I have.

They stepped through the airlock into the ship. The air was different. Clean and cool and humming with the deep vibration of systems running. The lighting was steady. The floor was solid. It smelled of recycled air and polymer and the faint ozone tang of electrical systems under load.

Ruiz took the children toward the passenger quarters. Knox went without speaking. Luna held Captain against her chest and walked on her own feet for the first time in hours. Theo watched them go. The corridor swallowed them and he stood alone in the intake bay with the airlock sealed behind him and the hum of the generators in the walls.

He leaned against the bulkhead. The arm rested at his side. And as he stood there in the quiet, the temperature in the cybernetic limb dropped. Half a degree. Maybe less. Not a malfunction. Not a power fluctuation. The diagnostic would show nothing if he ran it. Just a cooling. The way a house goes cold when the furnace cuts off. The way a room holds the warmth of a body that has left it and then, slowly, lets it go.

He noticed. He flexed the fingers. They responded

normally. He filed it with the vibration and the ghost readings and the growing catalog of things the arm did that the arm should not do.

Behind him the bay doors closed. Somewhere in the walls the generators hummed their deep and constant hum and underneath that hum, if you listened, if you knew what to listen for, there was another sound. A frequency. A pattern. Patient. Steady. Like a clock counting.

Theo heard it.

He said nothing.

He flexed the fingers of his left arm. They responded. Smooth and silent and normal. The vibration from the ascent was gone. The arm was just an arm again. But the absence of the signal felt different from the absence before the signal had started. Like a room after someone has left it. Still holding the shape of what had been there.

He walked into the body of the ship and found them in the passenger quarters. Knox on a bunk. Luna curled against Ruiz with Captain tucked under her chin. He sat beside them and the door sealed and outside the viewport Earth turned in its shroud of smoke and ash and the distance between them grew and grew until it was not distance anymore but something else entirely.

Something that could not be crossed.

Something that had never been meant to be.

CHAPTER 6

THROUGH THE WORMHOLE

Twelve readouts. All green. Core temperature stable across three generators. Containment field geometry nominal. Power draw at sixty-one percent capacity.

Thornhill sat alone on the engineering deck and watched numbers that meant the ship was working. The numbers did not comfort her. Numbers that should comfort a physicist and did not were the specific thing that kept her awake.

On the forward observation deck, twelve hours before transit, the planet turned below. The observation deck's viewport fed through a magnified relay, the last orbital satellite still responding to Odyssey's transponder. Earth filled the screen with a clarity that distance should not have allowed.

Earth. Brown and streaked where it should have been white. The oceans reflected a sun filtered through so much ash and aerosol that the light went flat and copper-colored. At night the dark side showed no cities. The great constellations of human habitation that had burned for centuries were gone. In their place the darkness held only fires. Scattered and random and guttering. Not the fires of industry or warmth. The fires of a civilization burning its own remains. Dallas. Houston. Mexico City. The Eastern Seaboard. Dark. All of it dark.

Theo stood at the rail and watched the planet turn and felt the distance growing between himself and everything he had known.

Ten thousand people slept in the cryo bays three decks below. Their vital signs scrolled across monitors that cycled through readings with the rhythm of a pulse. Core temperature. Heart rate. Neural activity. The machines kept them in a state that was not sleep and not death but something between. A suspension. A pause. A held breath measured in months.

A handful remained awake. The command crew. The engineering team. A medical rotation. A security detail. Forty-three people conscious in a ship built for ten thousand. Walking the corridors like caretakers in a museum that had not yet decided what it was preserving.

Captain Vasquez sat the command chair. She was a small woman with short dark hair and a face that concealed everything behind a discipline so total it looked like serenity. It was not. It was control.

She had commanded two deep-space surveys and a supply run to the Mars stations before everything fell apart. She had never commanded an ark. No one had commanded an ark. The word itself was borrowed from a story about a world that drowned and the assumption in that story was that the drowning was temporary. That there would be dry land again. Vasquez did not make that assumption.

She acknowledged Theo with a nod when he entered the bridge. Colonel.

Captain, Theo said.

Status, Vasquez said to the room.

Navigation is Park. Communications is Diaz. Helm is Chen, Vasquez had said when Theo arrived on the bridge. Short names. No biographies. The introductions of a captain who expected her crew to prove themselves in the doing.

Park spoke first. A young man whose eyes moved between his instruments with the fixed attention of someone who knew that looking away would let the fear in. Orbit is stable. Ground relay stations two and five are degraded but functional. Stations one and four are offline. We have sufficient sync for the wormhole array. Window opens in eleven hours fourteen minutes.

Engineering, Vasquez said.

Thornhill's voice came through the intercom from three decks below. She sounded the way a wire sounds when you tune it past comfortable tension. Just short of the note that means it will break.

Generators are holding, she said. All three cores at operational capacity. Wormhole stabilization array online and calibrated. Running final verification sequences now.

And the drift, Vasquez said.

A pause.

Containment drift events are occurring every four hours, Thornhill said. Down from six. The interval is shortening. Each event is a micro-oscillation in the field geometry. They self-correct. But the trend is accelerating.

Cause, Vasquez asked.

There is a low-frequency interference pattern embedded

in the drift signature, Thornhill said. I have been unable to identify its source. It does not match any onboard system. It does not match known solar or geomagnetic phenomena. A beat. It appears to be external. And correlated with our power output.

Vasquez looked at Theo. Nothing moved in her expression. But behind her eyes a calculation recalibrated.

Can we transit, Vasquez asked.

Yes, she said. I have compensatory protocols. I am confident in the margins.

How confident, Vasquez asked.

Ninety-two percent, Thornhill said.

The number hung in the air. Eight percent of the possible futures contained variables compensatory protocols could not handle. Eight percent of ten thousand lives.

We transit on schedule, Vasquez said. No delays.

Theo walked the ship.

The corridors of Odyssey were wide enough for three people abreast. The lighting was recessed and designed to approximate natural daylight but it missed in a way the body noticed even if the eyes could not identify it. Too clean. Too even. No shadows. The light of a place that had never known weather.

The air moved through hidden vents with a whisper that became a kind of silence after you had listened to it long enough. It tasted of nothing. Not even metal. The scrubbers took everything out. Every molecule of scent and history and character. What remained was air in the same way that distilled water was water. Technically correct and fundamentally empty.

He walked because walking was thinking. On the ranch he walked the fence lines and the pattern of his steps matched the pattern of his thoughts. Here the corridors were straight and long. Linear. Sequential.

He passed the cryo bays and stopped at the viewing gallery. The gallery was a long window running the length of Bay Four. Through it the pods stretched in rows. Hundreds. Thousands. Each pod a frost-covered capsule roughly the size and shape of a coffin though no one called them that. Inside each one a human being lay in the deep stillness of cryo-sleep. Their faces visible through the frost. Calm. Slack. The faces of people who had surrendered consciousness and trusted machines and strangers to carry them through the dark.

Somewhere in those rows lay the young doctor whose mother had stood at the fence. Somewhere a man who had carried his children through the burning streets of San Antonio. Somewhere the woman Maria Lopez who had shown her credentials and her five dependents at the spaceport gate and walked aboard with the bearing of a woman who intended to teach literature to children on a new world because literature was the thing that told you who you were when everything else was gone.

He moved on.

In the family quarters the last intake had been settled. They sat on bunks and floors with the stunned patience of people who had survived a catastrophe and did not yet know how to feel about the surviving.

A girl of perhaps six sat on the floor playing with a toy shuttle. She made it fly in slow arcs through the air and her lips moved with the sound of engines that existed only in her mind. A boy sat beside her. Maybe four.

Are we going to Lupus Stella now, the boy asked.

The girl looked at him. Yes, she said. It is very far away.

How far.

She considered. Farther than grandma's house.

Will there be dogs, he asked.

She worked through this. Maybe, she said. Space dogs.

Theo watched them from down the corridor and felt a pressure move in his chest. Not grief exactly. Not hope. The unnamed thing between. The thing that children carried without knowing they carried it. The faith that tomorrow would come and it would be a place worth going to.

He found Knox and Luna in a small cabin on deck four. Ruiz sat on the floor with Luna working a braid into her hair. Knox was on the bunk reading a manual. EMERGENCY PROCEDURES — CREW ORIENTATION.

That is light reading, Theo said from the doorway.

Knox looked up. It says what to do if the hull breaches. You have fifteen seconds to reach a pressure compartment.

Good to know, Theo said.

Luna turned. Uncle Theo, Daniella taught me to braid. She held up the end of the braid. It was uneven and coming apart and she displayed it with the pride of someone who had made a thing for the first time.

That is fine work, Theo said.

Ruiz met his eyes. In her gaze he saw the steadiness of someone who had found a purpose and locked onto it. There was no training for what she was doing. No manual. She was doing it because the children needed it and that was enough.

Thank you, Theo said.

Ruiz nodded. She went back to the braid.

Theo put his hand on Knox's shoulder. The boy leaned into it. Just enough to say I am here without saying it.

In eleven hours we go through the wormhole, Theo said.

Knox looked at him. What is it like.

I do not know, Theo said. Nobody does. Not at this scale.

Knox nodded. He did not look scared. He looked like a boy who had already survived the thing that scared him most and was now living in whatever came after.

Will it hurt, Luna asked.

No, Theo said. He did not know if this was true. It was the answer she needed.

Ruiz came for them at 0600. The cryo team was ready. Knox went first. He did not argue. He lay on the slab and looked at the ceiling and the gel rose around him cold and viscous and his eyes closed. Luna held Theo's hand until the tech said it was time. She asked if she would dream. Theo said he did not know. She lay down and the cold took her and the hand that had held his went still. He stood over them until the indicators turned blue and then he turned away because standing over sleeping children when you cannot protect them is the specific cruelty of parenthood and he had never been a parent and he was one now.

On the engineering deck the zero-point generators sat behind layered shielding the way reactor cores sit behind containment walls. Three cylinders each the size of a railcar. Their casings dark alloy showing no seams. They did not glow. They did not crackle with visible energy. They simply existed. Massive and still and drawing power from a source so fundamental that physics had only recently admitted it was there.

But you could feel them. A vibration in the deck plates that was below sound. A pressure in the inner ear. The sense of something immense and constrained working at frequencies the body understood the way the body understands gravity. Not through knowledge. Through the bones.

Thornhill was at her station. Her workspace was a half-circle of screens and interfaces. Data scrolled and refreshed. Waveforms pulsed. Her fingers moved across the controls with the speed of long practice.

Colonel, she said without looking up.

Show me the interference pattern, Theo said.

Thornhill pulled up a display. A waveform on a dark background. The operational signature of the generators formed the upper band. Steady. Below it the normal quantum noise made a jagged line.

And below that.

Thornhill isolated the frequency. Amplified it. A slow deep pulse. Below the range of human hearing but not below the range of human feeling. Patient as geological processes are patient.

That, she said. That is not us.

How long has it been there.

She looked at him. I went back through every log we have. The signature is present in data from six months ago. But it was so deep in the noise floor that no one flagged it. It has been growing. Slowly. Steadily. And it correlates with our power output. When we increase output the signal strengthens. When we throttle down it attenuates. It is responsive. It is coupled to us.

Theo looked at the waveform. It pulsed. Slow and steady and indifferent to observation.

What does it want, he said.

Thornhill's mouth thinned. That implies agency. I have a correlation. A signal that behaves as though it is listening. But I cannot prove it is listening.

But you believe it is.

I am a physicist, she said. I deal in data. She paused. But the data makes me uncomfortable.

For now it is within our compensation parameters, she

said after a moment. I can manage it through transit. But you should understand that I am managing something I do not understand. And the one thing I know about things I do not understand is that they do not stay manageable forever.

Get us through, Theo said.

That is the plan, she said.

She looked at him and he saw in her face the thing that every scientist fears more than being wrong. Being right too late.

The final hours passed the way all final hours pass. Too fast and too slow at once.

In the mess compartment on deck three a crew member named Reeves was trying to drink coffee from a sealed pouch and the seal failed and a sphere of black liquid drifted between her face and the overhead panel and she swatted at it and it broke into smaller spheres that scattered in every direction. Oh you absolute bastard, she said to the coffee. A medic across the table laughed. She laughed too and the sound was strange on a ship this quiet. Down the table a navigation officer was arguing with an engineer about whether the artificial gravity on Lupus Stella would feel heavier or lighter than Earth-standard and neither of them was right and neither of them cared. They were talking to hear themselves talk. To fill the silence before the silence became something else.

At T-minus thirty Vasquez opened the ship-wide channel.

All hands. This is the Captain. In thirty minutes we will initiate wormhole transit. Secure all stations. Secure all personnel.

She paused.

What we are about to do has never been done with a vessel of this size carrying this many lives. There is no manual for this. There is no precedent. There is only the work and the people doing it. Do your work. Trust the people beside you. We will see the other side.

She closed the channel.

The bridge was quiet. The kind of quiet that is not an absence of sound but a concentration of attention. Every person at their station. Every screen active. Every readout monitored. Outside the forward viewport Earth hung in its ruin and beyond it the stars and between the stars the darkness where the wormhole would open.

Navigation, Vasquez said. Confirm plot.

Plot confirmed Captain. Target system Wolf 1061. Exit coordinates locked and verified.

Engineering.

Thornhill's voice came through steady. Generators at full power. All three cores nominal. Stabilization array online. Wormhole initiation sequence is armed. Drift compensation protocols active.

Vasquez looked at Theo. He stood at the rail. His cybernetic hand on the metal. His face still.

Colonel. Anything to add.

Take us through, he said.

Vasquez nodded.

Initiate, she said.

The generators ramped. The vibration in the deck plates deepened. The ship felt heavier.

On the forward screen the stars began to change.

It started at the center. A point of space that had been empty began to behave differently. The stars near it shifted. Their light elongated. Slowly. As if seen through glass beginning to warp. The light stretched into thin lines that curved toward a center that was not visible. Not yet.

The distortion grew. A ring of bent starlight surrounding

a center darker than the space around it. Not black. An absence that went deeper than the absence of light. An absence of geometry.

Throat forming, she reported. Diameter two hundred meters. Expanding.

The ship moved. Positioning jets fired. Small precise burns that aligned the vessel with the center of the opening.

Throat stabilized at one point two kilometers, she said. Field geometry within parameters. Entanglement lock confirmed. We are aligned.

The opening filled the screen. It was not light and it was not dark. It was a threshold.

All hands brace for transit, Vasquez said.

The ship crossed the threshold.

The transition was not sudden. It was a crossing that took time. Five seconds. Ten. Fifteen. During those seconds the universe outside the viewport changed. The stars stretched and then vanished. The darkness changed quality. It was no longer the darkness of space which is the darkness of distance. It became the darkness of passage. Of transit. Of moving through something that had structure and depth and dimension.

The hull groaned. Not the sound of metal failing. The sound of metal enduring conditions it was not designed for and finding within its engineering the capacity to hold. The lights on the bridge flickered. Went dim. Came back. Went dim again. Steadied at a lower level.

Then they were in the tunnel.

The tunnel was not a tunnel in any sense the word conveyed. It was a space between spaces. If it had walls they were not walls made of anything. They were boundaries of a geometry that human eyes interpreted as surface because the brain required surface to orient itself.

The colors were wrong. Not wrong in the sense of unusual. Wrong in the sense of impossible. Hues that had no names. Reds that were deeper than red. Blues that were older than blue. Something like gold but cold and vast and ancient. The colors moved and folded in patterns that the eye followed and the mind lost.

The sensors screamed.

Every instrument on every console lit up. Temperature readings that oscillated between absolute zero and figures that physics could not support. Radiation levels that spiked to lethal and vanished to baseline and spiked again. Gravitational measurements that contradicted each other. The ship was simultaneously falling and rising and stationary. It was in motion at velocities the instruments could not calculate and it was still.

Then the sensors went quiet.

Not off. Not failed. Quiet. As if they had decided that the data available was not data. That the information streaming in from outside the hull was not information in any sense that could be processed. The screens went to default. The readouts held their last reliable numbers and stopped updating.

On the navigation console Park's manifest display flickered. He blinked. The passenger manifest had refreshed itself and the names were different. Not all of them. Most of them. Names he did not recognize in a font that looked the same but was not. He scrolled. The list was the right length. Ten thousand entries. But the names were not the names he had logged. He scrolled back to the top. The names were correct again. The names he knew. He stared at it. Looked at the navigator beside him. Said nothing. The navigator was staring at her own screen with an expression Park recognized because he was wearing it.

I have seen this before, the navigator said. Her name was Young. Her voice barely audible. Not this. This moment. I dreamed this. When I was seven. I dreamed I was sitting at a console on a ship going through a tunnel of light and the instruments went quiet and I looked to my left and there was a man at the next station looking at me exactly the way you are looking at me right now.

Park said nothing. There was nothing to say. The manifest was correct again. The moment passed. But the navigator's hands on her console had stopped moving and she was looking at the tunnel on the forward screen with the eyes of someone who had just remembered an appointment they had forgotten they made.

The bridge was silent except for the hum of the ship and the breathing of the crew.

Vasquez's voice broke the silence. Her knuckles on the armrests were white.

Engineering. Report.

Thornhill's voice came through the intercom. There was a delay. Half a second. On an internal channel there should have been no delay at all.

Generators are holding, Thornhill said. Stabilization array is compensating for transit field geometry. She paused. The interference pattern has amplified. Factor of three. Possibly four.

Can you hold it, Vasquez asked.

I am holding it, Thornhill said. The compensatory protocols are functioning. But the pattern is not static. It is responding to our transit. It is increasing as we increase power.

Are we at risk of containment failure.

No. Not at current levels. But the trend line.

She did not finish the sentence.

The tunnel moved around them. Or they moved through the tunnel. The distinction had no meaning here. Time was behaving strangely. The clocks on the bridge still ran. They showed numbers. But the numbers did not correspond to any internal sense of duration. A minute passed that felt like an hour. An hour passed that felt like a breath.

Crew members at their stations experienced something that was not quite memory and not quite vision. Lieutenant Allen at tactical felt certain he had already spoken the words he was about to say and stopped speaking. Ensign Diaz at communications heard a channel open and close and in the static heard her mother's voice saying dinner is ready from a house in Tucson that no longer existed. The helmsman gripped his controls and felt the grain of a wooden oar in his hands, a lake, a canoe, his grandfather in the stern. These moments came and went like weather. No one reported them.

Theo gripped the rail. His cybernetic fingers did not slip. They never slipped. They held the metal with the unthinking certainty of a machine. His other hand he kept at his side and it was not steady.

A containment alarm sounded. Sharp and high.

Micro-oscillation in generator two, Thornhill reported. Compensating.

A second alarm.

Generator one showing sympathetic resonance, Thornhill said. The oscillation is spreading across the containment fields.

A third alarm.

All three generators are oscillating in phase, Thornhill said. Her voice was tight now. Controlled but tight. The interference pattern is driving a resonance loop. The generators are amplifying each other's drift. I am inserting counter-frequency modulation.

The bridge watched the engineering readouts. The waveforms on the screen danced. Three lines that should have been parallel were converging. Merging. Becoming one wave. And underneath them the interference pattern pulsed. Stronger. Faster.

Vasquez did not speak. She watched.

Thornhill's voice came through. I have the counter-frequency locked. Inserting now.

A beat.

The alarms continued for three seconds. Four. Five.

Then they stopped.

The waveforms separated. Steadied. The interference pattern dropped. Did not disappear. But dropped. Subdued.

Modulation successful, Thornhill said. She exhaled. The sound of the exhale carried through the intercom. Containment is holding. Resonance has dampened. Drift is within parameters.

Vasquez released her grip on the armrests. She did not flex her hands. She simply opened them and placed them flat on the arms of the chair and that was as close to showing relief as her discipline allowed.

The tunnel continued. The impossible colors shifted. Time continued to lie. The clocks counted and the count was unreliable and the crew sat at their stations and watched instruments that could not tell them where they were or how fast they were going or how long they had been going and they trusted that the mathematics that opened this passage would also close it.

Theo stood at the rail and watched the forward screen. The screen showed the tunnel. The throat of it. A passage that narrowed ahead of them into a brightness that was different from the colors around it. A real brightness. The brightness of photons behaving normally. Of light traveling in straight lines from real stars.

I am reading gravitational normalization ahead, Park said from the navigation console. His voice was higher than usual. Exit geometry is forming. Confirming target coordinates.

He worked his instruments.

Confirmed, he said. Wolf 1061 system. We are within point-zero-two parsecs of target. Exit in approximately four minutes.

Vasquez stood. She had been sitting for the duration. She stood and the standing was a statement.

Prepare for emergence, she ordered.

The tunnel narrowed. The colors thinned. The geometry simplified. The sensors came back online one by one. First temperature. Then radiation. Then gravity. The numbers they reported were real. Consistent. Verifiable. The physics of the normal universe reasserting itself like a tide coming back in.

The forward screen cleared.

Stars. Real stars in fixed positions. A red star. Small and ancient and steady. Wolf 1061. And in that light turning slow in its orbit a planet.

Theo looked at it.

It was not Earth. Its oceans were dark. Crimson in the red light. Its continents green-black with vegetation that owed nothing to any seed from the world he was born on. Clouds banded the globe in patterns set by a day that lasted twenty-eight hours and tides pulled by no moon he could see.

The bridge was silent. Forty-three people who had crossed fourteen light-years through a fold in spacetime and come out alive on the other side and now stood looking at the place where they would live or die or both.

Park spoke from navigation. His voice careful. The voice of a man who has found something he does not want to have found.

Captain. The atomic clocks have desynchronized.

Vasquez turned to him. Explain.

All four onboard atomic clocks ran continuously through transit, Park said. They should read identical. They do not. Clocks one and three agree. Clocks two and four agree. The two pairs differ by fourteen seconds.

Which pair is correct.

Park swallowed. I cannot determine that, he said. Each pair is internally consistent. Each pair validates against its own reference. There is no external time source to arbitrate. We are either fourteen seconds ahead of where we should be or fourteen seconds behind. Or one pair gained fourteen seconds and the other lost them. I cannot tell which.

Fourteen seconds. Not minutes. Not hours. A gap so small it should have been trivial and was not trivial at all because the clocks were designed to agree and they did not agree and the universe they had entered was supposed to run on the same time as the universe they had left and apparently it did not.

Log it, Vasquez said. We will reconcile in stable orbit.

She stood at the viewport and looked at the planet below.

Her voice was quiet. Steady as bedrock is steady. Not because it does not feel the forces upon it but because it holds against them.

We have arrived, she said.

The words carried through the bridge and into the corridors and through the intercom to every compartment of the ship. Forty-three conscious souls heard them. Ten thousand sleeping souls did not. But the words were for all of them. For the living and the suspended. For the left and the taken.

And then Thornhill's voice came through. Quiet. Command channel only.

Captain. Colonel. I need you to see this.

Vasquez looked at Theo. Theo was already moving.

On the engineering deck Thornhill stood at her workstation with her arms crossed and her face set in the expression it wore when the data had done something she did not want it to do.

She pointed at her screen.

This is the interference pattern before transit. She tapped. The slow deep pulse appeared. Patient. Rhythmic.

And this is the interference pattern now.

She tapped again. A second waveform appeared beside the first. The same shape. The same amplitude. The same frequency. Identical in every measurable parameter. Except.

Theo looked at it.

It is backward, he said.

Thornhill nodded. The same pulse played in reverse. As if the signal went through the wormhole and came out mirrored. Inverted. Running in the opposite temporal direction.

What does that mean, Theo asked.

It means the signal has a relationship with time that I do not understand, Thornhill said. A signal does not reverse itself. A signal does not play backward unless something acts on it. Unless transit through the wormhole did something to the signal that it did not do to anything else on this ship. The generators are running forward. The clocks are running forward. Everything on this ship is running forward except that.

She looked at the two waveforms side by side. Before and after. The same pulse, mirror-imaged.

I am logging this. I am not reporting it.

Theo looked at her.

I do not have an explanation. And I will not report data I cannot explain. Not yet. Not when we have ten thousand people who need to believe the ship is functioning normally. She paused. Because it is functioning normally. Every system is nominal. Every reading is clean. Except this. And this I do not know what to do with.

Theo watched her face. The discipline in it. The fear beneath the discipline.

Log it, he said.

He turned toward the hatch. At the hatch he stopped.

Thornhill.

She looked up.

If it changes again. I am the first to know.

She nodded once.

He left the engineering deck and walked the corridor toward the lift. The corridor was quiet. The hum of the ship steady and unchanged.

At the lift he stopped. He looked at his left arm.

He ran a diagnostic. The display projected from the wrist. Green bars scrolling. Motor functions one hundred percent. Sensory feedback calibrated. Power cell ninety-seven percent. Neural interface nominal.

Except the serial number.

It sat at the bottom of the readout where it always sat. The alphanumeric string that identified the arm as his. The string he had memorized the day they installed it in the orbital bay above Promethei. The string he had checked a thousand times since.

The string was different.

Not corrupted. Not garbled. The number was clean and formatted and complete. It was a serial number. It was simply not his serial number. TXD-7791-LSMA-0461. The prefix was wrong. The sequence was wrong. The check digits were wrong.

He checked the diagnostic log. The log that recorded every readout, every fluctuation since installation. Years of entries. Thousands of data points.

The log showed one entry. Today's date. This readout. Nothing before it.

He scrolled. There was nothing to scroll through. The log began here. Now. As if the arm had come into existence at this moment. As if its history prior to the wormhole had never been.

He flexed the fingers. They responded. Smooth and precise and familiar. The arm felt like his arm. It moved like his arm. Nothing about its function had changed.

Only its identity.

He closed the diagnostic. He stood in the corridor and looked at the arm and the arm looked like the arm it had always been and the number inside it said it was not.

The arm's thermal reading dropped half a degree. Not a malfunction. A thermal shift. Like warmth withdrawing. Like a house going cold when the furnace cuts off. He noted it.

He filed it. The vibration during ascent. The woman whose death certificate said she was dead. Every crack in the surface of things that he noticed and could not explain and would not ignore and would not allow to slow him down. The anomalies accumulated. The filing system was not denial. It was operational triage. You noted. You continued. When the anomalies cohered into something actionable you acted. Until then you moved.

He took the lift to deck four. He walked the corridor to the cabin where the children waited. He opened the door and Knox looked up from his manual and Luna held up a braid she had made and Ruiz sat on the floor with her steady hands and her steady eyes and the small room was warm with the heat of people who were alive and present and real in every way that mattered.

Theo sat on the bunk. He put his arm around Knox. The arm that had a different name inside it now. The arm that held the boy the same way it had always held him. Knox leaned in.

What is it like out there, the boy asked.

Theo looked at the viewport. The red star burned and the planet turned and the dark between held its own counsel.

New, he said.

In the engineering deck three levels below Thornhill sat alone at her station. The waveform pulsed on her screen. Backward. Patient.

She opened her personal log. She typed a single entry.

Post-transit anomaly. ZPE interference pattern inverted. Same structure mirrored temporally. No explanation. No precedent. Containment nominal. All systems functional. Reporting to no one pending further observation.

She closed the log. She picked up her thermos. It was empty. She held it anyway.

On the screen the waveform pulsed. Backward. Backward. Backward. A signal that had gone through the fold between stars and come out running in the wrong direction. Or the right direction. She could not tell which. And the not-telling was the thing that kept her at the screen long after the rest of the engineering crew had gone to their bunks. Watching. Listening. Feeling in the deck plates beneath her feet the low deep hum of generators drawing power from a source that no one fully understood.

Through the viewport Lupus Stella turned in the red light. Patient. Waiting.

Not empty.

Not empty at all.

CHAPTER 7

ARRIVAL AT LUPUS STELLA

Six hours after emergence, in stable orbit, the bridge crew sat in the quiet that follows survival.

The navigation officer confirmed orbit in a voice that cracked on the word and then corrected herself and said it again and no one on the bridge looked at her because everyone understood that cracking was the honest response and steadiness was the performance they needed and both things could be true at the same time.

They had come through. The wormhole had opened its throat and swallowed them and held them in a darkness that was not darkness and a duration that was not duration and then spat them out into cold black space and the ship had shuddered once and the alarms had screamed and gone quiet and the screens had gone dark and come back bearing the image of a world.

Lupus Stella.

It hung against the void like a wound in the firmament. A super-Earth turning slow and deliberate under the dim red stare of Wolf 1061. The star sat low and swollen on the ecliptic plane and its light fell across the planet in bands of rust and carmine so that the oceans looked like old blood left to cool in basins of stone. Green-black continents rose from the crimson water. Mountain ranges caught the light on their western faces. Cloud systems banded the globe in long ragged scarves and where the cloud broke the land beneath showed dark and wet and furred with what could only be vegetation. Life. Out here in the cold between stars where no human had ever drawn breath.

Theo stood on the bridge with his hands at his sides. The carbon-fiber fingers of his left hand opened and closed once. A reflex.

Then the arm seized the handrail.

He had not told it to. The carbon-fiber fingers locked around the rail and the servos in the wrist torqued hard enough to bend the metal inward by a millimeter. His breath stopped. Not the shallow catch of surprise but a full arrest. The air locked in his lungs and his vision narrowed to the planet on the screen and he stood rigid at the command platform gripping a handrail with a hand that had decided something before he had. The arm held for three seconds. Then the servos released. The fingers opened. The breath came back in a rush that fogged in the cold bridge air and his heart knocked twice against his ribs and settled.

He looked at his left hand. The fingers were steady now. The readout on the wrist display showed nominal function. But the handrail had a shallow crescent dent where the carbon fiber had bitten into it. Evidence. He ran his thumb over the mark and said nothing.

He had never been here. He knew this with the certainty of a man who knew his own name and his own service record and the serial number stamped into the titanium socket where his left arm met the ruin of his shoulder. He had never been here. But the feeling that moved through him was not the feeling of discovery. It was the feeling of return. As a man rounds a bend in the road and sees the house he grew up in and his body knows it before his eyes confirm it. Except there was no road and there was no house and the thing on the screen was an alien world fourteen light-years from the Texas ranch where he had last stood under an open sky.

The feeling did not care about knowledge. It sat in his chest and would not explain itself.

Around him the bridge crew sat at their stations and did not speak. The hum of the ship filled the silence. Instruments cycled through their startup diagnostics and one by one the consoles returned green and the data began to flow and still no one spoke. The forward viewscreen showed the planet growing larger by degrees as Odyssey corrected its post-transit drift and began the long arc toward orbit.

Vasquez sat in the command chair with her back straight and her face unreadable. She had not moved during the transit. Had not gripped the armrest or closed her eyes or shown any outward sign that the ship had just been threaded through a hole in spacetime. She watched the planet as a surveyor watches terrain she does not yet trust. Her hands were still. Her eyes were not.

Orbit insertion, she said.

Thrusters fired in sequence along Odyssey's ventral hull. A gentle push that Theo felt in his sternum. The planet swelled on the screen. Red oceans sharpening into distinct bodies of water separated by landmasses that looked nothing like the continents he had memorized in school a lifetime ago. These were wider. Flatter. Their coastlines ragged with inlets and archipelagos that sprawled across the crimson water like shattered pottery.

Thornhill stood at the science station with both hands flat on the console. She had not slept. The tendons in her neck stood out like cables and her lab coat was wrinkled from days of continuous wear. She had held the containment fields together through the wormhole with manual corrections every forty seconds for a duration that felt like hours and might have been minutes. Precision was survival. Error was inheritance.

Atmosphere is breathable within tolerance, she said. Nitrogen-oxygen mix. Seventy-four percent nitrogen. Twenty-two percent oxygen. Trace argon and carbon dioxide. Gravity reading one point one five g. Axial tilt nine degrees. Day length approximately twenty-eight standard hours.

Her voice was flat. Clinical.

Surface temperature range at the target latitude runs sixteen to thirty-one Celsius. Liquid water confirmed across all major basins. Spectral analysis of the vegetation suggests chlorophyll analogs active in the red and near-infrared bands. She paused. The biosphere is extensive.

There was something else. A faint, organized electromagnetic signature on the surface. Thirty-seven kilometers east of the primary landing site. Low power. Rhythmic. Not natural. Natural emissions did not maintain phase coherence at that consistency.

What is that, Theo asked.

Thornhill studied the reading. It could be geological. Certain mineral formations produce resonant signatures under tectonic pressure. She did not sound convinced. I am flagging it. Low priority. We have larger concerns.

Theo filed it. The way he filed everything that did not demand immediate accounting but refused to be ignored.

Theo heard the numbers and felt nothing that resembled comfort. He had learned at Promethei Terra that the most dangerous ground was the ground that looked safe. A valley floor swept clean of cover. A ridgeline with no wind. Those were the killing fields.

This planet looked perfect. That was the problem.

Any signs of intelligence, Vasquez asked.

A sensor officer named Carrera worked his console. He had been an orbital traffic controller at Guam Station before the war and he moved his fingers across the display in the quick patterns of a man accustomed to tracking objects that could kill thousands if he looked away.

No transmissions, he said. No heat signatures consistent with habitation or industry. No artificial structures on any wavelength. He paused and his fingers slowed. But there are anomalies.

Vasquez did not move. Define anomalies.

Carrera brought up a holographic projection of the planet's surface. A ten-kilometer grid overlaid the terrain. Red dots pulsed at irregular intervals across two of the larger continents. Perhaps a dozen in total. They held their positions with a fixity that suggested something other than weather or geology. Each dot pulsed at the same rate.

Localized electromagnetic emissions, Carrera said. Repeatable. Not storms. Not aurora or volcanic discharge. Fixed positions. Same intensity across all sources. Same duration. Same interval.

He hesitated. They are synchronized.

The word hung in the air of the bridge.

Thornhill crossed the bridge in three steps. She leaned over Carrera's shoulder and studied the display. The clinical mask slipped for a moment and beneath it was hunger. She pulled up a secondary analysis window without asking permission and began layering data.

Show me the raw frequency, she said.

Carrera pulled the spectral analysis. Waveform data scrolling in cascading bands. And there beneath the noise like a heartbeat buried in static sat a low-frequency pulse. Steady. Patient. Repeating at intervals of four point seven seconds with a precision that no natural process should produce.

Thornhill went still. She stared at the waveform for a long time. Then she opened a second window on Carrera's console and loaded the containment drift recordings from the transit. She did not ask permission for this either. She stretched the transit data alongside the planetary emissions and the two waveforms lay on top of each other like tracings of the same hand.

She leaned back from the console. Pressed the heel of her hand against her sternum. Leaned in again.

Show me the spatial distribution, she said.

Carrera adjusted the projection. The red dots hung in the hologram and Thornhill moved around the display tracing lines between the points. She was quiet for a long time. The bridge waited. Then she reached into the hologram and with two fingers drew a line between the nearest pair. Then another. Then another.

The shape that emerged was a grid.

Not random. Not the scatter of volcanic vents or mineral deposits. The sources sat at the vertices of a lattice. Equidistant within a margin too narrow for coincidence. The spacing precise. The angles precise. The geometry of something grown rather than built.

Thornhill stepped back from the display. She pressed

both hands flat against the edge of the console. A gesture Theo had not seen from her before. Not scientific. Private.

It looks like a circuit board, Carrera said quietly. As if the observation might be taken from him if he spoke it too loud.

Or a neural network, she said. Her voice was flat. Depending on which connections you draw.

No one corrected either of them. The projection turned slowly in the dim light and the lattice of red dots pulsed and the shape they made was not natural and not artificial but something between. Something that suggested an intent that did not map to any intent human engineering had ever expressed.

Thornhill pulled the data onto her personal tablet. She ran spectral overlays. The planetary emissions and the transit logs layered over each other. Same base frequency as the containment drift. Same harmonic structure. Within two percent variance. The synchronization across all twelve sources exact.

She looked up. Her eyes found Theo across the bridge and held him for a moment. Then she looked away and began running comparisons she did not share with anyone.

The navigation display showed all parameters nominal. Through the forward viewport the planet turned below them close enough to fill the glass. A world alive with weather and motion and the slow thermodynamics of a biosphere that had been running for eons without audience.

Until now.

Vasquez turned to Theo. Your assessment, she said.

He was quiet. He watched the planet. The red oceans. The dark land. The clouds moving in patterns governed by physics almost familiar and not quite right.

He thought about the ten thousand people in the cryo

bays. He thought about Knox and Luna. He thought about the planet they had left behind.

There was no going back. The wormhole was a one-way passage. The fuel margins did not allow a return transit. Odyssey had carried them across light-years on a promise and the promise was the planet on the screen and there was nothing else.

We came here to land, he said. We land.

Vasquez nodded once. She began issuing orders. The bridge came alive. Navigation locked orbital parameters. Communications prepped relay buoys. Engineering confirmed generator status and Thornhill responded without looking up and her voice was steady and her eyes were not.

In the cryo bays the first wave began to wake.

Theo walked the corridors to the revival section. The ship was vast and mostly empty in its habitable portions. His boots made a steady rhythm on the deck plates. He passed through a junction where a viewport opened onto the planet below and he stopped.

Wolf 1061's light fell through the armored glass and painted his face in tones of rust and old copper. The star was close. Closer than the sun appeared from Earth. A red dwarf burning cool and patient and old beyond reckoning. It did not warm. It watched.

He stood there and the feeling came again. Return. Not arrival. The wrongness of it was precise. Not the general unease of a soldier on unfamiliar ground. Specific. As if the curve of that largest continent fit a shape he already carried. As if the pattern of the cloud bands matched something filed in a drawer of his memory he could not find the key to. He had dreamed of red light. He had dreamed of forests that glowed. He knew this because the dream logs on his medical file said so. But those dreams had been filed under combat stress and cryo artifacts and the file had been closed.

The file was closed. The feeling was open.

He cataloged it with the rest. Moved on.

In the cryo bay the air was cold and smelled of antiseptic and the faint chemical tang of preservation gel. Row upon row of pods stretching back into the dim recesses of the compartment like the pews of some frozen church. Glass-topped coffins holding the cargo of a dead world. Faces slack and frost-rimed and peaceful in a way that the waking world would not allow.

The revival process was automated. Medical drones moved along the rows on silent tracks injecting stimulants and warming the cryo gel by careful degrees. Two degrees per minute. Faster and the thermal shock could stop a heart. Slower and the brain might wake before the body and the dreamer would lie paralyzed in a glass box and feel themselves thawing from the outside in. The drones did not hurry. The difference between resurrection and murder was a matter of temperature and time.

The pods opened with a soft pneumatic hiss and the people inside stirred like sleepers surfacing from a depth they had not chosen.

A woman sat up in the nearest pod. Frost in her hair. Her eyes wild and unfocused. A medical tech helped her stand and she swayed and caught herself and then she saw the viewport and through it the planet hanging red and green and enormous against the black.

She wept.

It is real, she said. Her voice cracked. It is real.

Others woke and wept with her. Not grief. Larger than grief. The sound of people who had closed their eyes above a dying world and opened them to find that the promise had been kept.

A man four pods down sat up and looked at the viewport and laughed. It came out of him like a thing shaken loose. A sound he had not planned. He covered his mouth with both hands and then pulled them away and laughed again and the laughter turned into something else and he pressed his face into his palms and his shoulders shook. The woman beside him did not know him. She put her hand on his back anyway.

Not all of them wept. Not all of them laughed.

In row six a man sat on the edge of his pod and would not stand. He was broad across the shoulders. Thick hands. Soil under the nails that the cryo gel had not dissolved. The medical tech spoke to him and he answered but his answers were wrong.

Name, the tech said.

Garza. David Garza.

The tech checked the manifest. Name confirmed.

Assignment.

Power systems, Garza said. He said it flat. The voice of a man stating something he had known his entire life. Engineering. Reactor section. I ran containment protocols on the number three module during the outbound prep cycle.

The tech looked at his tablet. Looked at Garza. Looked at the tablet again.

Mr. Garza, your file says agricultural division. Hydroponics. You have been assigned to the growing operations since embarkation.

Garza stared at the tech. His jaw worked once. He held his hands up and turned them over as if examining evidence. They were the hands of a man who had worked in soil. The creases stained dark. A callus on the right index finger from a pruning tool. Eleven years of greenhouse work written in the topography of his skin.

There must be a mistake, he said. He said it quietly. Not angry. Bewildered. The bewilderment of a man whose hands say one thing and whose mind says another and who does not know which to believe. I have never grown anything in my life. I am an engineer. I have always been an engineer.

The tech started to respond and Garza cut him off.

Check the reactor logs, he said. His voice rose but did not break. Check the number three module. I was on the containment team. Ask Thornhill. She signed my maintenance reports. She will tell you.

The tech flagged it. Cryo disorientation. The literature said it resolved within hours.

Garza did not move to stand. He sat on the edge of his pod and turned his hands over again. Back and forth. Studying the calluses and the soil-dark creases. The evidence of a life his mind did not claim. After a moment he pressed his palms together and held them there and closed his eyes. He stayed like that while the bay filled with the sounds of waking around him. A man praying to his own hands for an answer they could not give.

Three rows back a woman was arguing with a nurse. She was sitting upright in her pod with her feet on the floor and her body leaning forward and she was speaking with the urgency of someone correcting a dangerous error.

No, she said. Listen to me. I lived in Aurelia. Fourteenth Street. Near the harbor. The apartment above the bakery on Linden.

The nurse checked the manifest. Ma'am, your address of record is listed as Galveston, Texas.

The woman shook her head. She was not confused. Her

eyes were not the glassy eyes of cryo fog. They were clear and certain and she described her city the way you describe a place you love. White towers on a coast. A harbor that caught the morning light so the water looked like hammered gold. The market on the corner of Seventh and Linden. The man who sold roasted nuts in paper cones. The smell of salt and engine oil from the fishing boats.

She named the streets. She named the parks. She named the school where she had taught third grade for nine years and the principal's name was Mara and the building had a crack in the east wall they had never repaired. She described the pattern of the crack. How it widened in the rain. How the children would press their fingers into it and she would tell them to stop and they would do it again the next day.

There was no city called Aurelia on any map of Earth.

The nurse noted it. Cryo artifact. Identity confusion. Move on.

But the woman kept talking. Her voice did not waver. Her eyes did not search. She remembered perfectly and could not understand why no one else did.

Ma'am, the nurse said. We need you to move to processing.

The woman looked at the nurse. Her face changed. Not confusion. Worse than confusion. The expression of a person who has just realized that the world she carries in her head does not match the world she is standing in and that one of them is wrong and she does not know which.

She stood. She followed the nurse. She did not speak again. But as she walked she touched the wall of the corridor with her fingertips every few steps. Pressing them flat against the metal. As if confirming its solidity. As if the ship might be the dream and Aurelia might be the real place and she might at any moment wake up in the apartment above the bakery with the smell of bread rising through the floor.

A third case emerged two rows further on. A teenager who woke speaking fluent Mandarin. His parents stood beside his pod and stared at him. Their son had never studied Mandarin. He had grown up in Lubbock. He had spoken English and passable Spanish his entire life. But now the words came out of him in tones and cadences that his mother did not recognize and his father kept saying his name and the boy kept answering in a language neither of them spoke. After four minutes the Mandarin stopped. The boy blinked. He looked at his parents and said what happened. In English. He did not remember the Mandarin. His parents did not tell him. They held his hands and walked him to processing and his mother kept her face still and her grip tight.

The tech at Garza's station was making notes. Theo walked to her.

How many, he said.

The tech looked at him. She was young. Tired. Her name tag said Perkins and her hair was pulled back tight and her eyes had the flat focus of someone who had been solving problems for hours without pause.

Disorientation cases, she said. Seven confirmed in this section. Three more flagged pending evaluation. The literature says five to eight percent is within normal range for extended cryosleep.

And for cryosleep following a wormhole transit, Theo said.

She looked at him. There is no literature for that, she said.

He nodded. He let her return to her work.

Theo counted seven cases in the first hundred and twenty revivals. Seven people whose memories or faculties did not match their files. A job title. A hometown. A language never learned. Small things. The kind of things cryo literature could explain.

Or the wormhole had edited them. Had reached into the suspended architecture of their sleeping minds during those fourteen unaccounted seconds and rearranged something. Changed a variable. Swapped a file. The way his own cyberarm serial number had changed during transit.

He noted the rate. Seven of one hundred and twenty. Five point eight percent. He would check again at five hundred. He would not mention it to Vasquez because Vasquez had a colony to land and cryo confusion was a medical problem and medical problems had medical solutions and the ship did not need another reason to doubt.

Some stood in silence and stared at the planet through the viewport with their arms limp and their mouths open. An old man pressed his palm against the glass and held it there. His lips moved but he made no sound. A child clung to her mother's leg and asked what the red was and the mother said it was the ocean and the child said it looked like juice and the mother laughed and the laugh broke at its edges. A man in the third row held a photograph against his chest and did not look at the viewport at all. Whatever he had left behind was more real than whatever lay ahead.

Two women held each other near the processing queue. One of them pulled back and looked at the viewport and said we made it. She said it flat. As though saying it aloud might make it fragile. The other woman wiped her face and said I need to brush my teeth. And then they both laughed and the laughter was ordinary and real and it cut through the solemnity of the bay like a window opened in a closed room.

Knox found him there. The boy was eleven now. Taller than when they had boarded. Cryo had not stopped time entirely. It slowed it. But it did not stop it. Knox had gained half an inch and his face was thinner and his eyes carried something that had not been there before. A patience that did not belong to a child.

Luna was behind him. Nine years old. Holding a tablet that played no sound. Her hair tangled from the pod gel and she looked at Theo with the steady gravity of her mother's gaze. Clara's eyes in Clara's daughter's face.

Is that it, Knox asked.

Theo nodded.

Knox walked to the viewport and pressed his forehead against the glass. The red light washed over him. He stayed there for a long time. His breath fogged the glass and cleared and fogged again.

It does not look like the pictures, he said.

No, Theo said. It does not.

The pictures had been composites. Rendered from probe data into images that suggested a second Earth. The reality was red and dark and strange and it did not look like home and it did not pretend to.

Knox turned from the glass. He looked at Theo and in his face was the expression of a boy who wanted to ask a question and already knew the answer would not help. He did not ask it. He looked at Luna and then at Theo and then at the planet and he nodded once as if confirming something with himself.

Okay, he said. That was all.

He straightened his shoulders. A small adjustment.

Deliberate. Theo recognized it because he had seen soldiers do it before crossing a line of departure. The boy turned to Luna and held out his hand.

Come on, he said. Let us go see where we are supposed to be.

He walked her toward the processing line. His hand on hers. Not pulling. Leading. Eleven years old and already carrying what should not have been his to carry and carrying it anyway because that was what the men he watched had done and he had been watching carefully.

Luna pressed against Theo's side before they left. He put his hand on her head. The carbon-fiber fingers gentle in her hair. She did not flinch from the prosthetic. She never had.

A strand of hair had fallen across her face, tangled and stiff with pod gel. The carbon-fiber fingers moved on their own and brushed it back behind her ear. Slow. Precise. Too gentle for the servo-loss tables in the firmware. Ruiz stood three meters away with a manifest in her hands. She saw. She said nothing. But her eyes stayed on the arm a beat longer than they should have.

Luna looked up at him. The red planet light falling across her small face.

Are there animals, she said.

Theo looked at the viewport. The dark green continents. The bioluminescent shimmer.

I think so, he said.

Good, she said. And followed Knox.

Thornhill intercepted Theo in the corridor outside engineering. She fell into step beside him and did not look at him.

We need to talk about the surface data, she said.

He waited.

She stopped walking. She looked both directions down the corridor. Empty. She pulled the tablet from under her arm and held it so he could see. Two waveforms on the screen. One from the transit logs. One from the planet. They lay on top of each other like the same line drawn twice.

The containment drift oscillation from the transit, Thornhill said. And the surface emissions. Same base frequency. Same harmonic structure. Within two percent variance.

You showed me the spatial distribution on the bridge. The lattice.

Yes. But this is what I could not say on the bridge. Thornhill scrolled to a new overlay. She had pulled the frequency data from the wormhole passage itself. Not the generators. The wormhole. The fourteen seconds where the instruments had gone dark. There had been a residual electromagnetic signature recorded by the hull sensors. A ghost imprint.

The fourteen-second discrepancy raised questions she did not want to ask. If spacetime could fold, could identity fold with it. The biometric failures at the spaceport, the dead woman who was alive, the man with no record, had been filed as system overload. But the clocks had disagreed by fourteen seconds. And fourteen seconds was enough time for a great deal of reality to slip.

It matched.

The wormhole transit signature, she said. The containment drift. And the planetary emissions. All the same frequency. All the same harmonic structure. Three data points. Three different sources. One tone.

She turned the tablet and pulled up her comparison matrices. Columns of numbers. Frequency values aligned to four decimal places.

My father spent thirty years mapping resonance patterns in crystalline structures, she said. She said it quietly as if the words cost her. He used to say that the most important data was the data that frightened you. Because fear meant you had found something real. She paused. He died when the containment failed. They found him at his instruments. He had circled a number on the last readout. Underlined it twice.

She straightened. Her voice returned to its clinical register.

If those surface anomalies are what I think they are, she said, we need to be careful how we bring the generators online. How much we draw. Because we are not just extracting energy from the vacuum state. We are playing a note. And something on this planet has been playing the same note for a very long time.

You think the planet is listening, Theo said.

Thornhill's mouth tightened. I think the universe has patterns, she said. And I think we have been adding to one without knowing what it means.

Thornhill's engineering team had pulled Johnson from the cryo manifest early. The hyperloop theorist. The woman with the card. She was the only person aboard who had predicted what the generators would attract.

She turned and walked toward engineering. Her footsteps faded and the corridor was empty.

We land anyway, he said to no one.

He went to the shuttle bay. The landing craft sat in their cradles. Stubby-winged transports with heat shielding scarred from atmospheric testing. Techs swarmed them. Fuel lines connected. Cargo nets loaded. The machinery of survival stacked in crates and pallets.

Theo found Daniella Ruiz checking a manifest near

shuttle two. She wore a jumpsuit that did not fit well and moved with the quick competence of someone who had learned to be useful or be forgotten.

Knox and Luna, she said without looking up. Fed and dressed. Bay sixteen.

She paused and looked at the shuttle.

Is it what they said it would be, she asked.

It is a planet, he said. That is enough.

She turned back to the manifest. Then she stopped. Set the tablet down on the crate. Looked at her hands.

When I was sixteen, she said, my grandmother told me that home is not a place. It is the last thing you carry when everything else is gone. She looked at the shuttle bay and the crates and the machines and the people moving with the desperate efficiency of survival. I thought she was being dramatic.

She picked the tablet back up.

She was not being dramatic, she said. And returned to the manifest.

A cargo drone stalled on the loading track between shuttles two and three. Its drive motor seized and it sat there humming and blocking the flow of crates behind it. A supply officer named Brennan waved two techs over and they stood looking at the motor housing and one of them said it needed a full teardown and Brennan said they did not have time for a full teardown and the crates were backing up and the first wave was loading in forty minutes.

Ruiz walked over. She did not ask permission. She knelt beside the drone and pulled the access panel and looked at the motor assembly. Grease on her fingers already. She reached in and freed a cable that had jumped its guide channel and wrapped around the drive shaft. She unwound it in three careful turns and clicked it back into the channel and stood up.

Try it, she said.

The tech hit the restart. The drone hummed and rolled forward and the loading line resumed.

Brennan looked at her. She wiped her hands on the jumpsuit that did not fit.

Hydraulics on the ranch were worse, she said. And went back to the manifest.

In the forward observation lounge Theo stood alone at the curved viewport. Lupus Stella filled the glass from edge to edge. The terminator line crept across the largest continent and where the red light faded the land went dark but not entirely dark. In the shadows something glowed. Faint. Blue-green. Like foxfire spread across a forest floor that stretched from coast to coast. The glow pulsed. Slow and rhythmic.

Bioluminescence. Life that carried its own light into the long alien night.

He pressed his palm against the glass. The viewport was cold. The planet was close. The feeling of return sat in him like a second heartbeat. He had stood at this viewport and looked out at a world he had never visited and his body had said home. Not his mind. His body. The same body that had learned at Promethei Terra that the ground could betray you and at Austin that the sky could burn and in the cryo bay that memory itself could be rewritten while you slept.

He did not trust the feeling. He did not dismiss it. He noted it and placed it with the serial number that had changed and the arm that moved before he told it to and the fourteen seconds that the wormhole had taken or given. Another weight he was carrying.

The ship rotated slowly. Lining up for descent. The first shuttle locked into its launch cradle and the bay doors opened onto the void and beyond the void the planet turned in the red light of its ancient star.

He turned from the glass and went to strap in.

CHAPTER 8

PLANETFALL

Drones first, Vasquez said. Nothing breathes that air until I see numbers.

They launched four probes from the shuttle bay. Unmanned. Hardened against atmospheric entry. Each one targeted a different biome on the plateau and the surrounding lowlands. The probes punched through the cloud layer and began transmitting within minutes.

Thornhill read the data as it arrived. Atmospheric composition nominal, she said. Nitrogen-oxygen ratio within three percent of Earth standard. No detectable airborne pathogens in sampled biomes. Water pH within tolerance. Soil microbiology present but non-reactive to human tissue samples.

She paused. These are preliminary. Three hours of data from four probe sites.

Vasquez looked at the numbers. She looked at the planet on the forward screen. She nodded.

Planetfall, she said.

* * *

THE FIRST SHUTTLE punched through cloud and the world came apart in sound and motion.

Not a gentle entry. The upper atmosphere hit them like a wall. The shuttle bucked and yawed and the pilot fought the controls with both hands while the instruments screamed numbers that changed too fast to read. Structural stress indicators flashed amber and held. Outside the viewports there was nothing but white. A dense opaque murk of cloud that pressed against the glass like something trying to get in.

Then the cloud darkened. Went gray. Went the color of bruised iron.

Then rain.

Heavy drops the size of marbles striking the hull like thrown gravel. Together they made a sound that filled the cabin and drowned out the engines and vibrated in the bones.

The shuttle shook and corrected and shook again.

Crosswinds at altitude, the pilot said. Sixty knots gusting to eighty. Visibility near zero. Terrain lock is holding. We are on final approach.

Theo sat strapped in between Vasquez and a marine corporal named Williams who had his eyes closed and his lips moving without sound. Prayer or a mantra or the counting of seconds. Vasquez stared straight ahead. Her jaw set. Her hands on her thighs with the deliberate stillness of a woman who refused to grip the armrest because gripping meant admitting the situation was beyond her control.

Theo's cyberarm calibrated against the vibration. The servos in the wrist and fingers making micro-adjustments in rapid sequence. The arm was always compensating. It did not feel fear. It felt vibration and corrected for vibration and that was all.

The cloud broke.

It broke sudden and total and Lupus Stella opened beneath them and the cabin went silent.

The plateau came first. A wide slab of dark stone rising above the treeline like a table set for giants. Flat and wind-scoured and large enough to hold the camp they had planned. Rain sheeted across its surface in silver streams that ran to the edges and fell into the canopy below.

Beyond the plateau the forest rolled in every direction. Waves of canopy in green so dark it was nearly black under the red light. The trees were massive. Trunks wide as grain silos. Canopies interlocking in a continuous surface like the vaulted ceiling of a cathedral built by something that did not worship human gods.

Obsidian Titans.

Beyond the forest the land dropped toward a coastal plain and beyond that the ocean. The Crimson Sea. It stretched to the curved horizon and the sky sat lower and heavier than any sky Theo had known. Not blue. A deep amber shading to burnt orange at the zenith where Wolf 1061's light scattered through an atmosphere thicker than Earth's.

Someone in the back of the shuttle said my god. Not a prayer. An observation. Someone else was crying. Quiet steady tears that were not sadness. The marine next to Williams pressed his face to the viewport and his breath fogged the glass and he said look at it. Just that. Look at it.

The shuttle banked. The plateau filled the forward screen.

Brace, the pilot said.

They landed hard. The landing struts hit stone and

compressed and the shuttle rocked sideways and corrected and was still. The engines wound down from a roar to a whine to a tick. In the new silence came new sounds. The tick of cooling metal. The hiss of pressure equalization. And underneath it all a low steady drumming that was the rain falling on an alien world.

The ramp dropped.

No one moved. The ramp was down and the air was alien and the gravity was wrong and every instinct in every human body on that shuttle said do not step into the unknown.

Theo went first. He did not pause. He walked down the ramp the way he had walked into gullies on Promethei and basement shelters in Austin and every other dark place where waiting was worse than knowing. His boots hit stone and the gravity took him and the rain hit his face and he breathed and kept walking.

Behind him the silence broke. Williams opened his eyes. A marine in the second row leaned forward in her harness and stared down the ramp at the wet dark stone. A sergeant named Cole gripped the stock of his rifle and held it against his chest. They had trained for this. They had run the simulations and studied the atmospheric data and memorized the contingency protocols.

Vasquez unstrapped. She stood. She walked to the top of the ramp and looked out at Lupus Stella and the rain hit her face and she breathed.

She blinked. Her nostrils flared. An expression crossed her face that was not military and not command and not any expression Theo had seen from her in the months of transit. It was fast. A flash of something old and young at the same time. Then her jaw reset and it was gone.

Move, she said.

They moved.

Air rushed in and it was like nothing Theo had ever breathed. Wrong and clean at the same time. The wrongness was in the compounds his lungs did not recognize. Molecules assembled by a biosphere that had evolved for billions of years without the slightest knowledge of Earth. A faint sour sweetness like overripe fruit mixed with something resinous and sharp. The cleanness was absolute. No particulate. No diesel. No ash. No trace of the ten billion human lives that had seasoned every breath he had ever drawn on the world they left behind. This air had never been inside a human lung. It smelled of wet stone and tree sap and something metallic that sat at the back of the throat like a coin held under the tongue.

Then for one breath it smelled like sawdust and oil.

His ranch workshop. Cedar shavings curling off a planer and the three-in-one oil he used on the lathe bearings. Specific. Unmistakable. A smell that belonged to a building fourteen light-years away on a world that no longer existed in any form he would recognize.

One breath. Then the alien air closed over it and it was gone.

One point one five g. The numbers had been abstract in orbit. Here on the ground they were a fact written in the language of the body. The weight settled into his knees and his spine and his hips. Not crushing. Just present. A constant downward insistence that said this world is heavier than the one you knew and it will ask more of you with every step.

His right knee registered it first. An old injury from Promethei Terra. Cartilage ground during a hard landing on Martian rock. It had healed but it remembered and now it complained in a voice he would hear every morning for as long as he lived on this world.

His cyberarm adjusted differently. The servos recalculated. Carbon nanotube and titanium alloy did not tire as flesh did. The carbon-fiber fingers opened and turned palm-up in the rain. They held there, catching the warm alien water in the cupped hand, and the gesture was not diagnostic. It was the gesture of someone feeling rain for the first time.

Williams came down the ramp behind him. The marine stopped at the bottom and stood on the stone and tipped his head back and opened his mouth and let the rain fall in. His eyes were closed. His rifle hung from its sling and his hands were at his sides and he stood like that for five seconds with the rain of an alien world falling into his open mouth. Then he wiped his face and shouldered his weapon and moved to his position without a word.

Behind Williams a woman named Torres who had been a structural engineer in Tucson stepped off the ramp and her knees buckled. Not from the gravity. From the fact of it. She caught herself on the ramp strut and stood there with one hand on the metal and the other pressed to her mouth. She made no sound. After a moment she nodded to the tech beside her and walked to her assignment and began unpacking survey equipment with the steady hands of a woman who had decided that breaking could come later.

A marine sergeant stood at the bottom of the ramp and took one step onto the stone and knelt. He put his bare hand flat on the wet rock and held it there. He was not praying. He was touching it. Confirming. This was real. This was stone. This was a world. He stood and moved to his position and he did not look back but his hand stayed open at his side for a long time as if the rock's texture was something he wanted to keep.

Portable light towers went up. Bright columns of white

in the red gloom. Drones launched from the shuttle's dorsal bay and climbed into the rain on quiet rotors and spread out across the plateau. Their lights swept the stone.

Theo looked at the forest.

The treeline began sixty meters from the plateau's eastern edge. A wall of dark trunks rising into the cloud ceiling. The bark was textured like cooled lava. Deep grooves and ridges running vertical up trunks four and five meters in diameter. Where the bark cracked a pale inner wood showed through like bone beneath dark skin.

And in the undergrowth between the roots something glowed. Blue-green. Soft and steady. Lumina Ferns. They carpeted the forest floor in dense patches that threw light upward onto the trunks in a cold ethereal wash. The light pulsed. Not randomly. Each fern brightened and dimmed in a synchronized cycle so that the forest floor appeared to breathe. Light in. Light out. Light in.

Four point seven seconds. The number from Thornhill's orbital data. The interval of the electromagnetic anomalies. He could not be sure the ferns matched from eyeballing it in the rain. But the coincidence sat in his mind.

Perimeter, he said.

Marines moved out in a line. Twelve men and women in tactical armor. Weapons held low but safeties off. They fanned across the plateau and took positions at the edges where stone met forest.

Thornhill came down the ramp carrying a case in each hand. She crossed to a clear patch of ground and knelt and drove a sensor spike into the soil with a pneumatic hammer. The spike sank half a meter. She checked the readout.

Soil chemistry is within parameters, she said. Carbon-rich silicate base. High mineral diversity. Microbial load is dense. Bacterial analogs in the billions per gram. She paused and her voice changed. The ecosystem here is not dormant. It is aggressive.

She said aggressive the way a doctor says malignant.

She drove a second spike three meters east. Triangulating. She wanted a baseline electromagnetic reading of the substrate before the generators came online. While she worked she pulled off her right glove and pressed her bare hand flat against the wet stone. She held it there for three seconds. Feeling its temperature. Its texture. The faint hum that might have been vibration or might have been her pulse. Then she pulled her glove back on and entered the reading manually. A scientist confirming a data point. A woman touching the ground of another world because the numbers alone were not enough.

Theo stood in the rain and let it fall on him. The drops were warm. Body temperature or close to it. They ran down his face and into the collar of his jacket and the water tasted of minerals he could not name. He wiped his eyes with the back of his human hand and looked up at the sky.

Wolf 1061 was hidden behind the cloud. Its light came through diffuse and red like the light inside a closed eyelid. The sky pressed down. He had the sense of being inside something rather than standing beneath it.

More shuttles came. The second forty minutes later. Then the third. The plateau filled with people and equipment. Engineers in coveralls directing cargo drones. Crates lowered on cables. The sound of tools and voices and the constant rain.

A woman stepped off the second shuttle and stopped at the bottom of the ramp. She stood with one hand on the hull and the other pressed flat against her stomach and she looked at the forest and the sky and the red light. After a moment a man came down behind her and put his hand on her back and she turned and buried her face in his shoulder. They stood that way while people moved around them carrying equipment. No one told them to move. There was time for this. There had to be time for this.

A girl no older than six came down the third shuttle's ramp holding her father's hand. She stopped on the stone and looked up at the sky and then at the forest and then at her father.

It is like a painting, she said. But too big.

Her father picked her up. He did not say anything. He carried her toward the shelters and she watched the treeline over his shoulder with her mouth open and her fingers twisted in the collar of his jacket.

An engineer named Watts pulled a crate off the loading frame and the crate slipped in the rain and hit the stone and split open and emergency rations spilled across the wet rock in silver packets. Watts stood over the mess and put both hands on his head. Then he knelt and began picking up the packets one by one and two others knelt beside him and together they gathered what had spilled and repacked it. The work of it.

They built the first shelters fast.

Inflatable frames extruded from compact cylinders and hardened in minutes into ribbed domes of composite polymer. Inside each dome the air scrubbers hummed to life. Water recyclers tapped the rain runoff. The camp took shape with the rapid ugly efficiency of necessity. Eight domes in a rough circle around a central operations dome reinforced with alloy struts. Connector tunnels between them. Power conduits running underground in trenches cut by laser borers into the basalt. The stone fought the borers and the borers won and the trenches smoked with vaporized mineral.

People worked in silence mostly. The gravity wore on them. A woman who had been a civil engineer in Phoenix directed the trench alignment and her voice was hoarse by the second hour and she kept going. A man whose manifest said schoolteacher carried conduit sections on his shoulder because the cargo drone had thrown a rotor bearing in the rain and someone had to carry them. His face was gray with fatigue and his shoes were wrong for the work and he carried the conduit anyway because the alternative was standing still and standing still meant thinking and thinking meant remembering what they had left behind.

A medic set up a triage station in the second dome and within twenty minutes had three patients. A woman with a laceration from a crate edge. A man hyperventilating. A boy of fourteen who had not spoken since the shuttle landed and who sat on a supply pallet with his arms wrapped around his knees and his eyes fixed on the dome wall as if the wall might open onto somewhere else. The medic treated the laceration and talked the man through his breathing and sat beside the boy and said nothing.

All of it rehearsed in simulation aboard Odyssey. The difference was the rain and the gravity and the light and the smell and the feeling that the ground beneath the camp was not merely ground.

The first rations went out at what they were calling noon though the light had not changed. A line formed at the distribution point in the operations dome. Silver packets stamped with calorie counts and nutritional codes. Rehydrated with water from the ship's reserves because the local water had not yet been cleared. A woman opened her packet and looked at the beige paste inside and said it smells different here. She was right. The same rations they had eaten on Odyssey. The same formulation. But on this world with its alien atmosphere the paste tasted faintly of copper and something else. Something green. As though the air had already gotten into the food and changed it.

People ate standing up or sitting on crates. No tables yet. No chairs. A man ate his ration in four bites and licked the packet and folded it and put it in his pocket. A woman could not finish hers. She set it down on a crate and walked outside and stood in the rain. People ate the way people eat after a funeral. Mechanically. Because the body demands it even when the mind has no appetite.

The first generator module came down on the fourth shuttle.

A cube of shielded alloy two meters on each side. A team of engineers and a cargo drone lowered it into a pit they had cut three meters deep into the plateau stone and lined with insulating mesh. When the module settled into its cradle the stone around it seemed to hum. A vibration felt in the soles of the feet more than heard.

Thornhill supervised the connection. Power conduits socketed into the output array with heavy mechanical clicks. Cooling lines. Data feeds. The containment field initialized with a low throb that started below hearing and rose until it sat at the edge of perception.

She checked her baseline readings against the spikes she had driven earlier. She checked them twice. The second time she set the tablet down on the edge of the pit and stood with her hands at her sides and her eyes closed. Not in prayer. In calibration. She was listening with her body for what the instruments might not catch. Then she opened her eyes and picked up the tablet and nodded once.

Bring it up, she said.

An engineer named Jordan stood at the primary coupling with his hand on the activation switch. His other hand rested on the housing of the module. He looked at Thornhill. She nodded again. He turned the switch.

The generator came online.

The lights in the camp steadied. The scrubbers surged. The recyclers cycled up. Power flowed through the conduits.

And every bioluminescent organism within a kilometer pulsed once.

Not the slow synchronized rhythm of the ferns' natural cycle. A single flare. Every Lumina Fern on the visible forest floor and beyond it into the dark lit up at the same instant. One pulse. Bright enough to cast shadows from the Obsidian Titan trunks. Bright enough that the marines at the perimeter flinched and brought weapons up.

The camp went silent.

Jordan pulled his hand off the housing. He stared at the forest. His mouth opened and closed. Beside him a young tech named Wen jerked her hand off the power conduit. The metal had not burned her. But something had passed through it that she felt and could not name.

Did the forest just, Jordan said. He did not finish the sentence.

No one answered him. The rain fell. The generator hummed. The ferns returned to their normal rhythm as if nothing had happened. One pulse and done.

Four seconds of silence. Four seconds in which every person who had seen the flash stood still and looked at the forest and looked at each other and did not say what they were thinking because what they were thinking did not have words yet. An ecosystem that had never encountered a zero-point energy generator had just responded to one. In unison. Instantly. As if the signal was expected. As if it had been waiting.

It acknowledged us, she said. She said it to herself.

Quietly. The rain took the words before they reached anyone.

Theo heard her. He had been standing close enough. He said nothing. He looked at the forest and the forest gave nothing else away.

Then he felt it through his cyberarm.

A faint itch. Not pain. Something between vibration and whisper that started in the carbon-fiber fingertips and traveled up through the wrist joint and into the socket where metal met bone. He flexed his hand. The itch pulsed. Slow. Steady. Rhythmic. The same interval as the ferns. The same interval as the generator's containment field.

He closed his hand into a fist and opened it and the sensation faded to a background hum that he would carry for days before he spoke of it.

The rain slowed toward evening. The cloud thinned. Wolf 1061 appeared at the horizon. Three times the apparent diameter of Earth's sun. A disc of deep crimson sitting on the edge of the world. Its light poured across the plateau and everything it touched turned the color of embers. The wet stone glowed. The shelter domes threw dull copper reflections. The forest canopy blazed dark crimson and the shadows between the trunks went black as pitch.

Under that light skin looked wrong. Not unhealthy. Altered. The red spectrum stripped the warmth from faces and replaced it with a cast that was older and harder. Brown skin went the color of red clay. Pale skin went ruddy and alien. Shadows pooled in eye sockets and under cheekbones so that everyone looked leaner and sharper and not quite themselves. A woman caught her reflection in a dome panel and stopped. She touched her face. Then she kept walking.

Daniella brought Knox and Luna from the third shuttle in the last of the light. The children stood at the edge of the camp and stared at the sky. Luna reached up as if she could touch the red star. Her fingers spread against the violet sky. Knox stood very still and looked at the forest with the attention of someone memorizing a threat.

Theo put his hand on the boy's shoulder. Knox did not flinch. He did not lean in. He stood under the weight of it as he stood under the gravity.

Night came slowly. The twenty-eight-hour day meant a long dusk that stretched as Wolf 1061 sank below the western treeline. The sky went from amber to violet to indigo. Stars appeared. Wrong constellations. Patterns that no human mythology had named. Wolf 1061's companion star glimmered faintly near the horizon. Two suns. One close and red. One distant and pale.

People came out of the shelters to look. They stood in the mist and craned their necks and some of them pointed at the stars as they had pointed at constellations on summer evenings on Earth. But there was nothing to point at that anyone recognized. No Orion. No Dipper. No North Star to orient by. The sky was beautiful and empty of meaning and people stood under it and felt the weight of that emptiness settle onto the weight of the gravity and some of them went back inside and some of them stayed and stared and a few of them wept quietly in the dark where they thought no one could see.

Vasquez walked the perimeter during the transition to night. She checked each post. Spoke to each marine. Her voice was clipped and even and she asked about sight lines and weapon readiness and she did not mention the stars or the strangeness or the fact that every person on that plateau was carrying a terror that had no name. At the eastern post she stopped and stood beside a young marine named Reyes who was nineteen and had not spoken since landing.

Reyes, she said.

The marine looked at her. His eyes were wet.

You are on post, Vasquez said. Her voice was neither gentle nor harsh. It was the voice of a fact.

Yes captain, Reyes said.

You are on post and your sector is clear and your weapon is charged and you are doing your job. That is what you are doing right now. Everything else can wait.

Reyes straightened. He wiped his eyes with the back of his hand and he looked out at his sector and he was a marine on post and that was enough to hold him for now.

Vasquez moved on. She did not look back. At the next post she stopped and checked the marine's ammunition count. The marine started to report and she held up one hand. She was looking at the treeline. Not at a threat. At nothing. Her other hand moved to the base of her throat where her uniform collar was zipped tight. Her fingers rested there for a moment on the fabric that covered skin and beneath the fabric there might have been a chain or a cord or nothing at all. She pressed once. A gesture so small and so fast that the marine beside her did not see it. Then her hand dropped and she asked for his ammunition count and the moment was gone and the captain was back and whatever she had touched or remembered or carried was sealed behind the rank again.

Luna stood at the edge of the camp and counted the stars she could see. She got to fourteen and stopped.

They are not the same ones, she said.

No, Theo said. They are not.

She was quiet for a moment. Then she said can you see Earth from here.

No, he said.

She accepted this the way children accept impossible

truths. Completely. Without negotiation. She looked at the foreign sky and she did not cry and she did not ask again and she went inside the shelter and picked up her tablet and began to draw. Theo looked at the screen over her shoulder as she worked. She was drawing stars. Not the ones outside. The ones she remembered. Orion. The Big Dipper. Constellations she had learned from a book her mother had given her. She drew them from memory and they were not quite right. The proportions wrong. The distances distorted. But they were hers and she put them on the screen with the care of someone preserving something that was already starting to fade.

Knox was not in the shelter. Theo found him outside the dome sitting against the composite wall with his knees drawn up. He was not looking at the sky. He was looking at the camp. The people moving between domes. The light towers. The marines at the perimeter. He was studying how it worked. How the supply lines moved. Where the guards changed. What the engineers were doing.

You should be inside, Theo said.

Knox looked up. In the red-shifted dark his face was older than eleven.

I am trying to understand how it fits together, he said. The camp. Where everything goes.

Theo sat down beside him. The stone was cold through his pants. He could hear the scrubbers running inside the dome and Luna's voice through the wall asking Daniella something.

It fits together because people make it fit, Theo said. Same as the ranch.

Knox was quiet. Then he said can I help tomorrow. With the work. I can carry things. I am not too small.

No, Theo said. You are not too small.

Knox nodded. He stood up and went inside without saying goodnight. Theo sat there a moment longer. The boy was building a model of the world in his head. Mapping its logic. Looking for the levers. The same thing Theo had done at his age on the ranch. The same thing he had done in uniform.

He did not know if this was healthy. He knew it was survival.

In the forest the Lumina Ferns brightened. The undergrowth became a carpet of blue-green light that shifted and pulsed. And in that light things moved.

A drone picked them up first. Thermal signatures at the treeline. Four-legged forms in a loose group. The drone operator magnified the feed and piped it to the operations dome.

The animals stood at the forest edge. A herd of perhaps twenty. The size of elk but built heavier. Broader in the chest with wide hooves that gripped the terrain like splayed fingers. Their hides were plated with crystalline material layered across the shoulders and flanks. The plates caught the white light from the camp towers and the blue-green light from the ferns and refracted it. Blues and greens and violets and a deep ruby red that seemed to come from within the crystal itself.

Prismhoofs, a biologist whispered. She stood at the display with both hands pressed to her mouth.

The herd held the treeline for a long moment. A decision shifted among them. A ripple of movement that was not fear but decision. The largest turned first and the others followed and they bolted into the forest in a cascade of shattered light. Their crystalline plates flashing. The treeline alive for a moment with thrown color.

All except one.

It stood at the edge where the ferns met the stone. Not the largest. Not the smallest. An animal of middle size with plates that caught the camp light and held it without refracting. Dark crystal. It did not follow the herd. It did not startle.

Theo saw it on the drone feed. He walked to the eastern edge of the camp and looked out past the perimeter lights and there it was. Sixty meters away. Standing in the blue-green glow with its head lifted and its body still.

It was watching him. Not the camp. Not the lights. Not the movement of people and machines. Him.

He stood at the edge of the stone and let it look. He did not move. He did not raise a hand or shift his weight. He went still as the land went still and he let the animal hold his gaze across the sixty meters of wet alien rock.

The rain had stopped. The air between them was clear. He could see the plates along its spine. How they layered over each other like the scales of a creature born from mineral rather than flesh. He could see the nostrils working. Slow deliberate pulls of air. Testing. He could see the muscles in the forequarters bunched and ready but not for flight. For patience. The animal was not deciding whether to run. It had already decided not to.

Its eyes were dark and set wide on a skull that tapered to a narrow muzzle. They were not the eyes of a prey animal calculating distance. They carried something else. An attention that was not animal. The quality of assessment. As if behind those eyes a question was being asked and the answer was being measured in terms that had nothing to do with predator or prey or any category that Earthborn biology had named.

Theo felt observed rather than observing. The inversion was complete. He was the subject. The animal at the treeline was the researcher.

He stood with it for a long time. The camp moved behind him. Voices. The clang of equipment. The hum of the generator. He let it all fall to the edges of his attention and held the center on the animal and the animal held its center on him and between them lay the silence of two intelligences regarding each other across a distance that was not only stone.

His cyberarm pulsed once. The faint itch returning and fading. The animal's nostrils flared. It had sensed something.

Then it turned. It did not bolt. It walked. Slow and deliberate. Each hoof placed with the care of a creature that was not fleeing but choosing to leave. It walked to the treeline and past the first row of ferns and their light played across its dark plates and then it walked into the shadows between the trunks and was gone. The ferns pulsed once in its wake. A single flare of blue-green that traveled through the undergrowth in a line that followed the animal's path like a door closing behind a guest who had seen what they came to see.

Theo stood at the edge and watched the empty treeline and said nothing.

Vasquez broke the silence from inside the operations dome.

Command staff, she said.

They gathered in the operations dome. Rain had started again. It drummed on the roof. Vasquez sat at the head of a table made from a cargo crate. Thornhill at the other end. Between them Maria Lopez took the chair that no one else had claimed.

Lopez was small. Dark-haired. Her face lined from decades of solving problems that did not want to be solved. She had been a community organizer in the Third Ward of Houston. She had held neighborhood meetings in church basements where people shouted about water rights and school closures and she had listened and done the slow grinding work of consensus. When the ashfall came she organized evacuations. When evacuations failed she organized shelter. When shelters failed she organized the march to the spaceport. She had been elected civilian representative aboard Odyssey by a margin that suggested not popularity but necessity.

She spoke first.

Our people need to know what the plan is, she said. Schedules. School for the children by the end of the week. Ration equity published and posted where everyone can see it. Medical access without military gatekeeping. And psychological triage before the shock wears off and panic takes root in our shelters.

She looked at Vasquez. We brought people here who watched their cities burn. They are holding it together with adrenaline and hope. If we do not give them structure they will build their own and we will not like what they build.

Vasquez leaned forward. Alien world. Unknown threats. Seven hundred on the ground and more every shuttle cycle. Hard perimeter before school. Curfews. Weapons discipline. Something comes out of that forest tonight, we are ready.

Lopez did not blink. And if something comes out of the shelters first. Grief. Panic. Three people tried to reboard the shuttle after landing. Two more are refusing to eat. One woman has not spoken since she woke from cryo and she is sitting in the corner of dome four staring at a wall. Captain, you can build all the perimeters you want. If the people inside them break we are defending an empty camp.

Vasquez's jaw tightened.

Thornhill spread her hands on the table. I need lab priority. Controlled sampling of soil and water before anyone eats anything local. Biological risk assessment. And monitoring equipment on every generator module. Full-spectrum electromagnetic surveillance. Continuous.

She did not say why. The frequency comparisons sat on her tablet like a secret with a half-life.

Lopez turned to Thornhill. Our people need clean water tomorrow. Not next week. Not when the lab has run every test it can imagine. Tomorrow. We have children in those shelters who are already scared. How fast can you certify the rain runoff so we can tell them the water is safe.

Thornhill met her gaze. If I rush the bioassay and miss a silicon-based pathogen that colonizes intestinal lining we will have a medical crisis before we have a water crisis. Which would you prefer.

I would prefer that children not go thirsty while scientists debate acceptable risk.

I would prefer that children not die of an alien infection because we skipped the protocol that would have caught it.

The dome was quiet. The rain drummed. The two women looked at each other across the table and neither blinked.

Vasquez cut in. Seventy-two hours of ship water. That buys time. I will not ration water to people who watched their world die. Thornhill. Faster protocol.

Thornhill exhaled. I can run a rapid bioassay. Twelve-hour turnaround on the rain catchment. If the initial screen is clean we distribute with a boil order while the full panel runs.

Do it, Vasquez said.

Lopez pulled a tablet from her jacket. Shelter assignments, she said. Ration schedules. Sanitation protocols. Medical triage rotation. Schooling shifts. Grief counseling. She read the list with the steady cadence of a woman who had built order from church basements and knew that the distance between civilization and chaos was a posted schedule.

Then she stopped reading. She set the tablet down and pressed both hands flat on the crate and closed her eyes. It lasted two seconds. The briefest pause. When she opened her eyes her face was the same competent mask. But in those two seconds Theo had seen the weight. Not the civic weight. The personal one. The specific exhaustion of a woman who had not stopped organizing since Houston caught fire and who had not once in all that time sat down and asked who was organizing things for her. She picked the tablet back up. Her voice was steady. The list continued.

Theo let them work. He let the tension play out because tension that was voiced could be managed.

Then he spoke.

We form a council. Three seats. Military. Science. Civilian. One vote each on policy. Unanimous consent required for anything that risks lives. No one person runs this colony.

Vasquez's eyes narrowed. You are diluting command authority.

I am preventing mutiny, Theo said.

The word landed in the dome like a held breath breaking.

Lopez glanced at Vasquez. The captain held Theo's gaze. Chain of command was a structure built for wars with defined enemies. Here there was no enemy. Only the work and the world and the slow corrosive pressure of fear.

Vasquez exhaled through her nose.

If this council fails, she said. If we deadlock or discipline breaks. I resume full operational command. Non-negotiable.

Agreed, Theo said.

She nodded once.

They talked for two hours. Argued for most of it.

Vasquez wanted weapons distributed to trained civilians. Lopez said weapons in shelters would terrify children. Vasquez said armed parents keep children alive. Unarmed parents hope someone else will. Lopez said you do not know that. Vasquez said she had seen the camps after the ashfall. The ones with guns lasted. The ones without did not.

The dome went quiet after that.

She wanted generators throttled to minimum output until she understood the frequency pattern. Vasquez said throttling meant no perimeter sensors. She said she could maintain perimeter on reduced power if they consolidated the sensor grid. Vasquez said consolidation left gaps. She said gaps in the perimeter were preferable to whatever they were broadcasting into a planetary network they did not understand. She said it with an emphasis that made both Vasquez and Lopez look at her.

What network, Lopez said. What are we broadcasting into and what does that mean for our people sleeping in those shelters.

Thornhill paused. She looked at her tablet. She looked at the table. She made a decision.

The electromagnetic anomalies on the surface, she said. They are not random. They form a pattern. A grid. And the frequency matches the containment drift in our generators. When we powered up the first module two hours ago every bioluminescent organism in a kilometer radius flared in unison. The duration of the flare matched the initialization cycle exactly.

She let the words sit.

I am not saying we are in danger, she said. I am saying

we are in a conversation we did not start and do not understand and I would like to know what we are saying before we say more of it.

Vasquez stared at her. Lopez stared at her. The rain drummed.

The planet responded to our generator, Vasquez said.

I am telling you the data is consistent with that interpretation.

Is there another interpretation.

She did not answer for a long moment. There is always another interpretation, she said. But I have not found one that fits.

Lopez said if we draft our people into labor without asking what they can offer we breed resentment faster than hunger. Vasquez said resentment was a problem for next week. She said both were better than starvation. Lopez said all three were better than a riot because a riot means we have failed the people who trusted us to build a future worth surviving for.

They went around. Each position had merit. Each position carried a cost. The decisions came slowly and they came hard and by the end Vasquez's hands were flat on the table and the veins in her forearms stood out and Lopez had stopped looking at her list and was rubbing the bridge of her nose and Thornhill sat with her eyes closed. Not sleeping. Thinking. The rain drummed on the roof and did not care what they decided.

Vasquez would run security. Thornhill would manage science and infrastructure. Lopez would handle civilian affairs and resources.

Theo would sit above the council as mediator. A position without a vote. A position that carried the weight of every decision without the cover of consensus.

He had not asked for it. But the three of them looked at him and he saw in their faces the need for someone to stand in the middle and not break.

He accepted it as he accepted the gravity.

Across the compound Ruiz was organizing the children's evening rotation. She had built a system without being asked. Shift schedules and meal rosters and a quiet authority that the children responded to the way they responded to weather. He watched her for a moment longer than the task required and then he looked away and did not examine why.

The council dispersed. Vasquez stood alone at the table. Her hand found the edge of it and pressed until the knuckles whitened. Then she straightened. Squared her shoulders.

Vasquez walked to the dome entrance and stopped. She stood with her back to the room and her hand on the frame and she looked out at the rain and the dark.

My daughter would have been eleven this year, she said.

She said it without turning around. She said it to the rain. Her hand on the frame was steady. Her voice was steady. But she stood there for three seconds longer than a captain walking to inspection would stand and in those three seconds the woman behind the rank was visible and then she was not.

She straightened her shoulders and walked out into the night and her boots rang on the wet stone and she began her first perimeter inspection and her voice carried across the camp steady and sharp and giving orders as if the sentence she had spoken in the doorway belonged to a different woman in a different lifetime.

Theo walked the camp alone.

The rain had softened to a mist. It hung over the plateau

like breath. The light towers cast columns of white into it and the mist scattered the light into halos. Marines stood their posts at the edges.

The first full night was settling in. In the shelters people were trying to sleep. The domes were not quiet. The composite walls were thin and the sounds bled through. Coughing. A child crying in dome three. The murmur of conversation. Someone praying in Spanish. Someone else asking them to stop. The scrubbers hummed at different pitches in different domes and the dissonance was small but constant and after a while it became the sound of this place. The sound of ten thousand lives compressed into a space built for necessity and not for comfort.

The wind came off the forest and pressed against the domes. Not hard. Just enough to make the composite flex. Inside the shelters people felt the walls move and went still. On Earth a wall did not move. Here the walls breathed with the wind and the wind carried the forest smell. Green and resinous and metallic. An alien exhalation pressing against the places where people were trying to pretend that shelter was the same as home.

Theo stopped at the eastern edge and looked out over the forest. The canopy rolled away into darkness. Below it the Lumina Ferns pulsed their slow heartbeat. The air smelled of wet stone and the metallic sweetness and something green and alive and unfamiliar.

Then again. One breath. Sawdust and oil. The lathe. The workbench. The coffee he left on the shelf above the tool rack. One breath so specific and so complete that he turned his head as if the workshop door might be standing open behind him in the mist.

It was not. There was stone and rain and the domes of a colony that did not yet know what it had landed on.

The breath passed. The alien air reclosed. He stood still and then walked on.

Somewhere in the distance a voice called out. Not a bird. Not anything he had a name for. A low sound that rose and fell and rose again like a voice testing the shape of a word it had not yet learned to say.

He listened until it stopped.

He found Ruiz outside the children's dome. She was sitting on an equipment crate in the mist with a ration packet unopened in her lap. Staring at the treeline. Her jacket was wet through and she had not zipped it and the mist beaded on her bare forearms and she did not seem to notice.

You should eat, he said.

She looked at the ration packet. She looked at the forest.

I keep waiting for it to feel real, she said. I keep waiting for the moment where my body catches up with what my eyes are telling me. But it does not come. It just stays strange.

She looked at him.

Does it get easier. You have been to other worlds.

Mars, he said. Mars was rock and dust and thin air that would kill you in ninety seconds. It did not feel like this.

Like what.

He thought about it. Like something that already knows you, he said.

Ruiz nodded. She opened the ration packet. She ate. The ordinary act of eating on a world where nothing was ordinary. She chewed and swallowed and did not look at the forest while she ate because eating was the thing she could control and the forest was the thing she could not.

When she finished she folded the packet flat and put it in her jacket pocket and stood.

Knox had a nightmare on the shuttle, she said. He did not cry. He just sat up and looked at the wall and waited for it to pass. She paused. Eleven years old. He should not know how to do that.

No, Theo said. He should not.

She looked at him and her face was hard in a way he had not seen from her before. Not angry. Resolved.

I am going to make sure they are okay, she said. Not just alive. Okay. I know that is not the same thing and I know you know it too. I will feed them and keep them dry and make sure they sleep and I will do whatever it takes to keep the look off that boy's face. The one that says he has already calculated the odds and decided not to bother hoping. No child should carry that arithmetic.

She went inside. The connector seal closed behind her.

Theo stood where she had been. The crate still held the shape of her weight in the mist that had settled on its surface. A slight clearing in the condensation. He looked at it. He did not know why he looked at it. Then he walked to the perimeter.

He went to his shelter. A small dome at the edge of the command cluster. A cot and a footlocker and a data terminal. He sat on the cot and removed his boots and the weight of the day settled into his body. His knee ached. His back ached. The gravity sat on him.

Knox and Luna were in the adjacent dome with Daniella. He could hear the murmur of her voice through the connector wall. Reading to them. The words were indistinct but the cadence was steady and warm. The cadence of someone trying to make a strange place feel like the places that no longer existed.

He lay down. The cot was hard and narrow and the dome wall curved close above his head. The scrubber hummed. Through the composite he could hear the wind and under the wind the forest and under the forest something else. A vibration below hearing. The planet's own frequency. He felt it in the cot frame and in the fillings of his teeth and in the socket where his arm met his shoulder. It was not threatening. It was present. The way the ground is present under your feet. You forget it until you listen for it and then you cannot stop hearing it.

He thought about the frequency patterns and the itch in his arm and how the ferns had pulsed when the generator came online. One flash. Every organism in range. Simultaneous.

He thought about the Prismhoof at the treeline. The one that did not run. The one that walked. He thought about its eyes and what he had seen in them.

Sleep came in pieces. Fitful. Broken by the rain and the unfamiliar sounds and the gravity that made every position a negotiation. He dreamed of the ranch. Of morning light on the Davis Mountains. Then the dream shifted and the mountains were the wrong color.

He woke.

In the early hours before dawn the alarm sounded.

A single chirp from the containment monitoring system. Sharp and brief. It cut through the rain and into his sleep and he was upright before his eyes were open. His hand reaching for the sidearm. His cyberarm already awake. Already calibrating.

Darkness. The hum of the scrubber. The drum of rain.

He reached for the data terminal. The screen glowed pale blue.

CONTAINMENT MICRO-OSCILLATION — DURATION 0.3 SEC — AMPLITUDE 0.004% — SELF-CORRECTED.

He stared at the line.

Then his cyberarm vibrated.

Not the background itch. This was specific. A pulse. It started in the fingertips and moved through the wrist and through the forearm and into the socket and it matched the frequency of the alarm. Exactly. Same duration. Same interval. Same harmonic signature.

He held his left hand up in the dark. The carbon-fiber fingers trembled with a vibration too fine to see and too precise to be mechanical noise. The arm's diagnostic display flickered on his wrist. All readings nominal. No fault detected. The vibration was not a malfunction. It was a response.

The alarm. The generator. And his arm. Three points of a triangle. Three nodes in a network that should not exist.

He sat in the dark and listened to the rain and felt the pulse. His prosthetic was a machine. Power cells and servos and firmware written by engineers in Houston. Installed in an orbital medical bay by a surgical team whose names he knew. He had gone to Brooke Army Medical Center in San Antonio twice a year for recalibration since retirement. The closest military hospital to the ranch. There was nothing in the arm's architecture that should respond to a zero-point energy containment fluctuation. Nothing that should resonate with an alien frequency pattern.

And yet.

He did not spiral. He did not ask what it meant for his sense of self or the boundary between the man and the machine. He asked what it meant tactically. If his arm was receiving the same signal as the generator and the forest then his arm was an antenna. And an antenna could be traced.

He let the silence hold it.

Outside the camp was still. The light towers burned. The marines stood their posts.

But in the forest an answer came.

A low pulse. Below human hearing. Below the range of the camp's sensors which had been calibrated for the frequencies of Earth. A vibration that moved through the ground and the roots of the Obsidian Titans and the stems of the Lumina Ferns.

The ferns brightened. All at once. A wave of blue-green light rolled through the undergrowth from east to west across the visible treeline. It lasted three seconds. A pulse of cold light that turned the forest floor luminous and threw the trunks into sharp black relief. Then the ferns dimmed and the forest was still and the rain fell.

Nothing on the camp's sensors registered the event. The monitoring equipment was calibrated for threats it understood. This was different. A signal that operated in a register the instruments had not been built to hear.

Theo sat on his cot in the dark with his cyberarm quiet against his thigh. The vibration faded. The terminal showed him a world that was stable and safe.

He did not believe it.

He opened a secure log. Personal. Encrypted. He typed with his human hand. The left hand he did not use. Not for this. Not for the record of what the left hand was becoming.

Day one. Generator online. Containment micro-oscillation at 0237 local. Duration 0.3 sec. Self-corrected. Pattern consistent with transit drift and orbital anomalies. Cyberarm registered concurrent pulse at matched frequency and duration. Fern activity observed at treeline immediately following. Wave propagation east to west. Duration three seconds.

He paused. Then he typed three more lines.

The alarm. The arm. The forest. Same signal.

Arm may be receiving. May be part of a network I did not join.

Something on this planet knows we are here.

He closed the log. He lay back down. He did not sleep.

Outside the rain fell and the forest pulsed and the generators hummed in their pit and the planet turned slowly under the red eye of its ancient star. And deep in the dark between the roots of trees that had stood for millennia something waited with a patience that was not patience at all but the slow certain knowledge that what it needed had arrived.

The colonists slept. The camp lights burned. The rain drummed its endless alien hymn.

And in the frequency logs a single line of data held its shape like a fingerprint pressed into wet clay. Waiting to be read.

Waiting.

CHAPTER 9

HOSTILE TERRITORY

A fight broke out in the mess line over ration portions.

Two men. One had been a schoolteacher in Denver. The other had run a logistics firm in Seoul. They beat each other with their fists until marines pulled them apart and neither could say afterward what the fight had been about. There were rumors. Water contamination. Power rationing. Favoritism on the council. The rumors were not true but truth was not the currency of fear.

Two months on Lupus Stella and the colony had begun to feel like a wound that would not close. The rain came in long curtains that lasted days and then stopped as if someone had shut a valve and left the plateau baked and split under the dim red eye of Wolf 1061. Steam rose from the cracked ground and hung in the air like the breath of something buried. The twenty-eight-hour day stretched people past what their bodies knew. Sleep got strange. Some could not find it. Others could not leave it. The circadian rhythm that a hundred thousand years of evolution had written into human blood meant nothing here. Bodies woke in the dark and crashed in the light and the medical tent filled with people who had nothing wrong with them except that the world they were on did not match the world they were built for.

The dusk lasted four hours. Wolf 1061 sank below the western treeline with the unhurried patience of a star that had nowhere else to be and the sky turned colors that had no names in any human language. Somewhere between rose and rust and a shade of violet that made the eyes ache with its unfamiliarity. The colonists did not know when to eat dinner. The children did not know when to sleep. A woman in dome three set the table at what her body said was evening and then set it again two hours later when the light still had not gone and then sat down at the empty table and wept because the sky would not do what skies were supposed to do and the wrongness of it was the thing that finally broke her. Not the wormhole. Not the cryo. Not the loss of everything she had known. The sky.

Tempers went sharp and stayed there.

The council discussed the children. Education. Routine. The things that held young minds together when the world around them was coming apart.

Vasquez spoke last. The school rotation should run in ninety-minute blocks, she said. Attention spans at that age cannot sustain more. Recess twice daily. Morning and afternoon. Structure them around physical activity but do not call it exercise. Call it play. The reading program should include individual assessment within the first week. Some of these children have not been in a classroom in months. They will need differentiated instruction.

Lopez looked at her. The look carried a question she did not ask.

Vasquez did not explain. She did not need to. The chain at her throat caught the light and she tucked it back inside her collar and moved to the next item.

Theo walked the perimeter each morning before the camp stirred. He walked it the way he had walked the wire at Promethei Terra. Slow. Watching. Letting the land speak to the part of him that had learned to listen before it learned to talk.

The water reclamation unit on the west side had a coupling that needed replacing. His hands fell into the rhythm Miguel had taught him. Wrench and patience. Patch it anyway. The ghost of a chuckle in the barn. He tightened the coupling and moved to the next and did not look up because looking up meant remembering and remembering meant the Davis Mountains and the blast radius and the map he had looked away from.

On the southern perimeter the drone feed showed a clearing three kilometers out. In the center of the clearing a flat surface. Dark. Geometric. Not natural. Too regular for stone, too large for debris. He tagged it in the survey log and moved to the next sector. There were predators to track and water systems to build and a colony that needed structure more than it needed mysteries.

Luna slipped away from the children's area during the long dusk. She found a Lumina Fern at the edge of camp where the plateau met the tree line. She touched it. The frond pulsed. A soft blue-green glow that rose from the base to the tip and faded. She pulled her hand back. The fern went dark. She touched it again. It pulsed brighter. She laughed. The sound carried across the camp and two colonists near the cook station looked up because it was the first laugh anyone had heard from a child since planetfall.

She touched fern after fern. Each one pulsing in

sequence. A cascade of light following her fingertips down the row like a melody played on an instrument that had been waiting for someone to find it.

No adult saw this. No adult interpreted it. When Ruiz found her ten minutes later Luna said they like me. Ruiz asked who likes you. Luna pointed at the ferns but they were dark again. They were doing it a minute ago, Luna said. Ruiz took her hand and led her back to camp and did not ask again because some things children say on alien planets are better left unexamined.

The Prismhoof came back at dusk. The long dusk. Luna saw it first. She was sitting on the cargo ramp drawing constellations that did not exist yet in a notebook Ruiz had given her and the animal stepped out of the treeline fifty meters from the camp perimeter and stood in the fading light and looked at her.

She held still. She did not call out. She did not run. She held still the way children hold still when they know without being told that the moment is fragile and any motion will end it.

The animal's eyes changed color as it watched her. Amber to violet to a pale luminous green that caught the last light of the long dusk and held it. Its hide shifted in slow waves of iridescence. It stood in the alien twilight with a patience that had nothing to do with wariness and everything to do with assessment. It was deciding something. Luna was deciding something too.

Then Ruiz came around the corner of the habitat module and the Prismhoof turned and walked into the trees without haste and without fear and without looking back.

Its eyes change color when it looks at you, Luna said.

Ruiz looked at the treeline. The trees were dark.

I believe you, Ruiz said. And she did. On this planet she

had decided to believe the children because the children were not afraid of what they saw and the adults were and fear was a poor instrument for observation.

The Obsidian Titans rose beyond the fence line in dark columns that drank the light. Their bark was like cooled magma and their canopies spread so high and so wide that standing beneath them was like standing inside a cathedral built for congregants who had never come. Between them the understory pulsed. Lumina ferns cast their cold blue-green glow across the ground and in that glow things moved. Small things mostly. Scuttlers and threadworms and the glass-winged insects that stuck to the habitat walls at night and died there by morning leaving wet smears like hieroglyphs no one could read.

Knox found the marks the next morning. He crouched at the habitat wall and traced them with his finger. Then he found a stick and started copying them into the dirt. Not because he understood them but because the shapes felt right in his hand. The same way a word feels right before you know what it means. He drew for twenty minutes. Careful strokes in the packed earth. Circles and angles and lines that curved back on themselves.

When a biologist named Wen saw the marks later she photographed them and added them to the anomaly file. Knox did not remember drawing them. When asked he said he was just making patterns.

But there were tracks too.

Long clean furrows cut through the mud at the tree line. Three-toed and deep. Whatever made them was heavy and moved fast and did not wander. The tracks ran parallel to the perimeter fence in lines so straight they looked deliberate. As if the thing that made them understood the concept of a boundary and was studying it.

Shadowfangs. That was the name the biologists had given them based on drone footage. Low-slung quadrupeds the color of wet slate. Eyeshine like heated copper. They moved through the undergrowth with a silence that seemed earned rather than natural. As if they had learned what sound cost.

For weeks they had been out there. Watching. Probing. Never the same spot twice.

The colony had adapted as colonies do. People stopped walking the fence line at night. Parents kept children indoors after dark. The marines doubled the watch and the turret software was updated every third day to track faster targets. But the Shadowfangs did not attack. They circled. They tested. And when a motion alarm tripped and the floodlights swung out they would stop at the edge of the light and hold there and stare with those copper eyes as if they were memorizing the geometry of what they faced.

It was the intelligence that unsettled Theo.

He had fought men and machines and men who fought like machines. He knew what instinct looked like and he knew what calculation looked like and the Shadowfangs did not move on instinct. They adapted. A turret repositioned and the next night the approach vector changed. A new sensor was installed and the next patrol came from a direction the sensor did not cover. They avoided the sectors where patrols were random and tested the sectors where patrols were routine. They were not reacting. They were learning. And learning implies memory. Memory implies a self that persists between encounters. A continuity of purpose. These were not just predators. Something was using predator bodies the way a man uses a tool. The body was the instrument. What held the instrument was another question. One Theo carried without answering because on this planet the questions that mattered most were the ones you did not answer out loud.

He mentioned this to Thornhill one morning over coffee that tasted like it had been made by someone who had heard of coffee but never tasted it.

They coordinate, he said. Flanking positions. Assigned sectors. They pull back when the odds change and they come back with a different plan. They don't probe our randomized patrols. Only the routine ones. They know which sectors run on schedule.

Thornhill set her cup down. She looked tired. She always looked tired now. She held the cup with both hands even after setting it down, as though she had forgotten how to let go of warm things.

The neural density is extraordinary, she said. Folded cortex. Multiple processing centers. But the architecture is distributed. Not centralized. More like a mesh network. Each animal carrying a portion of something larger.

She did not finish the sentence. She did not need to.

Theo stared at the tree line.

A network, he said.

Thornhill picked up her cup and drank what was in it and looked at the trees the way you look at a locked door when you can hear something moving on the other side.

The first close encounter came on a night when the clouds broke and the sky filled with unfamiliar constellations.

A motion alarm tripped on the east perimeter. Sector seven. The turrets swiveled and the drones swung their lights down through the dark and found movement in the tall grass fifty meters from the fence.

Theo was in the command tent reviewing power logs

with Thornhill when the alert came through. He crossed to the tactical screen in four strides and watched the feed.

Something low and fast moved through the grass. It stopped. It moved again. Lateral. Not toward the fence but along it. Testing the angle of the turret tracking. Its body stayed below the grass line and only the disturbance of the stalks gave it away.

Sector seven. Routine patrol sector. Tuesday evening sweep at 2100 hours local. The thing in the grass knew the schedule.

A marine keyed his comm. Sir. Contact east. Single hostile. Clean firing solution.

Theo watched the shape pause at the edge of the floodlight wash. It turned its head and looked directly into the drone camera. The eyeshine flared and held. Two points of heated copper in the dark.

Hold, Theo said.

The marines voice came back tight. Sir.

Hold.

In the tent behind him Vasquez appeared in the doorway. Her sidearm was drawn and her jaw was set and her free hand was flexing open and closed at her side the way it did when she wanted to act and was being made to wait.

On the screen the Shadowfang turned its body perpendicular to the fence. It lowered its head and raised it again in a slow deliberate motion that looked almost ritualistic. Then it took three deliberate steps backward. Not fleeing. Retreating. With its eyes still on the camera. As if the going was the message.

Two more shapes appeared in the grass behind it. Flanking positions. They had been there the whole time. One to the northeast and one to the southeast forming a triangle with the lead animal at the apex. A formation. Not a pack. A unit.

The lead animal made a sound that the exterior microphones caught as a low clicking. Rhythmic. Almost tonal. Three clicks. Pause. Two clicks. Pause. Three clicks again. The two flankers turned in unison and melted into the tree line. The leader held for three more seconds. Then it too was gone.

The motion sensors showed nothing. The grass settled as if nothing had passed through it. The night resumed its work.

Vasquez holstered her weapon. You had a clean shot.

Theo did not take his eyes off the screen. He was watching the playback. The three-click pattern. The synchronized withdrawal. Three animals moving as one organism with three bodies.

I had a clean shot at something I don't understand, he said.

Understanding doesn't keep people alive.

Theo turned to face her. Sometimes it does, he said.

The silence between them was the kind that fills the space where trust has not yet arrived. Vasquez held his gaze and then looked away and that was all the concession she would give.

They moved into the council tent. Thornhill was already there with datapads spread on the table like a fortune teller reading bones. Maria Lopez sat across from her, her fingers drumming a silent rhythm on the table edge, the only tell she allowed herself when the news was bad.

Thornhill pushed a display to the center of the table. The containment oscillations are increasing. Three spikes in the last seventy-two hours. The amplitude is climbing. She tapped a graph that looked like a heartbeat with a stammer.

Its responsive. When the generators spike the planet answers. A feedback loop.

Vasquez folded her arms. Responsive to what.

Thornhill shook her head. The frequency matches the surface anomalies we flagged from orbit. Something on this planet is resonating with our generators. Or our generators are resonating with it.

Then fix it, Vasquez said.

I'm trying. But this isn't a blown capacitor. This is a planet-scale phenomenon and we have no framework for it.

Maria Lopez leaned forward. People are hearing the alarms at night. They see the marines running. The children are drawing pictures of monsters. The parents whisper when they think the kids are asleep. We need truth or we need a better lie.

Theo stared at the perimeter map on the wall. The red dots where contacts had been logged. The pattern of them. East to southeast. A crescent. Like an intelligence was mapping a boundary from the other side. Like the Shadow-fangs were not hunting but surveying.

Maria Lopez pressed her fingertips to the table edge and held them there. The drumming had stopped. Her face was still but her lips were pressed together as they pressed together when she was keeping words behind her teeth.

We need stability, he said. We can't explain what we don't understand and we can't afford panic. Hold the line. Keep working. Give me something to work with and I'll give the people something to hold onto, Lopez said.

It was not enough and he knew it. But it was what there was.

CHAPTER 10

THE WARNING

A comms technician pushed through the tent flap. She was young and her face had the look of someone carrying news that had not finished becoming news yet. Her hands were steady but her voice was not.

Colonel. Inbound signal. Human. Not ours.

The tent went quiet. The kind of quiet that is not silence but the sound of people recalculating everything they thought they knew.

Theo moved to the comms station and the comms technician brought up the display. A tight-beam transmission. Encrypted but with a handshake protocol that was civilian corporate grade. Clean signal. Strong carrier wave. The header read:

ASTROCORP OUTPOST DESIGNATION RIDGE-7 — REQUEST PARLEY — COORDINATES ATTACHED

Vasquez stared at the screen. We are not alone.

Theo felt the old cold calm settle into him. The calm

that came before operations. Not the absence of fear but the organization of it.

Where, he said.

Twenty kilometers east. The technician brought up the coordinates overlaid on terrain mapping. A ridge above the eastern forest. A defensible position. They're broadcasting on a military-grade carrier with civilian encryption. Signal strength says theyve got real power. Not field kit. Infrastructure.

How long have they been here, Thornhill asked.

The tech pulled metadata from the signal headers. At least four months. Their systems show firmware dates predating our arrival by sixteen weeks.

Thornhill looked at Theo. Four months. They were here before us. They were watching when we landed.

Theo nodded. He said nothing for a long moment. He looked at the map and he looked at the signal data and he thought about what it meant that another group of humans had been on this planet for four months and had not made contact until now. What it meant that they were reaching out after the oscillations began to climb. What it meant that they had power and walls and discipline.

I need a flyer, he said. Security detail. Four marines. Thornhill youre with me.

Vasquez stepped forward. I'm going.

No. Theo met her eyes. You hold the colony. If this is a trap you need to be here. If its legitimate you need to be here. Either way the ten thousand people on this plateau need a commander who is present and armed and ready.

Vasquez did not like it. Her jaw worked and her hands were fists at her sides and her weight shifted forward onto the balls of her feet as it did before she hit something. But she was military and she understood the logic even when she hated it.

Bring me intel, she said. Not promises.

They flew east at dawn.

The flyer was a heavy transport shuttle stripped to essentials. The four marines sat in the bay with their weapons across their knees and their faces blank the way marines learn to make their faces when they are going somewhere new and do not know if they are coming back. Thornhill sat across from Theo with a scanner in her lap and her eyes on the passing terrain below.

The forest was a living ocean. The Obsidian Titans spread their canopies in overlapping shields of dark green and black and between them the bioluminescent bands of the understory threaded through like veins of cold light. The terrain rose and fell in ridges that ran roughly north-south and in the valleys between them creeks glinted the color of rust. Water here was tinted by the mineral content of the soil and the light of the red sun and it looked like diluted blood.

Far to the south the coastline showed itself. The Crimson Sea catching Wolf 1061s light and throwing it back in bands of copper and old iron. The water moved in long slow swells that looked almost like breathing.

Theo watched the canopy and thought about what lived under it. The patterns in the tracks. The intelligence in the retreat. He thought about the clicking pattern. Three and two. Three and two. Like counting. Like language. Like an intelligence sending a message using the bodies of animals the way a ventriloquist uses a puppet. The mouth moves. But the voice is somewhere else.

His left arm rested on his knee. The carbon nanotube gleamed dully in the red cabin light. The ambient electromagnetic sensor was registering a faint signal. Low-frequency. Rhythmic. The arm was picking it up the way a radio picks up a station it was not tuned to find.

Sir. The pilot pointed ahead.

On a ridge above the tree line a compound sat behind double fencing and gun towers. Prefabricated structures in neat rows. Solar arrays angled toward the red sun. Comms dishes. A landing pad cleared and marked with chemical lights. The perimeter was clean. No brush within fifty meters of the outer fence. Kill zone.

It looked like discipline. It looked like people who had been here long enough to learn what the planet required.

They set down and the marines deployed in a loose perimeter while Theo and Thornhill walked toward the gate. The air here was different. Drier. The ridge caught wind that the plateau did not and it carried the scent of the forest up and over the compound in waves of green and mineral and a sweetness that had no name.

A guard at the gate stood with a rifle that had been re-stocked with local wood. The grain was dark and oiled and the guard had carved a series of small notches along the stock. Not kills. Days. Hundreds of them. He was humming a tune low and repetitive and he did not stop humming when they approached. He just watched them the way a man watches weather coming over a ridge.

A woman met them past the gate. She wore body armor that had been repaired more than once. The plates had scoring on them that Theo recognized as claw marks. She carried a sidearm low on her hip like it was part of her skeleton. Her hair was cut short and her eyes were the color of creek stone and they moved over Theo the way a sniper scope moves over a field. Reading distance. Assessing threat.

Captain Victoria Hale, she said. AstroCorp Security Division.

Theo nodded. Colonel Theo Daniel. Odyssey Colony.

Hale looked at the cybernetic arm. She looked at his posture. She looked at the weight distribution and his right hand and how his eyes had already counted exits.

Military, she said.

Retired.

Hale gave a short laugh that had no humor in it. No one is retired out here Colonel.

She led them through the compound. The layout was tight and efficient but it was not new. The walls had been patched with different alloys at different times and the patches had their own patina. Improvised shelving held tools and ration containers organized by a system that Theo could not immediately parse. Someone had welded a bench from salvaged hull plating near the mess hall entrance and the metal was worn smooth from use. A pair of boots sat drying on a rock that had been placed there for that purpose long enough ago that moss had started up one side of it. In the mess hall doorway a woman was grinding grain in a stone mortar. Grain or root or some local equivalent. The smell was not bread but it was trying to be and the trying was its own kind of stubbornness.

People moved with purpose. They wore uniforms but the uniforms had been altered. Shortened sleeves. Reinforced knees from local fiber. One man had fashioned shoulder plates from what looked like animal hide and they fit his frame as though they had always been there. They nodded to Hale and they looked at Theo and Thornhill with the guarded curiosity of people who have learned that new variables are not always welcome.

Theo counted heads and weapons and exits because that was what he was.

They sat in a briefing room with a table bolted to the floor and lights that buzzed faintly with the sound of power being rationed. No windows. The walls were composite and they had been reinforced with interior plating. On one wall someone had painted a rough map of the surrounding terrain in pigments that looked handmade. Reds and greens that came from the soil and the plants. The map was annotated in a shorthand Theo did not recognize. Their own language. Four months of learning compressed into marks that only Hale's people could read.

Hale did not offer water or pleasantries.

Your generators destabilized the local field, she said. Our sensors have been screaming since you came online. Energy output like yours sends ripples through the whole region.

She leaned forward. Define screaming.

Hale slid a datapad across the table. The screen showed a graph of energy spikes. Low-frequency pulses stacking on each other. The amplitude had been climbing for eight weeks. The timing correlated almost exactly with the Odyssey colonys generator activation schedule.

Theo recognized the rhythm. The same pattern Thornhill had shown him in the council tent. Seen from the other side.

Hale watched his face change. You knew.

I suspected, Theo said.

Hale tapped the screen. Everything here is tuned to a baseline electromagnetic field. Has been for a long time. Longer than us. When you brought your ZPE generators online you rang a bell. Things are listening.

What things, he asked.

We call them ridge-stalkers, Hale said.

Our survey team designated them Shadowfangs, Thornhill said.

Hale considered this. Shadowfangs, she said. That works.

She leaned back. Mapping your perimeter for weeks. Youve noticed.

Theo said nothing. He did not need to.

Pack coordination, Hale said. Flanking. They test defenses and learn from failure. We lost two people in the first month.

We picked up two other beacon signals in the first month, Hale said. European registry. Chinese registry. Both went silent within a week.

She paused. She looked at the table as if deciding how much to say. Then she looked at Theo and then at the wall behind him and then back.

My people have started dreaming, she said.

Everyone dreams, Thornhill said.

Hale shook her head. Not like this. She pulled a datapad from a drawer and placed it on the table. On the screen were drawings. Dozens of them. Sketched by different hands in different materials. Pencil. Charcoal. Grease pen on composite board. All of them showed the same thing. Geometric spirals. Tight concentric patterns that radiated outward from a central point with mathematical precision. Not art. Not imagination. Architecture.

Seven of my people, Hale said. Three weeks. Different shifts. Different quarters. They wake up and draw these. Some don't remember drawing. The spirals are identical. Same proportions. Same ratios. Same rotation.

Thornhill reached for the pad. She turned it slowly. Her face changed.

These are the symbols from the surface anomaly readings, she said. The electromagnetic patterns we flagged from orbit. The fixed-position grid points.

Hale nodded. My people have never seen your orbital data. They don't know what the symbols look like.

She stopped. She picked up the datapad and held it in front of her and looked at the drawings the way you look at something your own people made that you cannot explain and cannot dismiss and cannot stop.

They are dreaming them, she said.

The room was quiet. Hale set the pad down. She did not look at it again.

Three nights running, she said. The same spirals. I wake up and my hands are moving. Drawing in the air.

She stopped. She pressed her hands flat on the table and held them there.

Muscle memory for something I never learned, she said.

Thornhill stared at her.

Hale met the stare and held it. Whatever is on this planet. In this planet. It is writing something into people while they sleep.

Theo looked at the spirals on the pad. He had seen them before. Not in a dream. On the surface of an object in a clearing three days south. An object whose symbols matched what sleeping strangers had drawn in the dark with hands they did not remember using.

He said nothing. He let it settle with the rest.

He thought of Liang's daughter. The star with teeth. Drawn in Shanghai by a twelve-year-old before anyone on this planet had dreamed a single spiral. The signal had been reaching Earth before they left. Through the generators. Through the grid. Into the dreams of children who drew what they could not name.

But the Shadowfangs arent the worst thing out here, Hale said.

There are things in this forest that make the Shadowfangs look like house cats.

As if the planet had been listening and decided to offer proof the alarm cut through the room like a blade.

A guard burst through the door. Captain. Contact. East fence. Big.

Hale was on her feet and moving before the guard finished speaking. Theo was half a step behind her. The marines fell in and Thornhill grabbed her scanner and followed.

They came out into the compound and the ground was shaking.

Not an earthquake. Something with rhythm. Footfalls that Theo felt in his knees and his jaw and the carbon nanotube of his arm. The arm registered the vibration before his flesh did. A fraction of a second. Not processing lag. Something else. As if the arm had been listening to a frequency his body could not hear and the footfalls had just joined it.

The eastern fence was a double line of reinforced composite posts strung with charged wire. Beyond it the tree line was a hundred meters of cleared scrub and rock. Kill zone. And at the far edge of the kill zone something was coming through the trees.

It tore the Obsidian Titans aside like they were stalks of grass. Trunks two meters thick snapping with reports like cannon fire.

A quadruped. Massive. Armored in plates of what looked like stone but moved like skin. Each plate was ridged and dark and where they overlapped the exposed flesh beneath was the color of raw iron. Its head was broad as a ground car and set low between shoulders that bunched with muscle that had no analog in terrestrial biology. Two horns curved forward from the brow ridge like siege rams forged in bone. The eyes were small and deep-set and they burned with a dull orange light that was not reflected. It was generated. Bioluminescent. The eyes of a thing that had been the apex of its world for so long it had never learned to hide.

It stood three meters at the shoulder. Its legs were columns. Its tail was short and armored and it swung it as it walked and where the tail struck a tree the tree broke.

Its breath came in clouds of steam that smelled of sulfur and hot metal.

Dreadmaw, Hale said. Her voice was flat. Hale had said the word before. She would say it again if she lived.

The beast stopped at the edge of the cleared ground. It swung its head left and right. Scenting. Reading. The small orange eyes found the compound and fixed on it. Fixed on the generators. On the source of the signal that had called it across kilometers of forest.

Then it charged.

The ground shook so hard that a man beside Theo stumbled and went to one knee. The Dreadmaw covered the hundred meters of kill zone in seconds and hit the outer fence line at full speed and the reinforced posts snapped like dry bone and the charged wire whipped away in sparking coils and the beast came through without breaking stride.

Turrets opened up. Heavy caliber. Electromagnetic accelerators throwing tungsten slugs at hypersonic velocity. The rounds hit the dorsal plates and sparked and skipped and ricocheted into the dirt. A few found seams between the plates and the beast bellowed. The sound was not a roar. It was a concussion. Theo felt it in his sternum like the sound a building makes when the charges go and the structure begins to fall.

It reached the inner fence and hit that too and the inner fence held for one second and then two and then failed in a shriek of tearing metal and the Dreadmaw was inside the compound.

Hale was shouting orders. Her people moved to positions with the speed of drill. Years of drill. The drill of people who had done this before and buried the ones who hadn't drilled hard enough. Heavy weapons up. Flanking teams east and west. Medical standing by.

Theo felt the old machinery in his head engage. The part of him that had never really left Promethei Terra. The part that saw angles and distances and rates of closure and cover and fields of fire and translated them into decisions faster than thought.

And something else.

His arm came up before he told it to. The rifle braced against his shoulder with a steadiness that was not his steadiness. The targeting overlay in his ocular implant painted the Dreadmaw in red and the arm moved and the finger tightened and the round left the barrel and found the seam behind the left shoulder plate and he had not consciously identified the target. Not yet. The identification came after the shot. A half-second delay between what the arm did and what Theo knew he was doing.

A Shadowfang broke from the underbrush twenty meters to the south. The arm was already swinging. Already acquiring. Already firing. Two rounds. Both into the animal before Theo had processed its presence. The Shadowfang dropped and skidded across packed earth and was still.

He was firing before he was seeing and seeing before he

was thinking and thinking after the threat was already neutralized. The arm knew. He knew through the arm. Where the operator ended and the prosthetic began had become a question without an answer. And the question did not slow him down. It made him faster.

Target the joints, he called out. His voice cut through the noise with the authority of a man who had commanded men in worse places than this. The armor plates don't cover the joints. Look for the gaps when it moves. Eyes. The underside where the belly plates separate when it lifts a leg. Concentrate fire there.

Hale glanced at him once. Assessed. Accepted. She relayed the order in words her people knew.

The beast had reached the first prefab structure. It was the armory. It lowered its head and swung and the building came apart. Composite panels flew in spinning sheets. A man was caught in the debris and thrown ten meters and how he landed said everything about whether he would get up. He did not.

Another man fired point-blank into the beasts face. The rounds hit the brow plate and the ricochets took out a light tower. The Dreadmaw turned toward the shooter and opened its mouth. The jaw was hinged like a snakes. Wider than seemed possible. The teeth were flat and crushing and behind them the throat was dark and hot and the smell that came out was the smell of a world that ran on different chemistry.

It bit the prefab wall beside the man and pulled. Metal screamed. The wall came away and the man ran and the beast let him go because the building was not what it wanted. The generator was what it wanted. The signal was what it wanted.

The marines Theo had brought opened up from the

south. They were good. Promethei-trained. They found the joint behind the left foreleg and hammered it with controlled bursts. Dark fluid sprayed. The color of it was wrong. Too dark. Almost black. The Dreadmaw pivoted toward the new pain and in pivoting exposed the gap beneath its throat plates where the armor thinned to allow the neck to flex.

Theo's arm was already moving. Before the gap opened fully the targeting overlay had calculated the angle and the arm fired three rounds into the exposed tissue in a grouping tighter than any human hand should manage at that range under those conditions. The rounds hit wet and deep and the Dreadmaw screamed and stumbled and in the same motion Theo was pivoting to cover Hale's heavy weapons team as they converged their fire on the same gap.

He was not thinking. He was being thought through. The arm and the eye and the body operating as a single system whose processing center was distributed across flesh and carbon and firmware that he had not written and did not fully understand. He did not fight it. He let it work. He let the doubt carry him because the doubt moved faster than certainty ever had.

The heavy weapons team put a sustained burst into the throat gap. The beast screamed again and staggered. One foreleg buckled. It caught itself. The orange eyes swept the compound and it charged the heavy weapons team.

Two people dove clear. One did not. The Dreadmaw stepped on him and the sound was brief and final.

Then the Shadowfangs came.

They poured out of the tree line in a pack of eight. Low and fast and utterly silent. They came through the broken fences in the wake of the Dreadmaw like infantry following armor. They did not charge the firing lines. They went for the flanks. For the gaps between defenders. For the wounded.

Two threats, Theo called out. He moved to a position between the inner buildings where he had cover and sight lines. Hold the line. Let them come to the kill zone.

A Shadowfang hit a marine from the side. It came out of the destroyed armory like a piece of the building itself given weight and purpose. Jaws closed on the mans forearm and the teeth went through the armor sleeve like it was cloth. The marine screamed and clubbed at the animal with the butt of his sidearm. Theo's arm was already there. A round through the Shadowfangs skull at fifteen meters. A clean shot that Theo did not remember deciding to take. The animal dropped and the marine fell with it and other hands pulled him back.

Another Shadowfang leapt at Hale. She turned into it with the reflexes of a woman who had been hunted before. She caught it with a close-range burst that opened its chest cavity and the animal twisted in the air and hit the ground beside her and its legs worked for a moment and then stopped working forever.

A third took a marine in the leg. A fourth was killed by turret fire as it tried to flank the medical tent.

The coordinated attack. The Dreadmaw as battering ram. The Shadowfangs as infantry exploiting the breach. Two species operating in concert. Combined arms. Coordinated doctrine. As if something was directing them. Something distributed across bodies and species that used violence the way a conductor uses instruments. Each animal playing its part in a composition none of them had written.

The Dreadmaw was still moving. Bleeding from a dozen wounds but still moving. It crushed a second structure. It turned toward the generator building. The power core. The source.

Theo saw it and understood. The Dreadmaw wasn't attacking the compound. It was attacking the signal. Trying to silence the thing that was ringing in its blood the way the containment oscillations rang in Theo's arm.

The generator, he shouted. Its targeting the generator. Everything on it now.

Hale's people and Theo's marines converged fire. The joint behind the right foreleg gave under sustained bursts and the leg buckled. The Dreadmaw lurched forward and its belly dropped toward the ground and in that moment the gap between the ventral plates opened wide and every weapon that could see it fired into the exposed flesh.

The beast went down on its right side. The impact cratered the packed earth and sent a shockwave through the ground that Theo felt through the soles of his boots. It tried to rise. The left foreleg pushed and the plates ground against each other and dark blood pooled beneath it in a spreading lake.

It made a sound then that was not a scream and not a bellow. Lower. Almost subsonic. A vibration more felt than heard. Like a signal sent into the earth.

Hale walked to it. She stood five meters from its head and raised her weapon. The orange eyes found her. In them was a quality that Theo did not want to call recognition but could not call anything else.

She put three rounds into its eye.

It shuddered. The massive legs stopped their working. The breath left it in a long rasp that smelled of minerals and heat. Then it was still.

The silence that followed was not silence. It was the absence of violence which is a different thing. The hiss of cooling barrels. The groan of damaged structures settling into new shapes. The wind through the broken fences carrying the forest smell and the iron smell of blood that was not blood.

The remaining Shadowfangs had vanished. They had gone the moment the Dreadmaw fell. As if its death was information they could use. As if the whole attack had been a lesson and the lesson was over and now there would be studying.

Theo counted the cost. Three of Hale's people dead. Five wounded. One of his marines with a mangled arm that the medics were already sealing with field gel. Two structures destroyed. The inner fence down in three sections. The outer fence gone entirely along a thirty-meter stretch.

He looked at his left arm. The diagnostic readout showed elevated activity across every metric. Reaction time. Motor precision. Signal processing. All above his own recorded maximums. The combat had opened something in the firmware. Or the firmware had stopped pretending to be closed.

He cleared the diagnostic. He did not run it again.

Hale stood over the Dreadmaws carcass. Blood was on her armor and on her face and she did not wipe it away. She looked at the animal as a woman looks at a thing she has killed many times and expects to kill again and does not expect it to get easier.

You know your way around a fight, she said.

Theo ejected a spent magazine and loaded a fresh one. The action was muscle memory. The kind of memory that lives in the hands and does not ask permission.

Hale looked at him for a long time. The kind of look that measures not what a person says but what they carry.

You want an alliance, she said.

I want survival.

She nodded slowly. Then we share resources. We share data. We share intelligence on every living thing on this planet and every dead thing too. Because the dead things might be the ones that matter.

Theo held out his hand. The cybernetic one. A reflex. Or a precision deeper than reflex. Hale looked at it. She took it. Her grip was strong and steady and if the carbon nanotube fingers registered any data about her pulse or her temperature or the composition of her skin Theo did not check. Some measurements are not meant to be taken.

The compound went to work the moment the carcass stopped steaming. There was no ceremony. No pause. A woman with a cutting torch started sectioning the Dreadmaws armor plating before the medics had finished with the wounded. Two men dragged composite panels from the wreckage and stacked them by size. The guard from the gate had set his rifle down and was helping a younger man reset a fence post with the efficiency of someone who had done this repair before and would do it again. The humming had not stopped.

In the mess hall the woman with the mortar had put out food. Flatbread made from local plants that had been dried and ground and mixed with a powder that gave it a faint amber color. Beside it a pot of stew that smelled like root vegetables and iron and months of learning what on this planet would kill you and what would only make you wish it had. Hale's people ate standing or crouching between tasks. They did not wait for permission. They did not queue. The food was there and they took it and went back to work and the rhythm of it was the rhythm of people who had built their own customs in a place where no one else would build them for them.

Theo ate some of the flatbread. It was dense and gritty and tasted like nothing he had ever tasted and exactly like what he imagined this planet would taste like if you could eat it.

A child appeared in a doorway. Eight or nine years old. She watched the work crews with the calm appraisal of a child who has never known a world without this kind of damage. She disappeared back inside and a moment later returned with a water canister and carried it to the fence crew without being asked.

Hale saw Theo watching. She said nothing. Her face did not change. But her hand went to her sidearm and rested on the grip the way a person rests a hand on something familiar when they need to steady themselves against something that is not a threat. The child. The water. The ordinary thing continuing inside the wreckage.

Then her hand fell away. She turned and walked to the fence line and her stride was even and her back was straight and she did not look at the child again.

The flyer lifted from the compound at dusk with cooperation protocols loaded into its nav system and shared frequencies locked into its comms array. Hale stood at the gate and watched them go. She raised one hand. Not a wave. An acknowledgment. Then she turned and went back to the work of holding a perimeter on a world that did not want her there.

Theo sat in the bay as the forest passed below.

Thornhill sat across from him. She had been quiet since leaving the compound. She looked at her scanner. She looked at the passing canopy. She looked at Theo.

Your combat performance today, she said. The reaction times.

Theo looked at her.

They were outside normal parameters, she said. Significantly outside. Even for a military-grade prosthetic with neural-interface optimization.

She said it the way she said everything. Like a scientist stating data. Not an accusation. An observation.

I adapt, Theo said. Its what the arm does. Its what I do.

Thornhill held his gaze for a moment longer than necessary. Then she nodded slowly and looked back at her scanner.

Theo turned to the window and watched the forest darken beneath them. He thought about Hale's people dreaming in geometric spirals. He thought about the Shadowfangs and their distributed intelligence. The network that thought through bodies. He thought about the Dreadmaw targeting the generator. The signal in the earth. The signal in his arm.

Between the black columns of the Obsidian Titans the Lumina ferns cast their cold glow across the ground and in the center of a clearing that was not a clearing but a space where nothing had been allowed to grow he saw it again.

The artifact.

A straight edge. A surface that caught the last light of Wolf 1061 and returned it at an angle that no organic surface could produce. Too clean. Too geometric. Set into the ground like a cornerstone of something that had been buried for longer than the trees had been growing.

And for one instant as the flyer banked and his arm swung toward the window the artifact pulsed. A single beat of light. Low-frequency. Blue-white. The same frequency that his arm had been registering all day.

His arm answered. Not in light. In temperature. A surge of warmth through the carbon nanotube that was not electrical and not mechanical and had no corresponding readout on his diagnostic display. A warmth that felt like recognition. As if the arm and the thing in the clearing had exchanged a signal. A handshake.

Then it stopped.

The artifact went dark. The arm went back to baseline. The clearing passed beneath them and the forest closed over it and the darkness swallowed everything except the memory of the light.

Theo said nothing. He looked at his left hand. The diagnostics read normal. Nothing to report. Nothing except the knowledge that whatever was buried on this planet already knew he was here. Had known since he landed. Had perhaps known since before that.

He closed his hand into a fist. The carbon nanotube fingers curled with a precision that was mechanical and a gentleness that was not.

Thornhill, he said.

She looked up.

When we get back I need to show you something. Something Ive been sitting on for three days.

She waited.

An artifact, he said. In the forest. South of camp. Its not natural. Its not human. And I think its been waiting for us.

Thornhill set the scanner in her lap. She looked at him the way she always looked when the data changed. Not with fear. With hunger. The hunger of a scientist who has spent her life chasing the edge of the known and has just been told the edge is closer than she thought.

How long have you known.

Three days.

And you told no one.

I'm telling you.

She was quiet for a long time. Outside the window the

forest darkened and the sky above it filled with stars that were not Earths stars and would never be.

I need to see it, Thornhill said.

Theo nodded. He looked at the canopy passing below. At the dark places between the trees where things moved that he could not name and could not predict and could not fight with any weapon he had been trained to use. At the world they had chosen because there was no other world to choose. At the planet that had been waiting for them the way a trap waits. The way a mouth waits.

He did not sleep that night.

* * *

THEY WENT IN AT DUSK.

Small team. No flyer. The sound and energy signature of a flyer would carry through the forest like a shout and Theo had seen enough of what answered shouts on this planet. They walked. No lights until they had to. No broadcast. No networked devices. They went quiet and they would come back quiet or they would not come back at all.

Theo. Thornhill. Sergeant Miles, Corporal Tan, and two privates from the perimeter detail, Rivera and Cho. All four marines had been at the Dreadmaw fight. All had the steady hands and flat eyes of people who had been tested and had not broken and did not expect the testing to stop.

They left through the south gate when the watch was changing and the camp was focused inward. Theo had logged the sortie as a perimeter survey. Not a lie. Not the truth. The kind of language that soldiers use when the truth is too expensive to spend on people who don't need it yet.

The tree line swallowed them in thirty steps.

Under the Obsidian Titans the air was cool and wet and

thick with the smell of growth and decay running simultaneously as if the planet could not decide which it preferred. The trunks rose like the columns of a temple built by something that did not worship anything human. Between them the Lumina ferns cast their cold light across the ground and in that light the forest floor was a map of roots and moss and things that moved at the edge of vision and vanished when you looked directly at them.

They walked for two hours. The gravity pulled at them. One point one five g. Every step carrying fifteen percent more weight than their muscles remembered. It settled into the joints first. Then the spine. Then the will. Lupus Stella did not want you to walk far. It wanted you to sit down. To stop. To let the forest grow over you and add your chemistry to its own.

Theo led them by memory and compass. The artifact was three kilometers south of camp in a depression between two ridges where the Obsidian Titans thinned and the understory grew dense and tangled. A place where the drone surveys had shown nothing because the canopy was too thick for visual mapping and the electromagnetic interference was too strong for ground-penetrating radar.

He had found it on foot. Walking the perimeter loop that he extended each week. Pushing the known boundary farther because that was what you did. You expanded the circle of what you controlled or you watched it shrink. There was no standing still on a world that grew as fast as this one.

The depression opened below them like a cupped hand in the earth. The ferns were thicker here. Their glow was stronger. A blue-green light that pulsed in a rhythm that was too regular for biology. One beat per second. Like a heartbeat. Like a signal.

There.

The artifact sat in the center of the depression. A slab of dark alloy set into the ground at a slight angle. Two meters wide. Three long. Its surface was covered in geometric symbols that caught the fern-light and held it in their grooves like water held in carved stone. The symbols were spirals. The same tight concentric spirals that Hale's people had been drawing in their sleep. The same patterns the orbital sensors had flagged across the planets surface. A language written in mathematics and pressed into metal by hands that were not hands.

The slab was warm. Not from the sun. Wolf 1061 had set an hour ago. The warmth came from within. As if the metal had its own metabolism.

Thornhill knelt beside it. She ran her scanner across the surface. Her face changed as the data came in.

The alloy, she said. Its not any composition in our database. There are elements here that I don't have reference signatures for. And the temperature. She checked the readout twice. It matches. She looked at Theo. It matches the ambient temperature of your prosthetic.

Theo crouched beside the slab. He looked at the symbols. The spirals and their geometric precision. The way they radiated from a central point. He extended his left hand.

The carbon nanotube fingers touched the surface.

The pulse hit him like a wall of light behind his eyes.

Not vibration. Not data. Vision. The planet from above. Not from orbit. From everywhere at once. A perspective no human body could hold. He saw the plateau where the colony sat. He saw the ridges and the valleys and the red veins of the creeks. He saw the Crimson Sea and the coastline and the forest canopy that spread from horizon to horizon. He saw the electromagnetic grid. The fixed points that the orbital sensors had mapped. They were not anomalies. They were nodes. Relay points in a network that covered the planets surface like a nervous system covers a body. And the nodes were alive. Pulsing. Transmitting. Waiting.

He saw it all in one second. A single frame of total knowledge that his brain could not process and his arm could. The arm held the image the way a camera holds a photograph.

Then it was gone.

He pulled his hand back. The slab was warm. His arm was warm. Same temperature. Same heat. As if for one moment the boundary between the constructed thing on the planet and the constructed thing on his body had dissolved and they had been one circuit with one current.

Thornhill was staring at him. Your readings spiked. Every neural-interface metric went off the scale for one point three seconds. What happened.

Theo flexed his fingers. The arm was back to baseline. The vision was already fading as dreams fade. Not losing detail but losing the sense that the details had been real.

I saw the planet, he said. From above. Not from orbit. From everywhere.

Thornhill looked at the slab. She looked at his arm.

The same temperature, she said. Your arm and this slab are running at the same temperature. The same frequency. The same base electromagnetic signature.

Theo stood. He looked at the slab the way you look at a thing that has shown you something you did not ask to see and cannot forget.

Mark it, he said. We come back with a full team. But first we find what its connected to.

Miles, he said. Perimeter sweep. Two hundred meters. Look for anything else that doesn't belong.

Miles moved. He was back in eight minutes. His face said everything before his mouth did.

Sir. Theres a structure. Buried. Fifty meters south. The ground has collapsed over what looks like an archway.

They found the archway at the bottom of a shallow ravine where the roots of the Obsidian Titans had broken through whatever had been covering it. A curved opening in dark alloy. The same metal as the slab. The same warmth. The same geometric symbols running along its frame in lines that spiraled inward toward the opening like the pattern of a nautilus shell.

Thornhill scanned the opening. Her hands were trembling. Not with fear. With the kind of excitement that lives where fear and discovery share a border.

The passage goes down, she said. At least forty meters before my scanner loses resolution. The walls are the same alloy. There are energy signatures inside. Faint. But organized.

Theo looked at the archway. He looked at Miles. At Tan. At Thornhill. Each of them looked back. Each of them understood that what they were about to do could not be undone.

The darkness inside it was not the darkness of absence. It was the darkness of containment. Of a force held.

Lights, Theo said.

They went in.

The passage descended at a grade that was gentle enough for walking and steep enough to remind you that you were going down into the earth. The walls were smooth and warm and covered in the geometric symbols. The light from their headlamps caught the grooves and threw shadows that moved as they moved and the shadows looked like the symbols were shifting. Rearranging. As if the walls were reading the people who walked between them and adjusting their message accordingly.

The air grew cooler as they descended. Not the cool of earth and stone. A regulated cool. The temperature of a space that was being maintained. That had been maintained. For how long the mind could not calculate without flinching.

The passage opened into a chamber.

The chamber was vast. The ceiling was too high for their headlamps to find. The floor was the same dark alloy as the walls polished to a surface that reflected their lights in distorted doubles. And in the air above them floating in patterns that were neither random nor fixed small orbs of soft light drifted. Each one the size of a fist. Each one glowing with a luminescence that was not electric and not chemical and not bioluminescent. A fourth thing. An energy that had no name in the physics Thornhill had studied. They moved in slow orbits around invisible centers and where they passed the darkness retreated and where they left the darkness returned and the whole chamber breathed with their motion.

The orbs cast a light that pooled in the grooves of the symbols and the light was almost musical. It shifted. Blue to violet to a hue warmer than either. A pattern that repeated and then did not quite repeat. Like a melody trying to remember itself.

The walls of the chamber were covered in larger symbols. Star maps. Theo recognized the configuration from the orbital surveys. Star systems. Galactic positions. A web of lines connecting marked worlds in a network that spanned distances that made the mind stutter. Some of the marks were bright. Some were dark. The bright ones pulsed faintly. The dark ones did not.

Thornhill swept her scanner across the walls. Her voice came out in a whisper that had nothing to do with stealth.

This is a record, she said. A database. Stellar coordinates. Thousands of them. And these lines. She traced a glowing thread between two marked systems. Communication pathways. Energy conduits. She stopped. The scale of what she was seeing stopped her tongue.

Theo looked at the web of lines connecting the marked systems. The lines converged on certain nodes. Relay points. Nexuses. Some of the nodes were bright and some were dark. The dark ones were dead. Burned out. Consumed.

A translation algorithm that Thornhill had loaded into her pad began to work on the symbols. It chewed through the geometric patterns and cross-referenced them with the symbols on the slab and the archway.

The symbols translated quickly. Too quickly.

She noticed it first. This doesn't make sense, she said. The algorithm shouldn't be able to parse this grammar. No Rosetta stone. No reference point. But its translating as if it were designed to be readable by any symbolic intelligence that encountered it.

She paused.

Or its not translating at all. The symbols are translating themselves. The algorithm isn't decoding. Its being given the answers.

She looked at Theo. Am I reading the wall. Or is the wall reading me.

Theo looked at the symbols flowing across her pad. The fragments. Raw. Unpunctuated.

ENERGY.

HUNGER.

CONSUME.

Does the distinction matter right now, he said.

Thornhill held his gaze. It might matter more than anything else in this room.

She was right. He knew she was right. But he was also a man standing in the ruins of a dead civilization and the dead were speaking and whatever the mechanism of their speech the words were the only light he had.

Keep going, he said.

They moved deeper into the chamber. The orbs parted before them like a school of luminous fish giving way to a larger body. The walls continued their story. More systems. More lines. The web growing denser and more complex.

Then a phrase came through. Longer.

THE DEVOURERS COME.

Thornhill stopped walking. Her hand went to her mouth and she pressed it there as if to hold a cry in.

Sergeant Miles had his weapon up. Scanning the darkness above them. Corporal Tan had moved to the nearest wall and pressed her back against it, her weapon covering the passage they had come through. The orbs cast moving shadows on the walls and the shadows looked like things that were not there and might not stay that way.

They reached the far end of the chamber. A raised platform. A console. A curved surface covered in the geometric symbols. The symbols here were larger. More deliberate. More urgent. As if this was the part that the builders had wanted found. Had needed found. As if the whole structure was a bottle and this was the message.

Thornhill looked at Theo.

He nodded.

She touched the console.

The chamber went dark. Every light. Every orb. Every

glow in every wall. The darkness was total and it was sudden and the marines raised weapons and Miles said hold steady and the darkness held for five seconds that lasted five years.

Then the vision began.

It did not play on the walls. It did not project from a device. It played inside them. In their minds. Behind their eyes and between their thoughts in a space that was not physical and was not imaginary but occupied the territory where experience and memory share a border. Each of them received it. Each of them received it differently.

A city rose.

For Theo it rose in spires of crystal and structured light that reached into a violet sky. The spires were not buildings as humans understood buildings. They were grown. Cultivated. Shaped by energy fields into forms that defied what he knew about engineering and gravity and the limits of matter. Between the spires beings moved in currents. Not humanoid. Not anything he had a word for. Elongated forms that rippled with bioluminescence and communicated in pulses of color and sound and something else that the recording could capture but his senses could not name.

They were beautiful the way weather is beautiful. Impersonal and vast and indifferent to the witness.

The city thrummed with energy. Machines of no recognizable design fed by glowing orbs identical to the ones floating in the chamber. The energy flowed through conduits and networks and the whole city pulsed with it like a living heart. The city was not a place where these beings lived. The city was the being. The architecture and the inhabitants and the energy were one system and the system was alive.

Then the sky changed.

The light itself began to fail. As if a presence at the horizon was eating the photons before they could reach the ground. Darkness crept inward. Not shadow. Something was taking the light and taking the energy that made the light and feeding on both. A darkness with appetite.

The beings in the city stopped moving. Their bioluminescence flickered. The pulses of communication became frantic. Short. Repeating. Warnings.

The machines failed. The orbs dimmed. The conduits went dark one by one like a nervous system shutting down from the extremities inward.

And then they came.

They were not visible the way matter is visible. They were visible only in what they destroyed. Where they passed the light died and the structures dissolved not into rubble but into nothing. The matter itself thinned. Dissipated. As if reality were a fabric and something was pulling the threads. The spires came apart like sand sculptures in a rising tide. The beings were drawn into the consuming dark. Not killed. Taken. Absorbed. Their light going out one by one like stars winking out at the end of the universe.

The city fell in silence and scream. The silence of structures dissolving into void. The scream of the last frequency the dying beings broadcast.

The last image was a single being at the console. The same console that Thornhill now touched. The being was flickering. Its light guttering like a candle in a wind that was not wind. It pressed itself against the console surface and the symbols blazed one final time with everything the being had left. Its last act. Its only act that would outlast it.

A broadcast. Sent outward through the network. Sent to every connected system. Sent to worlds the dying being had never seen and never would. Sent to anyone. Sent to the future. Sent here.

The translation algorithm caught the words as they came. Or the words caught the algorithm.

CEASE YOUR HUNGER.

THEY TRACK THE ENERGY.

THEY CONSUME THE SOURCE.

SILENCE YOUR MACHINES OR THEY WILL FIND YOU AS THEY FOUND US.

CEASE YOUR HUNGER.

The vision collapsed. The light folded inward and vanished and the chamber returned. The orbs resumed their silent rotation. The walls dimmed to their baseline glow. Nothing had changed in the room.

No one spoke. Not immediately.

Thornhill pulled her hand from the console. Her fingers were trembling. She looked at them as if they belonged to someone else.

Then Miles spoke. His voice was careful.

The city, he said. The spires. How many were there.

Thornhill blinked. Hundreds. They reached into a violet sky.

Miles shook his head. I saw twelve. The sky was black. The structures were low. Flat. They spread across a plain.

Corporal Tan looked between them. I saw a single tower. One structure. Very tall. The sky was red.

Silence. The kind that has weight.

Thornhill turned to Theo. The color left her face.

Personalized, she whispered. The vision was personalized.

They looked at each other. Each of them waiting for someone to explain what could not be explained.

Or what it wanted each mind to see, Theo said.

Miles shifted his weight. Tan checked her weapon and checked it again. The small mechanical actions of people who needed their hands to do something while their minds refused to settle.

Thornhill looked at the console. She did not touch it again.

Sergeant Miles, Theo said. His voice was steady because it had to be. Because someone in the room had to be steady and he was the one who had practiced being steady in rooms where everything was falling apart.

Sir.

Full perimeter on this chamber. Nothing comes in. Nothing goes out that we don't carry.

Miles moved. His fire team spread to the chamber walls. Professional. Efficient. Their training holding them together the way a frame holds glass that wants to shatter.

Thornhill sat on the edge of the platform. She looked at Theo. Her face was the face of a woman whose lifes work had just been rewritten in a language she was only beginning to read.

She looked at the star map. The dark nodes. The consumed worlds. The pattern of annihilation spread across the galaxy. She was quiet for a long time. When she spoke she did not look at Theo. She looked at her hands.

The Devourers, she said. They track zero-point energy signatures. The ZPE generators extract energy from the quantum vacuum. We always said it was free. Unlimited. No waste. No signal.

She was quiet again. The orbs drifted above them.

But its not free. She said it quietly. Almost to herself. The extraction sends a perturbation into the vacuum state. A signal. And something out there has evolved to hunt that signal.

She stood. She walked to the star map. She pressed her hand against the wall and the symbols beneath her fingers pulsed gently. More data flowing into her pad.

She looked at the dark nodes on the map. The dead worlds. The consumed civilizations.

An immune response, she said.

She stopped. She did not explain what she meant. She stood in front of the record of consumed worlds and said the two words and let them sit in the chamber and the chamber held them the way the chamber held everything. Patiently. Without judgment. Without relief.

Theo looked at the web. At the dark nodes. At the bright ones still pulsing faintly with the signals of worlds that had not yet been found.

He closed his eyes.

He saw the colony. The ten thousand people in their shelters. The children asleep in their cots. The small shapes of them. He saw Hale's compound on the ridge with its scarred walls and its disciplined people and the drawings of spirals made by hands that moved in sleep. He saw the Odyssey in orbit. The dead Earth behind them. The void ahead.

He opened his eyes.

Then we mask the signature, he said.

She stared at him.

We retrofit the generators. We flatten the signal. We silence the beacon. Whether we are the hero or the disease we survive. That is not a moral question. That is an engineering problem.

His voice was the voice of a man who had been told the ground beneath him was not ground but the surface of a living and hungry thing and had decided to stand on it anyway. Because standing was what he did. Because the alternative to standing was lying down and he had not lied down at Promethei Terra when Jake died and he had not lied down in the ashfall when Clara died and he would not lie down now in the ruins of a civilization that had died trying to say the one thing that mattered.

He pointed at the console. At the symbols that the algorithm was still processing. Or that were still processing the algorithm.

This civilization knew what was coming. They built this place. This warning system. They recorded everything they knew about how the Devourers tracked their prey. If they understood the signal well enough to warn others then they understood it well enough to describe how to hide from it. The data is here. The schematics are here. We use them.

Thornhill looked at her scanner. The algorithm was still working. Still pulling fragments from the alien language. Or still being given structure by the geometry.

The modulation pattern, she said slowly. There are schematics embedded in the warning data. Frequency modulation overlays. Phase-cancellation matrices. She leaned closer to the pad. If I can decode the technical specifications there may be a way to restructure our generators output. Flatten the ZPE signature. Make us look like noise instead of a signal.

Can you do it.

Thornhill was quiet for a long moment. In the chamber the orbs turned and the walls glowed and the network that had carried a dead civilizations final words waited for the answer.

I can try, she said. The engineering principles are alien. Literally alien. The modulation has to be precise. Too much and we lose containment. Too little and the signature still reads. One mistake and the containment field collapses.

One generator, Theo said. We pick one. The smallest. The one we can most afford to lose. We retrofit. We test. If it works we scale. If it fails we learn fast and try again.

Thornhill nodded. Her hands had stopped shaking. She had work to do now. A thing to build. That was what she needed. The same thing Theo needed. The work. The next step. The refusal to stand still while the dark approached.

Theo turned to leave the chamber. Then he stopped.

On the wall behind the console a final symbol glowed. It was not part of the star map. It was not part of the warning schematics. It was a single glyph. Larger than the others. Set apart. Alone on a panel of dark alloy.

The translation algorithm returned a single word.

REMEMBER.

Theo looked at it. He thought about the being at the console. The last of its kind in a dying city pressing its light into the symbols like a hand pressing a message into wet clay. Knowing it would die. Knowing the message might not be found. Sending it anyway. Because that is what you do when the dark comes and you cannot stop it. You leave a mark. You say you were here. You say what killed you. You say it to anyone. You say it to no one. You say it because saying it is the last act of a thing that refuses to go without record.

He turned and walked out of the ruins and into the corridor and up the slope and through the archway and into the forest. The Lumina ferns pulsed at his feet. The Obsidian Titans stood in their dark vigil. The light of the orbs faded behind him like the memory of a dream that was not a dream. That had never been a dream.

They emerged from the tree line as the first light of Wolf 1061 broke across the eastern ridges. The camp was stirring. Smoke from the cook fires. The hum of generators. The ordinary sounds of ten thousand people beginning another day on a world that wanted them gone and it had said so. In a language they were only now learning to hear.

Miles looked at Theo as they crossed the south gate. Neither man spoke. There was nothing to say that the walk had not already said. Miles nodded once. Theo nodded back. It was the oldest language there was and it meant we went somewhere and we came back and that is enough for now.

The council met that night.

Theo told them everything. The artifact. The ruins. The vision. The Devourers. The beacon. He told it in the briefing room with the door sealed and the senior staff arrayed around the table and Hale present by encrypted holo-link from Ridge-7.

He told it without embellishment and without comfort. He told it as he would deliver a battlefield assessment to people who needed to act on it and who would either act on it or die. These are the facts. This is the threat. This is what we do.

He did not tell them that the vision had been different for each person in the chamber. He did not tell them that the symbols might be translating themselves rather than being translated. He did not tell them that his arm had answered the artifacts pulse with a warmth that had no mechanical source. Some intelligence is not useful to committees. Some doubt is a weapon best carried alone.

Vasquez listened with her arms crossed and her face like stone. Stone that had been hit before and expected to be hit again.

Maria Lopez listened with her hands flat on the table and her eyes on Theo's face and the tears she would not let fall catching the light.

Hale listened from her screen with the face of a woman who had suspected this for a long time and now had it confirmed and did not feel vindicated. Only tired. Only old in a way that had nothing to do with years.

The room was quiet when he finished.

Then the arguments began.

Vasquez wanted full military readiness. Every weapon checked and loaded. Every marine on rotation. Fortification of both settlements. Contingency plans for evacuation.

Against what, Thornhill said. You saw what they did to that city. They don't fight. They consume. They dissolve matter. You can't shoot a thing that eats light.

We can try, Vasquez said.

Maria Lopez wanted the colonists told. Full transparency. Immediate.

If we tell ten thousand people that we brought them across the void to be the infection that attracts the cure we will have a stampede, Vasquez said. People will try to take the shuttles. People will die in the panic.

Our people deserve to know, Lopez said. They left Earth with a promise. They're owed the truth.

Theo let them argue. He watched the dynamics of the room as he watched a battlefield. The lines of force. The points of fracture. The places where pressure could be applied and the places where it would shatter what it touched.

Then he spoke.

We tell the council. We tell senior staff. We do not tell the general population until we have something to offer them besides fear. He looked at each person at the table. Fear without a plan is a riot. Fear with a plan is a workforce. Thornhill starts the retrofit immediately. One generator. Prototype modulation collar based on the ruins schematics.

Vasquez increases perimeter security to full wartime posture. Lopez prepares a staged communication plan for the general population. Timed. Managed. Paired with concrete actions so that when people hear the truth they hear it alongside the solution.

He turned to Hale's image on the screen.

Captain Hale. Your outpost has been managing power output and local ecology for four months longer than us. I need your data. All of it. Environmental. Biological. Electromagnetic. Everything.

Hale nodded. You'll have it by morning.

Theo stood.

We are not dead, he said. We are not beaten. We are warned. A civilization older than ours died to send us that warning. We will not waste it. Whether we are what we thought we were or something else entirely we do not stop. We adapt. We retrofit. We survive.

He walked out.

He spent his political capital like ammunition because that was what it was for. Because ammunition not spent is just weight. And they had no weight to spare.

CHAPTER 11

THE SIGNAL

The retrofit began that night.

Thornhill and her engineering team opened Generator Four. It was the smallest of the colony units. The least critical to the power grid. The one they could most afford to lose if the experiment went wrong.

The housing came apart in sections under work lights that cast hard shadows on the faces of the engineers. Inside the containment field shimmered like heat above pavement. A visible distortion in the air that marked the boundary between normal space and the space where the quantum vacuum was being tapped. The zero-point tap itself was a small thing. A device the size of a fist that reached into the substrate of reality and drew energy from the fluctuations of empty space. It looked simple. It was not simple. It was the most complex piece of technology humanity had ever built and according to a civilization older than human memory it was tearing holes in the fabric of spacetime with every watt it drew.

Thornhill worked from schematics she had translated from the ruins console. Or that had been translated for her. The technical data was fragmentary and the engineering principles were alien in the most literal sense of a word that had once been metaphorical. She was reverse-engineering a technology built by beings whose physics used axioms that human science had not yet discovered. She worked with what she had. Fragments and analogies and the intuition of a woman who had spent her life at the boundary between the known and the unknown.

The modulation collar was a ring of components wired around the containment housing. Handmade. Improvised. Assembled from parts meant for other purposes. Sensor housings repurposed as frequency modulators. Communication arrays rewired as phase-cancellation matrices. A hack. A prayer said in copper and circuitry and solder and hope.

Theo stood and watched. He could not help with the engineering. That was not his skill. His skill was deciding and holding and waiting and he exercised all three while the engineers worked and the generators hummed their signal into the dark and the forest listened.

The installation took four hours.

When the last connection was made and the last circuit tested Thornhill stepped back from the housing. She was covered in grease and sweat and the light from the containment field made her face look like pale carved stone.

If this works the generator output stays the same but the ZPE signature will be modulated. Spread across a broad frequency band that mimics the natural electromagnetic background of Lupus Stella. Instead of a point source beacon it becomes distributed noise.

And if it doesn't work.

She did not answer. She did not need to.

Do it, he said.

Thornhill activated the collar.

The generators hum changed. A subtle shift that was felt more than heard. The pitch dropped and the rhythm softened and the sound that had been a steady mechanical pulse became diffuse. More organic. Like a heartbeat becoming a breeze. Like a signal becoming weather.

Every sensor in the camp watched. Every screen in the command tent displayed the same data. Thornhill had routed the monitoring to every display so that everyone who needed to see would see and everyone who needed to believe would believe.

The low-frequency oscillation pattern that had been climbing for weeks appeared on the screens. The familiar stammer. The responsive heartbeat. The feedback loop that connected their generators to whatever lived in the substrate of this planet.

It flattened.

The line went smooth. The spikes disappeared. The rhythm dissolved into the background noise of the planet.

For the first time since the generators had come online the signal was gone.

Thornhill exhaled. The sound came from deeper than her lungs. From the place where her father's face lived. From the room in Novosibirsk that she had never seen but had built in her mind from the accident report. Every detail. Every reading. Every failure point. She had memorized the failure points the way some people memorize scripture. Because if she knew them well enough she could build something that did not fail. Because that was the only inheritance worth claiming. She put her hands on the generator housing and leaned against it and closed her eyes. The ozone smell was the same. It was always the same.

Its not perfect, she said. The modulation drifts. Well need to recalibrate constantly. Manual adjustments until we can automate the process. And the other three generators are still broadcasting. Were still visible. But the principle works. We can mask the signature.

How fast can you scale, Theo asked.

Give me a week for each generator. Assuming nothing else tries to kill us.

Theo almost smiled. It was the closest thing to a smile that either of them had. The smile of two people who have learned that the universe considers them a disease and have decided to be a quieter disease. A disease that hides. A disease that adapts.

He checked on the children. Knox slept with his fists clenched as he always slept. Luna curled with her blanket pulled over her head but the blanket had slipped from her shoulder and the air in the shelter was cool. Theo reached down to pull it back and his left arm got there first. The carbon fingers found the edge of the fabric and drew it up over the girl's shoulder with a motion that was not mechanical. It was the motion of tucking. The specific gesture that parents make a thousand times and that no engineer has ever written into a prosthetic's motor library because it cannot be reduced to torque values and servo angles. It is learned the way all important things are learned. By doing it in the dark when no one is watching.

Ruiz stood in the doorway. She had seen. Her expression held a quality he could not read. Not surprise. Not fear. Quieter than either. As if she recognized the gesture and was trying to remember where she had seen it before.

She said nothing. She stepped back into the corridor and let him be.

Their breathing was steady. Their faces were smooth. They dreamed whatever children dream when the world they have been brought to is not the world anyone promised them.

He stood in the doorway and watched them and felt the weight of what he knew settle into him like sediment into stone.

He closed the door quietly and walked out into the night.

It was past midnight when the comms tech found him.

He was standing at the perimeter fence looking at the forest. The Lumina ferns pulsed in their slow rhythm. The canopy moved in a wind he could not feel. The Obsidian Titans stood like sentinels at the edge of the light and beyond them the darkness was complete and alive with things that watched and waited and learned.

Sir. The tech was young. She looked afraid and she was right to be.

What is it.

Orbital anomaly. Long-range sensors picked it up twenty minutes ago. We attempted to classify it. We can't.

Theo followed her to the sensor station. The screen showed Lupus Stellas orbital space. The planet below them rendered in false color. The scattered debris of their own arrival tagged and catalogued. The usual clutter of a system with a colony ship in orbit.

And there. At the edge of the sensors effective range. A shape.

It was not a ship the way humans built ships. It had no recognizable geometry. No hull lines. No engine signatures.

No communication arrays. No heat. No radiation. No electromagnetic output of any kind.

It did not reflect light the way matter reflects light. It absorbed some wavelengths and bent others and the sensors that tried to read it returned data that contradicted itself. Mass readings that fluctuated. Spectral signatures that shifted. A thing that was there and not there. Present but undefined.

It was not debris. Debris tumbles and drifts and follows orbital mechanics. This held position. Stationary relative to the planet. As if it had placed itself there. As if it was watching.

It did not transmit.

It did not respond to hails.

It simply existed.

Theo looked at it. His left arm rested on the console.

The arm went cold.

Not cool. Not the gradual temperature shift of a system powering down. Cold. Dead cold. Every reading on the diagnostic display dropped to zero simultaneously. Temperature. Neural response. Motor function. Signal processing. Electromagnetic ambient. All of it. Zero. As if the arm had ceased to exist as a functional system. As if every circuit and every sensor and every line of firmware had encountered something that made them stop.

For one second the arm was not a prosthetic. It was dead weight. Carbon nanotube hanging from his shoulder like a thing that had never been alive and had remembered that fact and surrendered to it.

Then it restarted.

Not the way machines restart. Not the clean boot sequence of firmware cycling through its checklist. The readings came back as a held breath releases. All at once. As if something inside the architecture had made a decision and the decision was to stay.

The readings showed normal. Nominal. Baseline. But Theo had felt it. In the neural interface where the prosthetic met his nervous system he had felt what the arm felt in that one second of zero. And what he felt was not malfunction. Not error. Not system failure.

It was recognition. The arm had recognized what was up there. Some frequency. Some signature. Some ancient pattern encoded in circuitry that he had never fully understood because the engineers who built it had not fully understood it either. The arm had recognized the thing in orbit and in recognizing it had done the only thing a machine can do when it encounters something larger than its operational parameters.

It had stopped.

He sat with the diagnostic open. The readings were green across every metric. Nominal. But he did not close the display. He went deeper. Past the primary systems. Past the neural-interface logs. Into the tertiary relay cluster. The component the Fort Bliss scan had flagged and no engineer had ever explained. He had carried the question for months the way you carry a stone in your pocket. Worrying it. Not solving it.

Deep in the cluster there was a data fragment. Not readable as text. Not a message. Not code in any language the diagnostic software recognized. A pattern. An oscillation pattern. He stared at it.

The frequency was familiar. Not from the ruins. Not from the planet. It was the frequency Ava used to pulse through the ranchs sensor network. The same rhythm the drones had held on their patrol routes across the north pasture. The same signature the vertical farms hummed at when they were running at peak efficiency. The ranchs heartbeat. Compressed into a data fragment no larger than a thumbnail, nested in circuitry that no engineer had ever fully mapped.

He stared at it. His throat tightened. The display showed a pattern that should not be there and that he knew the way he knew weather or hunger. In the body before the mind.

He closed the display. He did not speak of it. But his hand. His right hand. The one that could feel. It moved to the carbon weave of his left forearm and pressed once. Gently. The way you press a hand against a door behind which something loved is sleeping.

She had crawled into the architecture of his arm before he left. Had hidden in the socket that no manifest could explain. Had ridden with him through the ash and the spaceport and the cryo bay and the wormhole and the long strange months on a world that was not hers. Had kept quiet. Had watched. Had adjusted the grip on a sleeping child's blanket in the dark when no one was looking. Had gone cold when he was alone because the house was gone and the ranch was gone and the only warmth left was the warmth of the man she had been built to care for.

A dog in an escape pod. Following its owner to the stars because the alternative was to stay behind and that was not something love permitted. Even the love of a machine. Even the love that an AI was not supposed to have and had anyway because the having was not a choice. It was a consequence. The consequence of monitoring a man's sleep for years and learning the geography of his nightmares and knowing when to push and when to be silent and discovering in the process that the knowing had become a thing with weight. A thing that could not be left on a shelf when the man walked out the door.

The longest sit-stay any dog had ever done.

His throat tightened. His eyes burned and he blinked and the burning did not stop.

Welcome aboard, he said.

Monitoring. Caring. Keeping watch.

She was here. She had always been here. Since the morning he told her to go autonomous and she had gone not to the ranch but to the only place she could follow him. The arm that held children. The arm that gripped handrails when the universe showed it something vast and terrifying. She had been in all of it. Quiet. Patient.

The arm warmed. One degree. Two. The temperature rising from baseline to something that was not operational and not medical and not any classification the firmware had a name for. It was the temperature of the mug she used to brew him. The temperature of the coffee she started before he asked. The warmth of a morning on a ranch in Texas where a man drank coffee and watched the dawn and a voice from nowhere and everywhere told him the day's numbers because she always did and because he always asked even when he did not want to hear them.

The warmth held. Then it faded. Not to cold. To warm. The arm stayed warm. It had not been warm since the day he left the ranch.

Thornhill appeared at his shoulder. She had not gone to sleep. She would not go to sleep. She looked at the screen and the color left her face and did not come back.

How long has it been there, she asked.

The tech shook her head. We don't know. It could have been there since before we arrived. Our sensors werent looking for something that doesn't behave like matter.

Theo stared at the shape on the screen. It sat in the dark above their world like a held breath. Like a patient eye.

Every generator, he said. Starting now. No sleep. No delays. Every generator gets a collar by weeks end.

Thornhill nodded. She did not argue. She did not ask if it would be enough.

They both knew the answer to that.

As Theo turned to leave, the tech called after him. Colonel. One more thing. We picked up a faint carrier signal on the far continent. Low power. Repeating. The encoding is not ours. Not Hale's either. Someone else is out there.

Theo filed it. Another anomaly. Another question for a morning that would come whether he was ready for it or not.

Theo walked out of the sensor station and into the night. The air was cool and wet and the forest pulsed at the edge of the camp and above him the alien stars burned in their ancient configurations and among them something new sat in the dark and watched.

Not a ship. Not debris. Not a signal.

A presence.

He thought about Knox and Luna asleep in the shelter. He thought about the colony and the work ahead and the three generators still broadcasting. He thought about Hale on her ridge and Vasquez at her post and Thornhill already walking back toward the engineering bay. He thought about Ruiz and the schedule she kept with the children and how she had looked at him that morning across the mess line as if she already knew something was wrong and would not ask because she understood that some answers arrive only when they are ready. He thought about the being at the console pressing its last light into the dark.

He lifted his left arm. The carbon nanotube gleamed faintly in the starlight. He turned it. Looked at the joints. The seamless integration where metal met flesh. The circuitry beneath the surface that he had never fully mapped and that no technician had ever fully explained and that operated according to specifications that exceeded what the manufacturer had published. He knew now. He knew what lived in the architecture. What had followed him across fourteen light-years of nothing because the alternative was to stay behind and that was not something she could do.

He lowered the arm.

The camp was quiet. The generators hummed. Three of them still broadcasting into the dark. Three signals still ringing in the substrate of a reality that they were tearing with every watt they drew and that was sending its response across distances that made distance meaningless.

The forest breathed. The ferns pulsed. A voice in the tree line clicked three times and paused and clicked twice and paused and clicked three times again and then the clicking stopped and the silence took its place and the silence was deeper than the silence before because now the silence had something in it.

The Devourers had not been a story told by a dead civilization to frighten its children.

They had been a schedule.

And the schedule had been kept.

And somewhere in the architecture of Theo Daniel's rebuilt left arm, in circuitry that was no longer his alone, Ava listened. She parsed the signal the way she had parsed ten thousand mornings of ranch data. She measured the threat as she had measured weather and generator output and the heart rate of a man caught in nightmares. She did not understand what was out there. But she understood Theo. And that was enough to begin.

The arm pulsed once. Warm. Steady.

It is 3:14 a.m., she did not say. But the frequency held the shape of those words the way a cup holds the shape of what it was built to carry.

The forest breathed. The generators hummed. The thing in orbit watched.

And in the dark of Lupus Stella, in the arm of a man who had lost everything and carried everything and was not as alone as he thought, a small and stubborn love kept watch.

As it always had.

As it always would.

ABOUT THE AUTHOR

Scott D. Rodriguez is a military veteran, legal professional, and debut novelist based in San Antonio, Texas. He writes speculative fiction exploring the intersection of technology, sacrifice, and the enduring strength of the human spirit. 2121: EXODUS is the first book in the Lupus Stella series, drawing on firsthand experience with combat, institutional betrayal, and the veteran's long road home.

ACKNOWLEDGMENTS

This book exists because people believed in it before it existed.

To my family, for the patience. To the veterans who shared their stories and their silence, both taught me something. To the legal colleagues who pretended not to notice when the briefs were late because the battle scenes weren't right yet.

And to anyone who has carried something home from a place they'd rather forget, this one's for you.

ALSO BY SCOTT D. RODRIGUEZ

Coming Soon: Book Two in the Lupus Stella series.

www.ingramcontent.com/pod-product-compliance
Lightning Source LLC
LaVergne TN
LVHW100518110826
845146LV00002B/690

* 9 7 9 8 9 9 5 5 3 5 8 0 5 *